THE **LIFE** AND
**(MEDIEVAL)**
**TIMES**
OF
**KIT**
**SWEETLY**

# THE LIFE AND (MEDIEVAL) TIMES OF KIT SWEETLY

JAMIE PACTON

PAGE STREET
PUBLISHING CO.

PAGE STREET
PUBLISHING CO.

Distributed by Macmillan, sales in Canada by The Canadian Manda Group.

24   23   22   21   20    1   2   3   4   5

ISBN-13: 978-1-62414-952-8
ISBN-10: 1-62414-952-9

Library of Congress Control Number:  2019948964

Cover and book design by Rosie Stewart for Page Street Publishing Co.
Cover illustration of Kit & Jett by Mina Price

Printed and bound in the United States

Page Street Publishing protects our planet by donating to nonprofits like The Trustees, which focuses on local land conservation.

# Dedication

FOR ADAM,

who walks with me through worlds imagined and real.

THE RED KNIGHT ONLY FIGHTS ON WEDNESDAYS, FRIDAYS, and Saturdays. Much to the everlasting chagrin of my boss, King Richard the Bold, aka Len Schwartz.

Tonight's Friday, and the Red Knight, my older brother, Chris, is running late. Again.

"Please, please, please let me fight." I pace across Len's tiny office, my skirts swishing. "I know all the moves, and I've been practicing. For years!"

"You're a Serving Wench!" snaps Len, not looking up from the—I shit you not—golden chalice he insists on drinking coffee from. "We've talked about this before. You serve the guests. Let the real actors take care of the story."

"Serving Wench" is my official job title, not just some sexist slur Len's throwing out. Well, it is sexist. But also correct in a history-is-painful-to-the-modern-feminist kind of way. When I applied, I had to list on the application what experiences I had that qualified me "to Wench."

Sigh.

Len shuffles through a pile of papers—schedules, bills, a stack of flyers from the Castle Corporate group festooned with Gothic script and lots of exclamation points—then shoves the flyers in my direction. "Hand these out to the other Wenches, will you? Corporate wants all of us thinking about how to get more butts into seats for the shows."

Snatching the flyers from him, I bang my hand on Len's desk and lean in close. I even drop into my best medieval English accent. "But I'm a real actor too! I've done drama for years. I go to forensic tournaments—"

"Yes, yes," Len says, and sighs. "I've seen your résumé every week since you started working here freshman year. You were in *The Crucible* and *The Secret Garden*."

"At the university," I snap.

"Whatever," says Len. "You're not fighting as the Red Knight. Women weren't knights in the Middle Ages. They didn't save the day then—"

"Wrong! What about Joan of Arc? Matilda of Canossa? Khawlah bint al-Azwar? Brienne of Tarth? Or even Arya Stark? She killed the Night King, in case you've forgotten."

Len takes another swig of coffee. Some of it runs down his chin and disappears into the hipster-musician beard that hangs past his collarbones. Gross.

"What about company policy, Kit?"

"It's the twenty-first century, Len."

"Not in here it isn't. And you know the Castle has a very strict hierarchy. Squires become Knights. You're not trained as a Squire—"

"Because you won't let me!"

"Irrelevant. Plus, Brienne and Arya are fictional."

I inhale sharply, counting to ten in my head as I search for patience. Getting angry at a guy like Len only makes him think he's won an argument. Of course I know Brienne and Arya are fictional. And Len knows I know because I'm the one who got him hooked on *Game of Thrones* in the first place. But even with the GoT ladies being made up, the other women were real. And badasses. They would've laughed if a guy like Len tried to stop them from fighting.

"Don't you think," I say through clenched teeth, "we should take every chance to show people what the Middle Ages were really like?"

This is a favorite soapbox of mine. History books have gotten the Middle Ages wrong for so long. And white supremacist groups have run with it. They've gleefully painted the Middle Ages as this world where everybody sticks to gender roles, white men in the West are heroes, and everyone else are bad guys to be conquered, subjugated, or killed. All in the name of God and country of course.

Ridiculous. Dangerous. And totally unnecessary at a place like the Castle.

Len rubs the space between his overgrown eyebrows, really digging his fingers into his skull. As if he could somehow make me disappear if he massages hard enough.

"Kit," he says in a weary voice. "While I appreciate your efforts, this place is a fantasy. It's more theme park than history lesson. We've got male Knights! A Princess! Serving Wenches! Horses! Turkey legs! Everybody has a job, and certain jobs are not open to everybody."

"That's unfair. And probably illegal." I cross my arms.

Len shrugs. "That's life, kiddo. Take it up with corporate when they visit next month if you're so worried about it."

"Maybe I will. When are they coming?"

Len narrows his eyes at me. His voice takes on an edge. "Don't. Even. Think. About. It. I mean it, Kit. They're already gunning for reasons to close this branch. The last thing I need is for you to give them more ammunition."

I hold his gaze. As I do, a plan begins to form in the corners of my mind. I brandish the flyers at him. "What if I can fill seats?"

He snorts. "Good luck with that. They're looking for easy solutions like coupon nights or senior brunch Wednesdays. If you want to keep your job, you'll keep your head down, work your shifts, and let it go."

"I can't believe you're being such a jerk."

Len stands up and adjusts the blue velvet cloak around his shoulders. Under the arena's torches, it almost looks regal, but here under the fluorescents, I can see all the places where the velvet has worn thin. Company policy also requires us to buy our own costumes, and even the King can't afford to replace his cloak more than once a year.

"If you weren't my niece, I'd fire you for talking to me like that. Now get back on the floor. You've got Eddy Jackson and his buddies in your section tonight. And the show's starting soon."

Eddy Jackson is a former NFL player who loves the Castle with an inexplicable passion. He's here at least once a month, and he always brings his kids or a bunch of his buddies (usually more former pro athletes). Having Eddy in my section means good tips, but that still doesn't mean I'm ready to give up the idea of knighthood.

Almost as if Len planned it, three loud trumpet bursts ring out from the speaker above our heads. That's our cue to get into places because the show starts in twenty minutes.

"We're not done with this," I say, shooting my uncle a look. "I'm gonna come up with a plan you can't veto."

"Get over it, kid. You'll be headed off to that fancy California college soon. I don't know why you care so much about being a Knight."

*I need the pay raise!* I want to scream at him. So I can afford that fancy college. And also, is it so wrong that I want to save the day for once? Or at least spend a shift getting cheers, not beers? Even if all we do here is fake?

"The California college just rejected me," I mutter as I push open the heavy wooden door of Len's office. "As did every other school so far. I'm holding out hope for Marquette."

Len waves a hand. "You'll get in somewhere. And you can always go to community college like Chris did."

I let out a frustrated noise, fighting my urge to punch Len in his smug face. It's a super low blow to talk about my brother's situation. When he's not being the Red Knight, Chris juggles two other jobs and takes night classes at the community college. He put his life on hold because my dad—Len's brother—walked out on us for good two years ago, cleaning out our college funds and leaving my mom with a mortgage payment and a bunch of bills.

I scowl at Len. He knows all this, but he has less empathy than a concrete block. Len the Bold prides himself on his ability to "tell it like it is."

Jackass.

A voice squawks through the walkie-talkie on Len's desk, cutting me off. "WE'VE GOT A BIRTHDAY AT TABLE 4-GREEN. NEED TO GET A KNIGHTING CEREMONY ADDED ASAP."

Len picks up the walkie. "Go get ready, Kit. Mingle with the guests and call your brother. Tell him to get his ass backstage immediately or he's fired."

ONCE I'M IN THE HALLWAY OUTSIDE LEN'S OFFICE, I TAKE a deep breath to steady myself. My moment of calm is interrupted by another trumpet blast from the loudspeaker. Almost showtime.

Right. Got to get rid of these flyers and find Chris. As I walk toward the employee bulletin board, I glance down at one, really reading its message for the first time.

## HEAR YE, HEAR YE!

GOT A SUGGESTION FOR GETTING MORE PEOPLE TO THE CASTLE? WE WANT TO HEAR IT! EMAIL US YOUR THOUGHTS, PLANS, DREAMS, AND SCHEMES BY APRIL 1ST. WE'LL CONTACT YOU SHORTLY AFTER THAT IF WE THINK YOU'RE ON TO SOMETHING. IF WE USE YOUR IDEA AT THE CASTLE, YOU'LL GET A CASH BONUS!

There's a generic email address at the bottom of the flyer, but no more details on what kinds of ideas they're looking for or how much the bonus might be.

Shoving the flyer into my pocket, I make a list in my head, because that's how I process things.

- April first is in two days, so I don't have much time.
- I need the cash. No matter how much it is, I could definitely use it for something.
- And I have an idea—maybe not a totally fleshed-out idea, but at least I know what needs to change around here.
- What I don't know is how to translate it into getting more people to our shows.

I mean, let's face it. I can't just tell the Castle higher-ups: "Hey, you should let anyone who wants to be a Knight try out. And also, maybe, let's do a little bit more to educate people about the truth of the Middle Ages."

I can hear them laughing at me already. What I need to do is something stronger. Something more concrete. Something that will *show* them this idea will translate to both audience excitement and raising the bottom line.

But who knows what that even looks like?

Wheels turning, I pin one of the flyers up on the employee bulletin board alongside a schedule for Knight training sessions, a bunch of notices from people looking for roommates, and a photo-heavy sheet of paper from someone trying to sell their old costumes. I drop the rest of the flyers onto the table under the bulletin board and look for my phone. Time to find my brother before Len can fire him.

My phone's not in my skirt pocket, meaning I must've left it in the employee lockers. They're on the far side of the basement. If I'm going to call Chris, it'll be much faster to find my best friend Layla, who always has her phone on her.

Cooks and dishwashers stream past me as I navigate the long hallway from Len's office. Shields, swords, capes, and other props line the corridor. A roar of noise swells as I pass by a door that swings open to the Great Hall. For a second I see the mob: crown-wearing guests moving in packs, taking pictures, buying souvenirs, and dragging wide-eyed kids toward the performers who are contractually bound to smile for the cameras. The door slams shut, blocking out the noise. Layla's out there somewhere, and I hope I don't have to wade through that mess to find her.

"Hey, look out!" I shout as a Squire in the Green Knight's colors nearly plows over me. He's carrying a pile of shields, weapons, and a messenger bag.

"Sorry, Kit," he calls out, shooting me a grin. It's Eric Taylor, man of two first names, who was a year ahead of me in school. "I thought Wenches weren't supposed to use this hall."

I scowl at him. "I thought Squires were supposed to be picking up horse poop."

As Len mentioned, the official way to become a Knight is to

work through the ranks and earn a place after being a Squire. Eric Taylor wants nothing more than to be a Knight and have his picture on the Castle website. He's even started growing his red hair out in anticipation of his knighthood. But he's got a long way to go, and right now it looks like he's wearing a Halloween mullet wig made from a red panda.

Eric scoffs. "That's just during the show. But you know that, right? Because I heard you were asking Len to be a Knight."

"How in the world do you know that?" My mouth falls open. "I literally just left his office. Do you have it bugged?"

"Word travels fast in the Castle," says Eric. "Jessica heard Len telling the MC that you—"

"Forget it," I say. I don't have the headspace for the Castle rumor mill right now.

"Let me be the second one to tell you," says Eric. "You'll never be a Knight. I'm up next for the role, and you know they won't go out of order."

"Get out of my way," I say through gritted teeth. I'm suddenly more determined than ever to become a Knight, if for no reason other than to knock the self-satisfied grin off Eric's face.

Eric steps aside, giving me a mock bow. "If you see Layla," he calls out to me, "tell her my offer is going to expire soon."

I spin around, temper flaring. "Let me be the first to tell you," I say, mocking his tone perfectly, "Layla will never go out with you!"

Eric laughs and then—the slug!—winks at me. "We'll see."

I grab for the closest thing, a foam chess piece shaped like a tower, and throw it at him. He laughs again as he dodges it and hurries away.

Eric's been trying to date Layla since we started working here three years ago. He's slime incarnate, but I worry he's starting to wear her down. Layla's love life is suddenly as pressing as my brother's truancy, so I push through one of the swinging doors, heading into the Great Hall.

Noise assaults me at once—laughing tourists, people ordering beer, upbeat medieval-style music playing through the speakers, hawkers calling out for people to buy souvenirs. The Master Falconer skulks in a corner with a hooded bird on his wrist. Above me, the vaulted ceiling is painted with shields, crests, and medieval heraldry. The heraldry is all sound and fury, signifying nothing, which is exactly the opposite purpose of medieval shields and crests. It's bothered me for years, but imagine Len's reaction if I threw my heraldry book onto his desk and demanded we fix it.

Yeah.

I have a heraldry book.

And no, not even the people at the Castle know. Some secrets are too much even for these premium geeks.

I squeeze through a crowd that surrounds Wallace, the Castle juggler and official Fool. He's got five multicolored balls in the air, and the crowd around him oohs and aahs as he throws them higher and spins around to catch them.

"Gadsbudlikins, Lady Wench!" he says, spotting me. The balls stay in the air, a twisting rainbow of color. "You're in quite a hurry for such a fopdoodling scobberlotcher!"

Wallace prides himself on being able to swear like they did in the Middle Ages. Usually, I'd stay and spar with him for a few rounds, but today I'm in a hurry. I rack my brain for a quick something to say back to him.

"I'm only racing to get past you, my dear muckspouting mumblecrust." I curtsy as I say it.

Wallace catches the balls and bows slightly to me. "Well played, Wench! Would you care to stay and exchange a few more choice words?"

I curtsy again at him. "Alas, my good Fool, I cannot."

"Go forth, and Godspeed!" He bows again and goes back to juggling.

I grin as I walk through the Great Hall, taking it all in. Despite my argument with Len, I really love the Castle. Which is why I've not left it for another job, even after years of laboring within a deeply flawed system.

The air smells like cheap beer, roasted meats, and too many bodies in too small a space. At least we get that part of the Middle Ages right. People back then loved their fairs and feasts, and despite being built on a foundation of illusion, here at the Castle we do a pretty good approximation of the loud, boisterous, excitement-in-the-air feeling those events must've held. In the Middle Ages, feasts, tournaments, and fairs were smelly, riotous, much-needed escapes for people whose lives were mostly toil, suffering, lice, and early death. So, when you got a break, you danced, laughed, and drank yourself stupid. You fought and did . . . other things.

We're a family-friendly place, so we (try to) limit the amount of drinks you can have, and as for the other things . . . well, the Castle staff does enough of those for all of us. But the giddy sense of abandon and fun we market, package, and sell at the Castle is one of my favorite parts of this job. So, despite the noise, my missing brother, and my need to find Layla and give her a come-to-Jesus about not ever dating Eric, I laugh in delight as I watch a tiny kid waving a light-up sword as he jumps up and down, looking for the King.

For a moment, it's ten years ago. I'm seven and clinging to my dad's hand as he brings us here for the first time. His brother, Len, had just gotten a job at the Castle. Chris and I couldn't wait to go. Back then, on the first night, it was just me, Dad, and Chris, all of us stunned by the epicness of the Castle. He bought a sword for Chris and a flower crown for me. I felt like a princess but secretly wanted a sword too.

"Excuse me." Someone touches my shoulder, dragging me back into the present. "Could you take a picture with us?"

"I'm not really a—"

Before I can protest that I'm just a Serving Wench, I'm shoved into a family photo. A skinny woman clutching a terrified-looking girl child digs her nails into my forearm, pushing through the thick fabric of my costume.

"Say 'Middle Ages,'" calls her husband, a round man in a yellow polo shirt and athletic shorts, whose paper crown is balanced precariously on his bald head.

I grin, the shutter clicks, and the woman releases my arm.

"You should go meet the Princess." I point toward the back of the Great Hall, where Jessica stands in a shiny gown, a smile plastered on her face.

The girl's face lights up and her mom shoots me a grateful look. They don't need to know Jessica's a royal bitch who just broke up with Chris after a year of dating so she could go out with the Green Knight, who's richer than a lord in real life. No need to spoil the beautiful dream of Princess Jessica.

I smile back at the girl. "Have fun."

She squeals happily and pulls her mother and father away.

"Nicely done, Sweetly," says a voice from behind me. I turn around and see Jett, my second-best friend at the Castle.

He's wearing the purple-and-silver tunic that marks him as part of the King's court, and a golden trumpet rests on his shoulder. But his hipster haircut and sneakers place him firmly in this century.

"Oh God, it's good to see you," I say, leaning into his shoulder for a quick hug. "How's your night going?"

He shrugs and slings an arm across my shoulder, hugging me back. "Pretty good so far. Len's raging because you want to be a Knight, but I haven't had any tourists ask me yet why there's a brown guy in the King's Court."

Jett's dad is a physicist from India, and his mom's an anthropology professor from Russia. Predictably, with parents like that, Jett's smart, funny, and ridiculously gorgeous. In fact, at this very moment, a pack of girls our age is openly staring at him, each of them looking like they can't find the courage to say hello.

Jett and I have known each other since the start of freshman year. In that time, we've developed a few Unbreakable Rules: (1) Never speak about that time sophomore year when I tried to take us on a shortcut through the country and his car ended up in the middle of a farmer's field surrounded by angry cows; (2) we always pay for our own food and movies because (3) friends don't date friends because if it all falls apart, then everybody loses.

Both of us learned that lesson the hard way when Layla dated Jett's best guy friend a few years ago. After they broke up, our friend circle imploded as he found "cooler" friends and demanded that Jett choose between him and us. After that mess, Jett and I decided we liked each other far too much to ever date.

Which, if I'm being honest, seems like less and less of a great idea every time Jett and I are alone together lately. At least from where I'm standing. But I'm pretty sure he's okay with staying friends forever. I'll probably end up best woman at his wedding or something.

Ugh.

Pushing that depressing thought and all notions of how good Jett smells tonight—did he get new shampoo?—way down, I focus on what he's just said. Right. Stupid tourists who think there were only white people around in the Middle Ages.

"Next time someone asks you that, send them my way," I reply. "I'll cram some real history through their thick skulls."

"You're my hero," says Jett with a smile. "Hey, did you get through the math homework?"

"It's Friday night." I quirk an eyebrow at him. "You know that, right?"

Jett laughs. "I know, but I like to get a head start on these things."

"Next week is spring break. Why would I do my homework now?"

"So you won't have it hanging over your head over break?"

"Spoken like a true nerd." I laugh with him. "I haven't even looked at it. I got home and then pretty much had to catch the bus to come here."

A frown creases Jett's forehead. "Where's your brother? Why didn't he give you a ride?"

"That's the million-gold-pieces question. I've been looking for him, which is why I need to find Layla. . . ."

"She's stuck behind the registers over in admissions," says Jett. Another trumpet blast rings through the loudspeakers, and Jett and I jump. Our hands brush for a moment. It's a feather of a touch, but it sends heat throughout my body.

Good grief. There's a washerwoman in my stomach, twisting it into knots.

I squeeze his hand once in a hey-best-friend-glad-we're-close-but-remember-our-rule-about-not-dating-each-other kind of way, then let go.

"Want to get coffee after the show?" he asks, as he slips his hands into his pockets. He sounds totally unfazed by our hand contact. Which makes sense, since he's the one who suggested the Unbreakable Rules in the first place. "Promise we won't talk about math homework."

"Absolutely. Meet you here afterward. Have a great show and don't forget to blow hard!" My reply comes out in a rush, but I try to make it sound cool and relaxed.

He raises the trumpet at me. "You're hilarious. Wench your heart out."

"You know I will."

I most certainly don't sound cool or relaxed. Lucky for me, though, my reply is lost in the hum of the crowd.

As I make my way toward the front of the Castle, I run my finger over and over the spot where Jett's hand brushed mine. Feeling the planes of it like it's a worry stone, wishing he'd come back and do more than hold my hand.

Which is stupid and not even remotely a good idea. I know this. But that doesn't mean I want it any less.

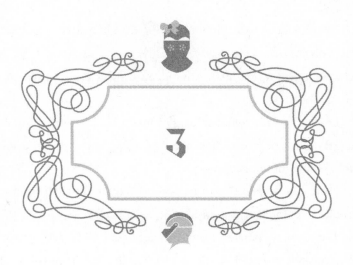

3

THE ADMISSIONS DESK IS CROWDED WITH LATE ARRIVALS, and Layla stands behind the counter. Doodles and caricatures of people at the Castle cover the sheet of paper in front of her. Layla's art is astonishing, and she's already been accepted into a graphic design program in New York City next year.

"Uh-huh, yes, I understand." Layla nods, her face a mask of customer care, as a woman in a polka-dotted dress and gold heels waves a ticket at her. "I see you do have a ticket here. But this was for the four thirty show, not the seven thirty, and we can't do any refunds. You can sit in an open section if we have anything left . . ."

The woman's face starts to turn pink as she begins a Veruca Salt–level tirade. I grab a handful of table cards and shove them across the desk toward her.

"Here, just go to section four, Blue Knight's cheering area."

"Thank you so much," says the woman. "I'm glad I didn't have to take it up with your manager. I mean these tickets are expensive."

Layla's mouth twitches as she holds back a smile. We've heard all this before: tickets are expensive, it's a special occasion, you want your money's worth . . .

"You can step on over to photo," Layla says. Her smile breaks free, making the dimples in her cheek pop.

The woman pauses for a moment and considers Layla. "Did anyone ever tell you look just like the girl from *Game of Thrones*, the Khaleesi's friend?"

At least once a night someone tells Layla she looks like "the Khaleesi's friend." People rarely know the character's name— Missandei—or remember the fact that she's fierce and super smart in her own right. Or that she was a slave initially, so maybe it's not something you should get into with your seventeen-year-old African American cashier who's just trying to do her minimum-wage job with a smile on her face.

Layla digs her nails into the countertop. "Dracarys," she hisses under her breath.

A confused look passes over the woman's face. Like she can't quite place the fact that *dracarys* was the last word Missandei uttered before being executed. Or the fact that it was a signal to her bestie to burn it all down. It's also Layla's and my latest BFF code for "Get this person out of my face now before I lose it."

I squeeze Layla's arm once and point the woman toward the Great Hall. "This register is now closed," I say. "Please move on to photo."

Once the woman is gone, I turn to Layla. "You okay?"

"That was the third time tonight," she says, exhaling sharply. Her fingers unclench. "Give me strength to withstand fandom tourists."

"You handled it beautifully. Just a few more months and then you're out of here."

Layla smiles at me again. "Thanks for the rescue. So, what brings you this way, m'lady?"

"Chris. He's MIA and Len's threatening to fire him if he doesn't show up. Can I use your phone?"

Looking over her shoulder to make sure none of our bosses are around, Layla hands me the phone. It's a super expensive, just-released iPhone. Light-years cooler than my shitty pre-paid knockoff one.

Chris's phone goes straight to voicemail, so I leave a message: "Where are you, dude? Len's going to lose it if you don't get here. I'm on Layla's phone. Call me!"

As I hang up, a text from Eric comes in. Without reading it, I delete it before Layla sees it. Probably terrible, I know. But these are the things you do for your best friend.

"Chris will turn up," says Layla, giving me a sympathetic smile. "He's probably back there getting ready and you just missed him. Did you see Eric at all?"

Feeling slightly guilty about deleting his text, I shrug. "I ran into him earlier. He's still the worst in case you're wondering."

Layla laughs and pulls a crumpled note out of her pocket and hands it to me. "He shoved this into my hand earlier."

I read it out loud: "Hey, princess, want to get coffee sometime? My treat . . . call me." I pretend to barf into the garbage can under the desk. "Ugh—even his notes are greasy!"

"C'mon, you're not being fair, Kit. He's not that bad."

"Not that bad? NOT. THAT. BAD?"

"He's kind of cute—"

"In what? A small-mammal-wildlife-documentary sort of way?"

She laughs. "Now that he's graduated, he's chilled out a lot. And it's just coffee."

"I can't believe you. This is the same Eric Taylor we're talking about? Man of two first names who's been stalking you for years?"

"He's just persistent," says Layla. "He's not a stalker."

"Don't go out with him. Please. For the love of all between us."

"Stop being so dramatic. Besides, you've never given him a chance."

She's not wrong. I've hated Eric ever since the first day he started working here, when I caught him making fun of a guest with a disability. But Layla's heart is bigger than mine, and she's convinced people can change.

"You can do so, so much better."

Layla rolls her eyes at me. "Thanks, Mom," she says. "How's your love life? You and Jett still drowning in sexual tension?"

"Shut up." I glance over my shoulder to make sure no one else has heard her. "We're just friends. I can't date him."

"You can and you should."

"Dating is against the Unbreakable Rules. You know this."

"He's adorable, smart, and totally into you. Plus, hanging out with Jett isn't going to derail the rest of your life."

"He's not into me like that. And it could ruin our friendship. I'm not risking it."

"What if it works out?"

"It wouldn't. We're seventeen. There's no way we're one of those best-friends-who-date-and-end-up-getting-married couples. That's like the plot of a bad movie."

Layla smacks me on the arm. "Those relationships work out sometimes. My aunt married the guy she met in eighth grade."

I roll my eyes at her. "Don't you have a cash drawer to count?"

"Don't you have a section to wait on?"

I do. And I should be helping guests get settled now. Especially Eddy Jackson and his crew of big drinkers and big tippers.

"Can you get them started?" I ask. "I'll split the tips with you. I'm going to run back to the stables and make sure Chris is here."

"No problem at all," says Layla. She's been angling to move up from cashier to Wench for months, so taking my section is a great way to show Len she can do it.

Before I can thank her, a pimply Page wearing a frumpy velvet tunic and—poor thing—ancient tights that are a sort of hazing for the Pages runs up to the desk.

"Kit," he says, trying to catch his breath. "Fight. In the stables. Your brother and the Green Knight. They're gonna kill each other. . . ."

4

I DUCK INTO THE EMPLOYEE HALLWAY THAT CIRCLES THE Great Hall and race toward the stables. Bits of sawdust and sand cover the floor. The rich, earthy smell of horses fills the corridor. When I burst into the indoor stable yard behind the castle, I'm stunned. We're so close to showtime that everyone should be lined up near the door, but chaos reigns. Grooms, Squires, and backstage hands have formed a ring around two Knights who circle each other. Over the heads of the crowd, I see flashes of red and green cloth. My brother's long brown hair swings like a fan around him as he ducks a punch thrown by the Green Knight and spins away. Although they're fighting for real, some of their stage training still makes its way into the battle.

Sensing the furious energy of the crowd, the horses paw

at the ground of their stalls and make nervous noises. Some of them are saddled, but most of them still need to be dressed for the show. The Blue, Yellow, and Black-and-White Knights stand at the edge of the ring in costume, but the Purple one still has on his Chuck Taylors. The Master of the Horse leads a gorgeous gray stallion away from the chaos, heading into the arena to do the horse-tricks part of the evening.

"Get your brother under control," he hisses as he passes me, nodding his head back toward the ring where Chris and Dalton—the Green Knight—throw punches.

"I'll try my best," I say, pushing my way through the circle of onlookers. The smell of BO assaults me as I squeeze between two particularly large stable hands, both of them sporting ponytails longer than my forearm.

Right as I arrive at the front of the crowd, Chris pushes Dalton to the ground. The Green Knight scrambles to his feet and throws a handful of sand up at Chris. Then, while Chris is blinded, Dalton punches him in the face.

Chris stumbles backward, clutching his cheek.

"Not fair!" I shout, breaking into the ring and running to Chris. "You can't do that!"

"Chivalry's dead, Kit," says Dalton, sneering at me. "We can fight however we'd like."

"Your words, douchebag," says Chris, wiping his eyes. A bruise rises on his cheek. "Let me kill him, Kit."

With pleasure. But that's a sure way to get fired.

"No, you will not." I drag Chris away from the center of the ring. "Jessica's not worth it, and you have to get into the real arena soon."

"Walking away from a fight," shouts Dalton behind us. "Typical! This is why she broke up with you. Because you're afraid to stand up for yourself."

Chris whips around, breaking free from my grasp. I'm strong after my years of training with Chris, but he does blacksmithing as a hobby. I don't stand a chance as Hurricane Chris whips past me.

He's on Dalton in a moment, tackling him down to the sand. He sits on his chest.

"She. Did. Not. Say. That." Chris marks each of his words with a punch.

Dalton squirms beneath him, turning away from each of the punches. His white-blond hair is filthy from the sand, and I pray Chris rolls him into the pile of manure a few feet away.

Before the fight can escalate, Jessica's voice breaks through the crowd. The soft British accent she uses in the show is replaced by her usual grinding South Side of Chicago drawl.

"Get off of him, Chris!" she shouts, stepping into the circle with her white silk skirts held high in her hands. She shoves Chris off Dalton, and he falls to the sand. "I did say that, and I said that you're too worried about your own self to think of me."

"Baby, that's not true at all," says Chris, standing up.

"Get away from me!" snaps Jessica. "We're over. We've

been over for a long time. Don't talk to me again. Don't call me, and don't try to beat up my new boyfriend."

"He wasn't beating me up," says Dalton. He stands up and wraps his arms around Jessica. She leans into him and they kiss, a long, sloppy number that makes the Pop Tart I shoved into my face before my shift threaten to come up. Chris turns away from them.

"Everybody back to work," shouts Len over the stable intercom. He's probably in the royal box, but news of the fight must've reached him already. "Showtime in five minutes."

We're already running behind, and the crowd scatters. I grab Chris's arm and lead him into a corner at the back of the stable.

"You okay?" I ask. His face is sweaty and his hands shake as he runs them through his hair.

He takes a deep shuddering breath. "I'll be fine," he says. "She doesn't have to rub it in, you know? And Dalton is vile. If she wanted to date someone else at the Castle, fine. But Dalton? C'mon."

"He's a troll. But you can't let them get to you. You'll find a better girlfriend. You're incredible."

Chris looks up at me, and for a moment, he looks much older than nineteen. Dark circles ring his eyes and his body slumps into the wall.

"I don't know about incredible. All I am right now is exhausted," he admits. "Between this job, the one at the coffee shop, the Uber driving, plus school, and now Jessica, I don't have much left in me."

"Have you been sleeping?"

He shakes his head. "Maybe an hour or two every night for the past week. My anxiety's been terrible and I just lay there awake, trying to see a way ahead for all of us."

"You're going to hurt yourself if you fight out there tonight," I say. "Make you a deal: You do the initial scenes where you have to ride around and play the games, I'll do the fighting scenes."

Chris looks at me, and a yawn splits his face. He knows how badly I want to be a Knight. And how much we could use the money. "Len tell you no again?"

I nod and make a face. "Company policy, blah, blah, blah . . ."

"He's a dinosaur," says Chris. He gives me a lopsided grin. "You remember the moves? How to use the jousting pole to catch the rings? All the fighting stances? Think you could do it?"

I nod, excitement coiling in my belly. Chris and I have gone through the moves so many times, I could do them in my sleep. He's a few inches taller than me and definitely buffer, but with all the pads and armor on, it won't be too noticeable.

"Then, fuck it. You can do the entire show," says Chris. "Ride out in the helmet for the whole thing."

Except for my curls, our hair is about the same length and same shade of reddish brown. And since my boobs are reluctant A cups at best, that won't be a deal breaker.

"This could work. But how do we make the switch?"

Approximately half the cast and crew linger in the stable, waiting for their cues. Most of them keep looking at Chris, like they hope he'll come at Dalton again. Dalton sits astride his horse, head turned forward. He wears a rose that Jessica tucked into his tunic when she stopped kissing him.

Chris grabs a walkie-talkie from a passing stagehand and radios Len: "Hey boss, my face is looking like a bunch of grapes that fell down a flight of steps. You okay if I fight this one with my helmet on?"

"I don't care how you do it," growls Len. "But you better be on that horse and in the arena by your cue."

"Done," says Chris, grinning at me as he hands back the radio. "Follow me. We don't have much time."

CHRIS GIVES ME A HUNDRED DIFFERENT PIECES OF ADVICE AS we step out of the main stable and run toward the Knights' dressing room.

I try to take it in: *Don't get into the Blue Knight's guard; be sure to fall when the Yellow Knight grabs a mace in the third round of the tournament; sit still on the horse, but be commanding; and, above all, tonight's the Green Knight's turn to win the tournament, so you have to let him.*

Chris scowls as he says the last bit.

"I can beat him if you want," I say, popping my head out of the dressing room door. Chris watches, back turned, for stray performers, but no one lingers in this area.

"Don't do anything I wouldn't do."

"Message received," I say, my mind already racing with ways I can bring the Green Knight down.

I trade my dress for a long tunic and faux chain mail leggings; then, I pull my super anachronistic Converse—the same ones I Wench in—over my Maleficent socks and attach holders for the jousting pole to them. Next comes the breastplate, shield, scabbard, and chain mail hood. Thankfully, it's made out of spandex and has a hole in the back for my hair to flow out of, since flowing hair on Knights is a big part of the Castle's brand. Last comes the metal helmet, which pinches my cheeks and narrows my vision.

"How do I look?" I ask as I step out of the dressing room. The armor weighs like nine thousand pounds and sits awkwardly. Surely anyone can see I'm not Chris from a mile away.

Chris smears some saddle grease in my hair, smoothing the curls, and then he paints some under each of my eyes like I'm a football player. It smells like leather and stinky feet all at once.

"What's that for?"

"You're prettier than me. I'm just trying to make it less obvious."

"Can you tell I'm not you?"

"You're going to do great," says Chris, sidestepping the

question. He hands me a sword and pats me on the back. "Now go find Shadowfax, and get out there."

I love that my brother named his horse after Gandalf's. Solid nerd move.

"Are you leaving?"

Chris grabs a gray sweatshirt out of his bag and pulls the hood over his head. "Of course not. I'll be in the audience, cheering you on."

"Sit in my section—Layla was filling in until I found you, but can you ask her to cover for a bit longer? She won't tell anyone if she sees you."

"I'll meet you back here," says Chris. "Then we can change clothes like it was me all along."

For a moment, part of me wants the glory myself, wants everyone to know that me—a girl—is out there with the Knights.

But Joan of Arc was burned for such things, and I can't afford to lose this job.

"See you after the tournament."

"Fight well, Red Knight."

I grin beneath my helmet, but Chris can't see it. So, I salute him and then hurry toward the stables, where a groom waits with Shadowfax. Like Gandalf's horse, Shadowfax is beautiful, strong, and smart. Unlike Gandalf's horse, he's a sort of weird yellow-gray color, but details, schmetails. Close enough.

Trumpets blast again. Len starts his welcome speech. It's time.

In one fluid movement, from years of secret, after-hours practice with Chris, I swing into the saddle. The Red Knight's Squire, a pimply-faced kid with a shaved head (totally against company policy), hands me a red-and-white-striped lance. He's got his phone tucked into his sleeve and is frantically texting without looking at me. He doesn't seem to notice anything is different about the Red Knight.

"Excellent fight, dude," he says without looking up at me. "You would've had Dalton if it hadn't been stopped."

I grunt my thanks and then sit up straighter on my horse, going over the order of the tournament in my head: The ring catch is first, then tokens from the Princess, then races, then the joust and the hand fights.

I can do this.

ISTORY DOESN'T TELL US HOW JOAN OF ARC FELT AS SHE sat on her horse, eyeing the besieged town of Orleans, planning her first military mission. Did her mind drift back to her village and the girl she was before the visions? Was there someone she loved before God told her to lead the French to victory against the English? (Which is a very Franco-centric view from God, if you ask me.) But really, who was Joan? Mystic? Mad? Fiercely brave? Or just the right girl for the job at perhaps the wrong time?

Maybe her stomach turned like mine was doing and her armor pinched her elbows and sweat ran in a sticky thread down her back, soaking her shirt.

"Right girl for the job," I whisper to myself, tightening my grip on the lance. "Right girl for the job."

And then, it's my cue.

"GIVE A CASTLE-WORTHY CHEER FOR YOUR CHAM-PION, THE RED KNIGHT!"

Our MC sounds more like a WrestleMania announcer than usual tonight, but his words wipe all fear from my brain. I kick my heels into Shadowfax and pound through the arena tunnel. Bright lights and loud cheers greet me. Beneath the purple stage lights and the mist that smells vaguely like mildew, the faces of the crowd blur. Another trumpet blast sounds, and I glance over my shoulder. Jett stands on the royal platform, looking glorious and much more majestic than beer-bellied King Len next to him.

Kit!

Focus.

Time to ride. Not time to think about the way Jett's eyes crinkle at the edges when he smiles.

KIT!

I dig my knees into Shadowfax and we pound across the pitch.

The first pass is easy. Once around the arena, hands on the reins, head up. I stop in front of the red cheering section and stand in my stirrups. I wave and bow toward the king. The crowd erupts in cheers from my section and boos from the others. In the front row, Layla turns for a moment, her arms laden with a drink tray and basket of rolls. She gives me the smallest of waves, but there's no time to acknowledge it because a horn sounds.

Ride!

The MC announces the Blue Knight, and I turn away from the crowd and focus on the game at hand. Chris and the Knights make it look so easy every shift. And afterward, they laugh with each other as they talk about who cruised a cute boy or girl in the crowd, who managed to maintain the best posture while on horse, whose section cheered the loudest.

But that's hours and several battles away. Right now, all I know is I really should have peed before agreeing to this.

Even that thought disappears as the horns sound again and the Knights gallop in a circle around the arena. So much of this job is showmanship. . . . I dig my heels into Shadowfax, and together we move toward the rings that hang in the middle of the oval arena.

The task is simple: lower my lance, put it through a hoop, and then retreat to the Red Knight's part of the crowd.

I miss the first one.

Which is something my brother would never do. My section groans loudly, and I bite my bottom lip as I ride. The warm, metallic taste of blood rises in my mouth.

Dalton hits two in a row on the same pass, and he makes a point to gallop past me on the way to his own section. "Can't see out of that black eye?"

I want to flip him off, but instead I ignore him, kick my heels into Shadowfax, and head back for another pass. My shoulders ache as I steady the lance, but I imagine Joan, waving her sword and calling soldiers to arms. I think of Chris, watching in the audience, exhausted and proud all at once. I remember myself at seven and the tiny girl I met in the Great Hall.

*This is for you all.*

I pinch my thighs together and drive Shadowfax forward. One ring clatters onto my lance and then the second one slips on easily.

I want to punch the air and cheer, but that's not what Knights do. Instead, I ride back to my section and drop the rings into my Squire's hands. A quick glance at the crowd shows me Chris, way up at the top of my section, standing behind Eddy Jackson and his buddies, all of them waving red banners. Even though Chris can't see it, I wink at him.

I've got this.

The tournament goes on. We race each other up and down the arena, horses kicking up sand and the crowd cheering. Although I have to stay alert, some part of me is on autopilot, outside my body, going through the motions. Sweat pools in my helmet and streams down my back. This is every-Knight-for-themselves, and the races aren't scripted. The Blue Knight wins most of them, soundly trouncing Green, Yellow, and me.

We take a small break, and I grin to see Eric Taylor rushing out with the other Squires to clean up the horse poop that's scattered about the sand of the arena. They use long rakes, which look almost exactly like what you'd use to clean a cat's litter box, and I secretly hope that Layla's reconsidering her opinion of Eric while she watches him work his pooper scooper.

By the end of the races, it's time to get favors from the Princess to throw into the audience. My thighs ache from holding myself upright in the saddle, and my back and arms scream at me. Although I've trained, I've never gone through an entire show. And we're only halfway there.

"Medieval warrior women, give me strength," I mutter, thinking of all the female warriors I've read about as I researched what the Middle Ages were really like. If they could fight like this in real life, I can stay on my horse for another thirty minutes for the sake of a show.

I ride up to the King's Platform. Princess Jessica, most treacherous of them all, stands at the edge, throwing fake flowers to each of the Knights. She doesn't look at me as a white carnation drops from her hand. For the sake of the show, she can't ignore Chris (well, me) entirely, but she doesn't have to smile at him. I reach up a spent arm and grab at the flower. It almost— almost—slips through my fingers, but I snatch it out of the air at the last second and turn Shadowfax's reins. With a quick sprint back to my section, I fling the flower into the audience. Then, I join the line of other Knights galloping back to the royal box. This time, Jessica slips colored scarves tied to rings onto the edge of each Knight's lance. When I approach her, lance held straight, she deliberately misses and the scarf flutters toward the ground.

I swear, more loudly than I mean to, and fumble for the

scarf, nearly dropping my lance in the process. Mercifully, I hang on to it, but this sloppiness is the last thing the Red Knight would do.

Jessica's already turned away from me, but Jett stands at the edge of the royal box. His mouth drops open when he sees me fumble and hears me swear. "Kit?" he mouths.

Our eyes meet and I give him the smallest of nods. He smiles and glances quickly at King Len.

"Rock star," Jett mouths, before putting his trumpet back to his lips.

Buoyed by his confidence, I readjust the lance and race back to my section, the scarf waving from my hand. I fling it into the audience and a young boy in the front row catches it. He waves at me, grinning. I smile, confident again.

There's not time to really do more than smile, though, because the trumpets sound again and it's time to joust.

HAVE YOU EVER THOUGHT ABOUT JOUSTING?

It's basically the medieval version of chicken, but with ten-foot wooden sticks pointed at the other person. And, rather than swerving away at the last moment, you have to just sit there and take it.

It's stupid, brutal, and jolly good entertainment, both five hundred years ago and today.

The Yellow and Blue Knights race toward each other, and then there's a hollow, thunking, splintering noise as Yellow's lance shatters into Blue's shield. Blue fake falls off his horse and they take the combat to the ground. Dodging, weaving, swords crashing—this is what the crowd is here for!

Blue topples Yellow—as he's supposed to according to the script—and their hand-to-hand fighting ends with Blue's sword balanced on the edge of Yellow's throat. They grin at each other, and then Yellow rolls away. Together, they bow to the audience quickly, and then it's my turn. Green is supposed to win tonight, which means I need to unseat Green on his horse and then let him beat me in the floor combat.

Except that's not what's going to happen today.

I can tell from the first pass, Dalton is still pissed about his fight with Chris. Right before our lances meet, I straighten my back and steel myself. He's supposed to pull back on his lance, so it just barely glances against my shield. But, instead, he drives his arm forward, ramming the lance into my shield. I dig my heels into my horse to steady myself as my shield shatters and I nearly fall off.

I can't help it; a scream breaks out of me as I turn my horse around. Luckily, it's lost in the roar of the crowd. Green stands up in his stirrups and raises his arms to the crowd. They shriek approval as he parades around.

I grit my teeth and trade my lance for a sword and a new shield.

The choreography of this fight is meant to be simple: Green falls off his horse as we ride past, and then I jump down to the ground to face him in the sand. The Castle has been doing this same show for three years now, and I've seen it twice a night, four nights a week, for all of those years. That's 1,248 shows, and each time the same thing happens—the last two Knights duke it out with swords, maces, and spears until the Knight of the Night (if you will) emerges triumphant.

But Green is out for blood tonight.

On the next pass, he dodges my blow, jumps from his horse, and knocks me down. While I'm on the ground, he advances, raining blows on me. I hold up my shield, arm aching, as he batters it with his sword. I roll out of the way, dropping my shield as I do so, and dance away from him. Inside my helmet, sweat stings my eyes.

My Squire hands me a mace—really just a prop made of balsa wood and aluminum, nothing like its hardier iron cousin, which could do real damage.

"What's wrong with him?" he asks, nodding at Green. "Did he do coke before the show or something?"

"Just Dalton being his usual self," I say in as Chris-like a voice as possible.

Before I can turn around, Green swipes my legs out from under me. My Squire jumps out of the way, and as I try to get to my feet, Green whacks me on the shoulder with his shield—totally illegal, off-script move—and pain shoots down my side.

From the stands, I hear Chris yelling, "Cheater!"

The crowd is half boos and half cheers, and I can't tell if they're on my side or not. But I don't care. In acting there are cues and maybe a bit of improvisation. But, in a fight, there's only action and reaction. And I'm done just reacting.

My shoulder throbs as I skitter out of Green's path and swing the mace at him. He's supposed to block it with his sword, but I aim lower, winging the end of it between his legs. It's a dirty move, but certainly one a medieval warrior, desperate for any advantage, would've used. I make certain to cover the move with my shield as I do it, however, so the audience just sees the mace hit Dalton's leg, and then his fall.

With a cry of pain, Dalton crumbles, clutching his groin. His sword falls out of his hand and then he flops onto his back.

I step a booted foot onto his chest and raise my arms. Triumph.

The crowd goes wild, and I turn to the royal box. Len's mouth hangs open, and he knows something is wrong.

We. Don't. Go. Off. Script.

It's rule number one at the Castle.

But I've broken like a hundred others tonight, so why not one more?

The MC tries to bring things back. "AND SO IT SEEMS THAT THE BEST MAN WON TONIGHT!"

I remove my foot from the Green Knight and stride toward the royal box. In that moment, I'm Éowyn in *The Lord of the*

*Rings* as she faced the King of the Ringwraiths. I tear the helmet from my head. My hair's probably standing up in every direction, but I don't care. I grin and raise my arms.

"I AM NO MAN!" I yell. It's my favorite line in all of *The Lord of the Rings*, and I deliver it perfectly.

In the royal box, Jessica scowls, Len's mouth is a thin line of fury, and Jett's dropped all pretense of staying in character and is clapping for me.

"Get it, KIT!" he yells.

The MC stammers, his usual narration cut short by what's happened. But, professional that he is, he picks right back up. "LADIES AND GENTLEMAN, MAY I PRESENT OUR VERY FIRST EVER FEMALE KNIGHT, KIT OF THE CASTLE!"

I bow to the King and then to the crowd. They're stunned at first and then a loud hoot splits the arena. Layla rescues me with her classic ear-shattering whistle, the one she perfected when we were kids.

As if awakened from a spell, the crowd loses it. They're on their feet, stomping, cheering, and throwing their colorful scarves and cheering cloths into the arena. Eddy Jackson and his buddies are whooping and raising their pitchers of beer in my direction.

Dalton's gotten to his feet and he stands with Eric, his Squire, shooting me death looks. I want to stay there and bask in the crowd's praise, but Len looks like he's ready to fire me then and there. I grab Shadowfax's reins from my Squire and swing myself into the saddle. With one last wave and a bow, I gallop out of the arena.

CHRIS WAITS FOR ME BACKSTAGE, A TAKEOUT CONTAINER IN his hands and a grin on his face. There's a roar from the arena signaling that more of the Knights have appeared to finish up the show.

I slide off Shadowfax as a groom takes the reins. Adrenaline pumps through me. I want to dance and barf at the same time.

"That was amazing!" I say, gripping Chris's arms. "You never told me how FUN it is to be out there. Or how good the crowd feels!"

He grins at me ruefully. "You were supposed to leave your helmet on."

"I couldn't help it!" I fling a hand across my heart. "Éowyn called! I mean, that setup was perfection!"

"You are such a dork," says Chris affectionately. The last notes of the show play, and then there's a loud bunch of applause. Chris steers me out of the stables and toward the back door. "I'll go get your stuff out of your locker; you go to the car. I'll deal with Len once I drop you off at home." He plops his keys on top of the takeout container.

"But I'm supposed to meet Jett," I say, peering over his

head. Two Serving Wenches—Lizzy and Mags—walk past us lugging tubs full of dirty plates.

"Nice one, Kit!" says Lizzy. She's a tall, pretty white girl who plays volleyball and just got voted "Most Likely to Dress like a Librarian for the Rest of her Life" in our senior class. Quiet and bookish in real life, when she's at the Castle, she trades her cardigans and patterned dresses for a low-cut Wench dress that hugs her curves.

"Epic," Mags nods, giving me a high five as she walks past. Mags's parents are from China, and she's got short black hair and dark eyes. Her piercings and tattoos (which she started getting the minute she turned eighteen) are never covered, as they should be under company policy. "Are you going to be out there every show?"

"I wish," I say.

"Well, if you figure it out, let me know. I've always wanted to fight as a Knight!"

Before I can reply to her, Chris opens the back door.

"Go," he hisses. "Before anyone else sees you."

Waving to Mags and Lizzy, I stumble outside, stunned for a moment by the contrast between the loud, smelly Castle and the warm spring night. The moon rises beyond the office buildings in the east, pale yellow, like the moonfaced girls who were so popular in the Middle Ages. When I get to Chris's car, an ancient tan Volvo that was old when our mom bought it fifteen years ago, I consider myself in the reflection on the window.

Hero? Loser? Knight? My face is sharp and chicken pox scars remain on my long nose. "Striking" is what my grandmother used to say, but that was just polite.

Exhaustion hits me and I have no more time to contemplate my stupid face. As I drop into the passenger seat, my adrenaline crashes. I think of only one thing: Have I just gotten myself fired?

HOME IS NOT A CASTLE. IT'S A PEELING-PAINT, ROTTEN-roof, split-story ranch on the edge of the freeway. Prime property when my parents bought it fifteen years ago. Before the Fall. The Separation. The End of Times.

Now, we're the working poor. Mom makes barely enough to pay the mortgage and weeds long ago took over the land-scaping. We're the ones who lower the property value of all those around us.

Chris's Volvo rattles into the driveway. I glance at the house. No lights on, even though it's nearly ten at night.

"She'll be home soon," says Chris. "Don't say anything to her until I talk to Len. I'll head back to the Castle and do some damage control."

My bones ache and the beginning of a headache eats at

my brain. I've taken off Chris's armor, but I'm still in the faux chain mail leggings, tunic, and my boots. I look like I'm ready for yoga at a Marilyn Manson concert.

"I'll just shower and wait up for you," I say, grabbing my backpack. There's a nagging feeling in the pit of my stomach, like some part of me knows I really, royally screwed up. But the rest of me is too tired, bruised, and hungry to dwell on it.

Chris waves as he pulls out of the driveway, and his headlights make my shadow huge against the house. Once he's gone, I look up. Far above us, almost hidden by the light pollution of the suburbs, the stars wink their centuries-old message. I could be seeing light from stars that burned out during the Middle Ages. Light that's been racing for seven hundred years across the galaxy to shine for a moment on me.

That's a heavy thought. That we're just the souls of stars in exile, as Plato says. Or that some girl might be alone on a night seven hundred years from now, waiting for a sign from the universe. And all she's got is starlight from tonight.

Overwhelmed suddenly by my smallness, I sit down on the driveway. It's damp from the rain we had earlier, but still warm. Bumpy asphalt rises under my fingers, and I remember the many times my dad would stand out here, slopping driveway sealer on the stones, making a mess that always somehow came out tidy and better looking by the end.

I lean back, resting the takeout container on my stomach, and stare at the stars. They blur together in my vision as I let my eyes go out of focus. As I lie there, I'm still half in the arena, my ears full of the crowd's shouting. Almost like a long road trip—where you drive all day, and then when you close your eyes to sleep it's more of the same: road and highway all the way through your dreams. Suddenly, I'm back on my horse, and the lance sits heavily in my hand. Resting the take-out container on the ground, I hop to my feet.

I can't help it. I grab a stick from the ground, like a seven-year-old fighting imaginary dragons—and yes, I was that kid; I even made a scabbard for my imaginary dragon stick—and brandish it like a sword.

The moves come to me like music rising. Back, forward, and into the other Knight's guard. It's a dance, and each step must be placed just so.

I've sword fought my way nearly to the mailbox at the end of the driveway when an Audi station wagon drives past the house, music blaring.

"Freak show!" a girl yells as the car races past. She throws a bottle out the window. I leap out of the way as a green long-neck shatters against the mailbox.

I flip them off, but their headlights are just red smears—a Balrog's whip, my inner nerd chimes in unhelpfully—in the night. I drop the stick, grab the mail and my takeout container, and stomp up the stairs to the front door.

When I'm inside, I fumble around in the dark for a moment, then flick the switch closest to the door.

Nothing.

Shit.

Did our power get shut off again?

I shine my cell phone down the split-level stairs. Chris's basement bedroom is dark, none of the telltale lights of his thrift store electronics shine.

Heading up the stairs, I try every light in the living room and kitchen. Nothing. And the stove clock is out. We had power this afternoon before my shift, so that means that the food in the fridge might still be okay. I drop the mail on the kitchen table and put my phone on the counter, so its light makes a column in the dark kitchen. Good grief, I hope no one calls the cops because they think I'm breaking into my own house. I light a few candles using the lighter my mom left on the counter. Then I pull out the cooler we keep under the table for occasions like this and start stuffing all the food from the freezer into it, hoping to make a cool bottom layer. Fridge stuff—a half-eaten pack of bologna, a bag of apples, and some leftover gas station burritos—goes on top, layered like a portrait-of-poverty lasagna. I empty two ice trays over the food for good measure and slam the cooler shut.

My stomach grumbles, and I take a candle to the table with my takeout container. Inside are two turkey legs, roasted potatoes, a pile of garlic bread, and some lemon cake. Layla, bless her, must've filled the box for me and then handed it off to Chris. For one selfish moment I don't want to save my mom any of it, but I can't do that. She never takes time to eat when she works a double shift. And this is far, far more appetizing than the other stuff in the cooler. Or the expired cans from the food bank in the pantry. One of them is silver—no paper label—and it just says BEEF underneath the silhouette of a cow. None of us have been brave enough to open that one yet.

No one's watching, so I tear into the turkey leg, licking my fingers and nibbling on the bone like a puppy. I don't slow down until I've devoured my turkey leg and started in on the potatoes.

I almost choke on a laugh when it occurs to me that despite my job, eating a turkey leg in the flickering light of a guttering candle is probably the most medieval thing I've done all day.

Except most people back then didn't eat meat and most of them didn't have candles. It's easy to forget such little details about the Middle Ages when the pageantry of it all sweeps me away, but they really were the Dark Ages in the sense that the world was pitch-black when the sun went down. Maybe you had a fire in your castle or hut, maybe not. Candles, torches, and lanterns would've kept the darkness at bay a bit, but just beyond the circle of your light lurked beasts, real or imagined.

And the meat thing? Forget ninety-nine-cent burgers from McDonalds to feed poor kids like me. Meat was mostly the privilege of the upper classes. Regular eating of it was such a class-based thing that some churchmen saw eating too much roasted meat as a gateway to hell. I read a book once where there's this great exchange between a friar and a noblewoman on her deathbed.

To paraphrase liberally, he says to her, "So, you're pretty much dead, do you think you're going to heaven?"

She replies, "You better believe I'm headed there."

Then, he—big jerkwad—says, "Yeah, probably not. Let's face it. You've lived in castles and eaten roasted meats every day of your life. Don't you think that's going to count against you?"

Wherein (in my mind) she gives him a withering look, like the Dowager Countess in *Downton Abbey*, and says through clenched teeth: "Maybe you haven't noticed, but my husband is a terrible asshole. I don't care how much roasted meat I've eaten. I'm going to heaven for putting up with him for all these years."

History doesn't tell us the clergyman's response, but roasted meats were definitely up there with fornication, witchcraft, and dancing too much.

It was a different time.

My mom's headlights illuminate the kitchen windows as she pulls in. I jump up from the table. I'm still in my fighting clothes. She's been sewing these fighting outfits for Chris for years, so she'll know immediately that something has happened if she sees me in them.

I shove the takeout container into the cooler and head to the bathroom. There's nothing left on the toilet paper roll, but by the sink, Mom's left a pile of napkins she swiped from a fast food restaurant. I'll be lucky if there's any hot water at all, but at least I get to bathe.

I shove aside the army of medieval-themed rubber duckies that line the tub's edge (a present from Jett last Christmas) and twist the faucet. As hot water pours out the tap, I say a silent prayer of thanks to the gods of hygiene and public health. One thing I'm always forgetting about the Middle Ages is how badly everyone must've smelled. Sure, it was no match for a few hundred years later when the Industrial Revolution turned cities and countryside alike into cesspools and cholera-breeding grounds, but it was close. The medieval church undid centuries of Roman bathing habits and convinced people that baths were immoral and basically one-way tickets to all sorts of sins. Washing your face was thought to weaken eyesight, and kings and queens were applauded for the claim that they'd only ever bathed twice in their lives.

Twice! In their lives!

Imagining the stench of a crowded medieval royal court on any given summer day boggles my modern-plumbing and four-different-types-of-body-wash (thank you, Layla for the birthday set) self.

When I'm done showering in nearly total darkness, I throw on the first things I can find in my clean laundry basket—thrift store PINK sweatpants with holes in the knees and a Wonder Woman T-shirt—and twist my long hair into a bun on top of my head.

Five texts have come in since I got into the shower. Layla, twice. Jett, twice. And Chris.

Before I can open any of them, Mom calls for me.

7

SHE SITS AT THE KITCHEN TABLE, STILL WEARING HER diner uniform. It's supposed to be an adorable throwback to the 1950s, but coffee and ketchup stains cover the yellow-and-white dress, and it's stretched across her chest, like it's about to pop open. Mom's only forty-five with a strong jawline, dark eyebrows, and a head of reddish brown curls like I have, but the circles under her gray eyes are deep trenches of fatigue.

"Hello, darling," she says as I walk into the room. She's lit a bunch of candles and turned on an ancient camping lantern.

I kiss her cheek, get the Castle leftovers from the cooler, and sit down beside her. "Long day?"

She covers her teeth as she laughs her smoky, tired laugh. She's not had dental insurance in years and her teeth are broken and stained. She sends Chris and me to a dentist rather than go herself.

"It was rough. Got the worst section because I was late after dropping off a money order at the electric company."

I look around. "Why don't we have lights if the electric company has your money?"

She shrugs. "They'll cash it on Monday. Until then, we'll have to make do."

It's only Friday, but that's okay. We "make do" a lot. Luckily, we're all pretty crafty and there's a lot of "making" possible. Mom sews; Chris makes blacksmithing stuff he sells online; and me, well, I don't do much of any of that. I mostly study and go to work. Because part of my Big Plan is to get a good job to get us all out of this mess.

"It'll be fine," I say. "I can stay at Layla's tomorrow night and get a jump on my homework and charge my phone over there."

Mom nods. "How was your night? Anything new from the Castle?" As she talks, she takes out a wad of fives and singles from her apron pocket. A few coins also fall onto the table. "Count it, will you?"

In the candlelight, I smooth out all the dollars and fives and divide them into piles. "Eighty-five sixty-eight," I say.

"From a double shift." Mom swears, shaking her head. "That place is getting slower and slower every day. How much did you make?"

She picks up the cash and stuffs it into a Mason jar on the

table. We all put our tips in the jar to pay for food, groceries, toilet paper, and things like that. Mom's day job as a custodian at an office pays the mortgage. Barely.

"I haven't counted it," I say quickly, hating myself for lying. "I'll put it in later."

"How's school? Still going to graduate?" She grins at me, a forkful of potatoes halfway to her mouth.

It's one of our oldest jokes. But it's not funny. Mom dropped out of high school to marry my dad and follow his band around the country until she had Chris. Basically her life was one long music video as she hitchhiked around the US and couch surfed through the Pacific Northwest before it was cool. She's asked me every day since the start of freshman year if I was going to graduate. The answer is always, of course, yes. But the implication is always that I wouldn't make her mistakes. Which is really all she wants for me. But it just makes me want to hug her and tell her I know she's doing her best.

"It was good. AP exam results will come back soon, and the guidance counselor says I should hear about colleges in the next few weeks."

I haven't told Mom about all the rejections yet. She doesn't need the stress.

A worried look crosses Mom's face. I know she's thinking of tuition bills, room and board, and all the other things we can't afford. College is ridiculously expensive. I used a month's worth of tips from the Castle just to pay for my AP exams. I have no idea where I'm going to come up with thousands of dollars a semester.

"I hope you get those scholarships," she says. "We can't ask your father for help."

We probably could ask my dad. In fact, on nights like this, when we're eating secondhand poultry in the dark and I'm thinking about which fast-food place I can steal more napkins from to use as TP, I'm really tempted to ask my dad for help. Last I heard he was a musician at a megachurch a few towns over. His weasely face no longer hangs in photos around our house, but sometimes I see him on giant ads at the bus stop and on the TV late at night, doing infomercials and praying for old ladies to send him money so he can give it to Jesus. Scammer to the core. Like the Pardoner in Chaucer's *Canterbury Tales*, my dad is as oily as a bunch of sardines in a can and has about as much of a moral compass as those dead fish.

He refuses to divorce Mom, because the Lord told him divorce is wrong, but he also refuses to pay any child support or his part of the bills unless we come to church with him. Mom says she'll be deep in the ground before that happens. So, we "make do."

Mom offers me a piece of cold garlic bread and I take it. We chew in silence for a moment, when my eyes fall back to the mail. One of the letters has a return address from Marquette University. It's skinny and in a normal-sized envelope. My heart skips a beat. My other rejection letters looked like that too.

I can't open it now because I don't want Mom to ask me about it until I know what it says. And because some part of me doesn't want to know yet. Plus, disappointment goes down easier for me when I don't have to share it with anyone. But it's all I can do to sit there, eyeballing the letter.

Mom's phone rings, and she puts her turkey leg down. "I'm going to get changed. You can have the rest of the food." She points to what's left in the takeout container.

She answers her phone as she walks down the hall. I grab the letter from Marquette but pause when I see another letter beneath it. "FINAL MORTGAGE PAYMENT NOTICE" is stamped on the envelope in bright red letters. My hand trembles as I turn it over. I open it without thinking twice.

**Dear Mrs. Sweetly:**

**Consider this your final notice for payment on the mortgage. You are now three months behind, and we will move into short-sale proceedings if you do not pay the full balance of $3,800 in a month's time. . . .**

The letter drops from my fingers. With shaking hands, I put it back in the envelope. Mom hasn't said anything about not paying the mortgage. Why hasn't she been making payments? Are we really not making enough together to cover it all?

The letter from Marquette stares at me, ready to deliver even more bad news.

I can't face it yet.

If this isn't an acceptance, then I'll have to go to community college. Which is fine, except I really, really, really want to study history at Marquette and then go on to law school there. It's a great school, close enough to home that I can commute to the Castle on the weekends, and I can still help Mom and Chris around the house. Plus, they have a collection of J. R. R. Tolkien's original manuscripts (aka nerd heaven) and a chapel Joan of Arc was supposed to have prayed in, and their history professors are famous. I read about one of them who's traveled all over the world to do things like drink beer out of barrels from the ninth century and study rats in the sewers of Paris. To get to work with someone who—

"Courtney Love Sweetly!"

I cringe as my full name—the unfortunate by-product of my parents' love of '90s grunge music, too many drugs, and their desire to have a different last name than either of their families—comes charging at me down the hallway. Mom stomps into the kitchen in her bare feet, her face nearly pink. The cheap prepaid cell phone in her hand trembles. Did I mention that the reason we all still have cell phones is because they're essential to life? I mean, you can always swipe an extra roll of TP from a public bathroom, but you can't always use someone else's phone. It's Poverty 101.

Mom drops the phone on the table. "That was Len." Her voice is very precise. Each word measured and furious.

I exhale sharply. There's no way this can be good. "Yeah? How is he? He had a good show to—"

"Kit. Don't pretend like you don't know what he said. He told me you fought! As a Knight. Where's your brother and how could he let this happen?"

"It's not Chris's fault, Mom! I wanted to fight. And I'm good at it. I won! Did Len tell you that?"

"He told me you got your ass handed to you! And that he's probably going to have to fire you because of company policy. Apparently somebody made a video of it, and it's all over the Internet. His boss called him, raging. You might've lost not just your job but also your brother's and uncle's."

My stomach churns at the thought. But a part of me is righteous and insistent.

"But, Mom, it's not fair! They should get rid of the gender restrictions at the Castle! To just let guys fight is outdated at best and illegal at worst."

My mom lets out a slow breath through her teeth.

"This isn't some political march or history lesson, Kit. Take a stand where it matters. This is real life, and we don't have enough insurance to cover you if something happens. Our deductible is five thousand dollars! What happens when you break your leg?"

I can't think of anything to say to that. "I'm not going to break my leg." I hate how petulant my voice sounds. "I'm really good at it."

"I don't care if you're the world champion of jousting at some crappy theme restaurant! You're not going to fight again.

And you're grounded."

"It's not crappy, Mom." I stomp my foot, which doesn't help my position as not actually a toddler. "You can't ground me! I need electricity to do my homework. I have to go to Layla's."

Mom makes a frustrated noise and picks up the lighter from the table. She quit smoking a while ago, but she still needs something to do with her hands when she's upset.

"Fine," she says at last. She flicks the lighter on and off. "You can go to Layla's tomorrow afternoon and spend the night. But don't leave the house before that. And I want the yard mowed. And call your uncle and figure this out. Beg him for your job back if you have to."

She stomps off to bed without saying good night, and tears fill my eyes as I slump at the table. I ask for so little; I want so little. And most of the time when I go for something I want, I get punished. It's not Mom's fault. She's trying to keep me alive and in one piece, but I think she's wrong. Busting up the gender restrictions at the Castle could be a big deal. And it is important. Not just because I want to fight, but also because I'm sure there are tons of other people there who want to work in roles outside those prescribed by their gender.

But what can I do about it?

I turn the question over and over in my mind, certain there's an answer. But it feels too big to tackle from where I'm sitting—in the dark of my kitchen, with what's got to be a rejection letter from my dream college in hand.

As I try to figure out a way to make things better at the Castle, a text comes in, lighting up the small screen of my phone.

Layla: CHECK THIS OUT!

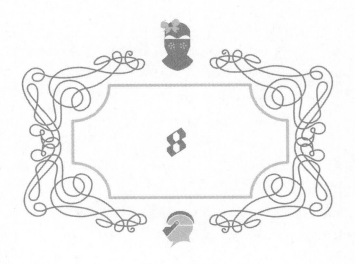

A PICTURE, DRAWN IN HER QUICK, MANGA STYLE, FILLS MY screen. It's me, in full armor, sitting astride my horse. Underneath the picture is a caption: **KIT OF THE CASTLE VANQUISHES HER FOES!**

It's so ridiculously perfect it makes me laugh. Which does wonders for breaking up the heaviness of my thoughts. I text her back immediately.

Kit: I LOVE IT!

Layla: There's more where that came from. Stay tuned.

Something moves in my brain. The merest shadow of an idea. Before I can nail it down, more texts come in.

Layla: How are you feeling?

Kit: Sore, tired, exhilarated. Also my mom is pissed.

Layla: You were badass out there!

Kit: I loved it. Do you think I'll get fired?

Layla: Len's mad, but don't worry about it. Talk to him before your next shift. I'm sure it'll be fine.

Kit: ✌️ How was waiting tables?

Layla: 🙂 I made $300 in tips!

Kit: Bless you, Eddy Jackson?

Layla: The man is a saint, and also, I've never seen anyone eat so much turkey.

**Eddy holds the current Castle record of most turkey legs ordered by one person.**

Kit: He's a legend.

Layla: 😂 😂 😂 I'll bring your half of the tips tomorrow.

Kit: Those are yours, keep them.

Layla: We agreed to split them. And I don't need them, so no worries.

**Layla's mom is a brain surgeon and her dad is CEO of an international corporation. Her house is like a museum, and she gets $800 a month in allowance. So, no, she doesn't need the tips. But I don't like to tell her how poor I really am.**

Kit: Cool. Can I come over tomorrow afternoon and spend the night?

**Spending the night at Layla's is like what I imagine it feels like to sleep in a luxury hotel. With the addition of my kickass best friend.**

Layla: YES! 😉 Good (k)night!

Kit: 'Night (and totally see what you did there).

I'm smiling by the time I pocket my phone. Mom's door is closed and Chris still isn't home. I grab a candle, throw out the remains of the takeout—just bones and some bread crusts—and take my letter from Marquette and my phone into my room.

Kicking aside a pile of dirty clothes, I set the candle on my bedside table. It flickers, casting looming shadows. One of my walls is taken up by a screen-printed reproduction of part of the famous medieval tapestry *The Lady and the Unicorn*. I found it in a thrift store, complete with troubling stains in the upper right corner and a set of cigarette burns where the unicorn's eyes should be. On the other wall, framing my window, are two bookshelves overflowing with fantasy novels and history books. A photo of Layla, Jett, and me from the Castle sits on my dresser, and the rest of the room is a riot of knockoff medieval stuff. My bras hang from a concrete knight that's supposed to be a lawn ornament. I got him at a yard sale for a dollar. I've put plastic films on my windows, so they look like stained glass. A stuffed dragon sits on top of one of the bookshelves, a present from my dad long ago. Two reproduction swords that I bought at a Renaissance faire lean against my desk.

Above my desk is a collage I've been adding to for years. "Fierce Ladies of the Middle Ages," it says in bold letters. I got the idea from some list I saw online, and I've been doing research on these women ever since. Now, they hang in my room like some odd family tree or something.

There are the famous ones most people have heard of: Lagertha (thank you, *Vikings* the show for cosplay inspiration for days); Joan of Arc; Boudicca.

And then there are hosts of other woman who did remarkable things, but who most people don't know about: Matilda of Canossa, an Italian countess who battled for 30 years against kings. Caterina Sforza, another Italian woman who said, "If I must lose because I am a woman, I want to lose like a man." Sichelgaita of Salerno, a Norman woman who commanded sieges. Khawlah bint al-Azwar, sister to a Muslim commander during the Islamic conquest who led a troop of women against the Byzantine army (oh! to go back in time to that battle!). And so many others. Each of them brave. Fierce. And heroic.

"What should I do?" I ask the faces that stare back at me.

They're silent, as always, so I turn away from my favorite ladies and toward what hangs on the other wall above my bed. It's a giant sheet of poster board with "KIT'S BIG PLAN" written at the top in gigantic letters. Big plan, big letters. I can't help it. I'm a planner, literalist, and sucker for a pun. Beneath the title are ten tidy bullet points and rules for living that will get me from where I'm at to where I want to be. It's half bucket list and half dammit-universe-I-will-wrestle-my-destiny-from-your-cold-unfeeling-hands.

As I do every night before I get into bed, I recite the bullet points. To remind myself of the direction I'm heading and what I have to do to get there.

First point:

- Get a better job, preferably KNIGHT!, to save money for college.

Chris tells me that some Knights can make close to $50,000 a year, which is more than I need, but even just working a few shifts a week as a Knight would net me more than the tips I make as a Wench. You'd think wenching at a place like the Castle, with the sheer number of guests we have, would bring in a lot of tips, but most guests leave small tips because they've paid so much for admission and then blown the rest of their money on souvenirs and beer.

Next point:

- Get into a great college to study history. Options: ~~Stanford, Yale, UPenn, Harvard,~~ Marquette.

Marquette sits out there alone, like the last fragile leaf on a tree before the autumn wind comes along. I glance at the letter on my nightstand. I can't open it and risk marking through that last hope. Not tonight.

After the college plan, the bullet points get more abstract:

- Study in Paris—so much history! Musée de Cluny! The Louvre! Notre Dame! (A whole bunch of hearts and exclamation points follow this one, and hopefully it will be repaired by the time I get there).

- Get into law school, join fancy law firm, take care of Mom. . . .

I can't read the rest of the bullet points after that like I usually do because instead of getting closer to the first one, after my stunt at the Castle tonight, I'll probably have to start over and get a new job.

Not part of my plan at all.

After brushing my teeth, I crawl into bed, ignoring the Big Plan. My bones ache as I settle onto the pillow.

Another text comes in as I'm falling asleep.

Jett: You okay?

Kit: Erm . . . I got grounded. And I got my letter from Marquette. . . .

Jett: Well?

Kit: Well what?

Jett: Did you get in?

Kit: I didn't open it. I'm preparing myself for a rejection.

Jett: KIT!

Kit: JETT!

Jett: What if it's not a rejection?

Kit: I'm not ready to take that leap of faith just yet.

Jett sends me a GIF of a squirrel leaping from one branch to the next. I reply with one of a dog trying to jump over a kiddie pool, failing miserably, and landing in the water.

Jett: Ye of little faith.

I can almost hear the teasing tone in his voice.

Kit: Promise I'll open it tomorrow. Just can't handle any more drama tonight.

Jett: You get in trouble for fighting as a Knight?

Kit: To be discussed later.

Jett: Call you tomorrow. Oh, and did you see this?

He sends a link that takes me to a YouTube video. It's titled *Kickass Girl Knight Takes On the Castle!*

My heart speeds up as I recognize myself in the arena. This is definitely not flying under the radar.

Kit: Did you have anything to do with this?

Because of course he did, since Jett's planning on studying filmmaking in college and he's seen like a million documentaries. This video also looks like it was shot from the royal box.

Jett: ☺ ☺ ☺ Maybe.

Kit: I can't decide if I'm mad or delighted.

Jett: Sleep on it. Tell me what you think in the morning.

I risk one heart emoji and promise I'll watch it tonight. After I say good night to Jett and blow out the candle, I click on the video.

It starts with my "I am no man" moment, then has a bunch of clips from the show. I watch it three times in a row, still not quite believing it's me on the screen.

It's fierce, badass, and fun.

I think my wall of medieval ladies would be proud.

The number of views keeps jumping as I watch.

It's only been up for an hour, but it's already been viewed more than four thousand times. And the number keeps climbing.

Holy shit.

That's a lot of people watching my video.

That's a lot of people who could be watching at the Castle in real life.

That's a lot of people who I should tell the Castle Corporate Group about.

Where is that flyer?

Using the light from my phone, I find my backpack. My wenching dress is shoved into it. I fish the flyer out of the pocket.

"Email us your thoughts, plans, dreams, and schemes," it says.

And I suddenly know exactly what I need to do.

I scrawl notes into my bullet journal until my phone's low-battery light flashes at me. Before I go to sleep, I click back to my video one more time.

Six thousand views and still climbing.

This might actually work.

SEVEN FORTY-FIVE SATURDAY MORNING. I WAKE UP SORE and with a head full of foggy dreams. In them, I was a cartoon character, fighting in the arena . . . and then someone buried me in the ground.

Ground.

Right.

Grounded.

I roll out of bed and get myself dressed in yard-work clothes. Scrubby T-shirt, jeans with holes in the knees, and torn sneakers.

As I brush my teeth, I space out, thinking about being grounded.

Mom's punishment reminds me of a part of the Middle Ages that's always sat badly with me. Lots of women were basically grounded back then. Unless they had the moxie (and fists) of the Wife of Bath, travel beyond a small sphere was limited.

Other women, though, were grounded in a more literal sense. Like scary Edgar Allan Poe bury-you-alive style. These unfortunate souls were anchoresses, nuns whose primary duty in life was to "anchor" the convent or church community they lived in. And where do you put an anchor? At the bottom of things. So, these women were walled into a small cell below the ground. The cell had a few openings that looked onto street level: one for delivering food and water, another for hearing the prayers of the faithful, and (hopefully) at least one for getting rid of waste.

But that was it. That was their life for years and years. Subsisting on whatever crusts of sunshine and fresh air made their way through the cracks. Shivering in winter, baking in summer. Peering out at the bustle of the street and imagining all the what-ifs had their lives gone differently.

I'm not that grounded, and it's disingenuous to say so. But it does make me think.

The chime of the doorbell startles me out of my teeth-brushing history-fanatic space out.

Mom's door is open and her bed empty as I pass. I heard her leave for her early-morning shift hours ago. Guilt stabs at my belly as I think of our fight. We'll make up later—we always do—but fighting with her makes me sick because everything she does is to help Chris and me get ahead. Hence the reason why one of the bullets on my Big Plan is taking care of Mom.

I fling open the front door and my mouth falls open when I see Jett standing there. His hair's wet and slicked back. His skinny jeans, black T-shirt, leather jacket, and Doc Martens make him look like a movie star.

"Stop being so cool before nine in the morning," I say, and groan.

"I'm amazingly cool," he says, moving aside and pointing to the rusty red minivan in the driveway. Jett's the oldest of four boys, all of whom are usually crammed into the van.

"No motorcycle today?" I try to smooth out the nest that is my hair.

Usually Jett drives a vintage black Triumph. He saved up a year's earnings at the Castle, bought a broken-down bike, and fixed it. His dad told him if he could fix it, he could drive it. But only around town. And he's not supposed to have passengers, but his parents make an exception for me because I'm sort of like family.

"Super cool ride, I know." He grins. "You had breakfast yet? I thought we could go out for celebration coffee and donuts. You're over ten thousand views this morning."

"I cherish you," I mutter, my voice still full of sleep. My only other breakfast option is stale Pop Tarts or something from the cooler of doom. "But I'm grounded."

Jett raises an eyebrow. "Grounded? The first Lady Knight

of the Castle is grounded?"

"C'mon," I say, giving him a little shove. "My mom will kill me if I leave."

"Is she here?"

I smile at him. "No, she's on a double today and won't be home until eight or so."

"Then we've got tons of time. Let's go. My treat."

"Uh-huh. No buying my food. Against the Unbreakable Rules."

"Just this once?"

"Nope."

"Fine."

I glance over my shoulder. Chris's door is cracked, and his snores carry up the stairs. He probably got drunk on cheap beer after having it out with Len. I can go out, get coffee, and be back with time to spare before I have to mow the lawn. "Let me grab a few things."

"I'll be waiting in the van," says Jett.

I take the stairs two at a time. I could change, but it's coffee and donuts with Jett. He doesn't care if I look like I just crawled out of bed. I grab my purse—a giant designer tote with a glittery unicorn and embossed castle on it that I got from Layla for Christmas and that I love with a fiery passion—the letter from Marquette that I still need to open, and my dead phone.

On the kitchen table, there's a note from Mom.

Sorry about the fight, Kit-Kat. I think you're brave and fierce, but I don't want you to get hurt or get your hopes up. Get your chores done and have fun at Layla's. I'll see you tomorrow.

XOXO, Mom

I grab a pen and scrawl at the bottom.

Sorry too, Mom. See you tomorrow.

—K.

The Mason jar full of tips sits on the table where we left it last night. I only pause for a moment before I reach in and take out a twenty. Although I'd love for Jett to buy me breakfast, I can't let him. Beyond our Unbreakable Rules, I don't want him to know that this money is kind of way too much to spend on breakfast. Jett and Layla know I'm poor, but I've worked hard to make sure they don't know how broke we are. Like I'm planning on stealing a roll of TP and some of the free tampons that are tucked into a cabinet in the local Dunkin' Donuts bathroom, just so I don't have to buy more before payday. That's a ridiculous level of poor and the kind of things that are hard to explain to your well-off best friends.

Jett smiles as I get into the van. I plug in my phone to the charger, and the brassy horns and lilting melancholy of Beirut fill the car. Jett loves this band for the horns, but I love it because it makes me think of cities I've never visited. Of Paris before the wars and Istanbul at twilight. We're quiet on the ride to Dunks, but it's not weird. Just a nice silence. The cozy kind that's like snuggling into a blanket on a cold day or wearing your favorite PJ pants. When Layla and I are together, we chat almost the whole time. Which thrills and exhausts me, but with Jett it's always been relaxed and easy.

I'm pouring more sugar into my extra-large coffee when he asks to see the Marquette letter.

"Don't make me open it." I groan, and hand it over. I bite into a chocolate Long John. Sweetness fills my mouth. Donuts are my kryptonite, and of course, the history nerd in me knows that in the Middle Ages, they were a favorite treat before Lent.

"You can do it!" he says, sliding a finger under the lip of the envelope.

I snatch it back. "Too soon. Let me have a few more minutes of suspended disappointment. Please."

He raises an eyebrow at me. "You're not being very kick-ass Girl Knight."

I drink more coffee. "Leave me in peace. I promise, I'll open it today."

"Pinky swear?" He holds out a finger.

I curl mine around his. "Pinky swear. Also, I haven't done this since I was like nine."

And I love the way our fingers fit together.

Jett laughs, unhooks his finger from mine, and finishes his donuts. "You know what you need?"

"A day of yard work at my mother's insistence?"

Jett shakes his head. His brown eyes glow in the morning light. Goddammit, he's gorgeous. "Road trip. To Marquette. Now. It'll be like a pilgrimage. And you can open your letter there."

"I can't. I'm grounded."

"And I've got to be back for my shift at the Castle tonight. You'll be home with more than enough time to mow the lawn. I promise."

I think again of all the women in the Middle Ages, especially of the Wife of Bath. Bold, brave, saucy, and spirited. Traveling to pilgrimage sites was kind of her thing. Exactly the kind of woman I want to be. Minus the six husbands and all that.

"Let's go."

We leave the donut shop before I have time to pilfer the bathroom for supplies, but that's okay for now. Pilgrimage awaits.

**10**

ARQUETTE IS IN MILWAUKEE, A LITTLE OVER AN HOUR and a half away from my house. Driving into the city always takes my breath away. Lake Michigan sits in the east, an endless stretch of sapphire to the horizon. Then, skyscrapers, smokestacks, and the steeples of the city's many churches and breweries stab at the clouds.

We find parking a few blocks from campus and stroll along the street. It's mostly empty and quiet this morning. A homeless guy pushes a shopping cart past us. Jett puts a five-dollar bill into his outstretched hand. The guy thanks him with an elaborate blessing. It's too much, but Jett just smiles and waves as we walk away. Only a few students stroll (or stagger) across campus. It's Saturday morning after all. Even still, I wish I had changed. Most of the early-morning students have expensive bags and wear North Face pullovers. It's almost like a uniform.

"I'd never fit in here," I say as we walk.

"Don't be ridiculous," says Jett. "You're brilliant, hard-working, and nice. You'll be fine." He takes my hand and gives it a squeeze. I squeeze back and then drop his hand.

Without meaning to, we've moved toward the center of campus. There's a terraced garden where a riot of tulips and other flowers bloom. At the center of the garden sits a small, medieval stone chapel. It looks impossibly out of place among the nineteenth-century ivy-covered brick buildings and the more modern shapes of the Engineering Hall and the Wehr Life Sciences Building.

"St. Joan of Arc Chapel," I say, a little awestruck. I've seen pictures of it, but I've never been here. My heart kicks inside my chest as I think about teenage Joan of Arc, standing here, just like me, looking for some direction.

I'm not religious, but I do love connecting to the past. And this is about as real as it gets.

We take a couple of selfies in front of the chapel.

"Did you know some rich lady brought this chapel over here stone by stone?" says Jett. "I did a bunch of research last night."

"Bless your little nerd heart," I say. "Can you imagine that, though? Stone by stone?"

"She actually brought a whole château over, so this was literally a drop in the stone-by-stone bucket."

Rich people. SMH.

"This is like Disneyland for history geeks," I say, pushing on the wooden door. It's surprisingly heavy—as I suppose doors had to be back in the days of Viking raids and Inquisitions—and Jett and I step into the shadowy nave.

It's so perfect it's almost a cliché.

Dust motes dance in slivers of sunlight that filter through the row of arched windows. Threadbare tapestries cover the walls and wagon-wheel wooden chandeliers dangle from the star-shaped ceiling. Behind us an armless Christ figure hangs above the door, flanked by carved cherubs. An altar stone sits at the front of the chapel, solid beneath the distracting whimsy of the round stained glass window above it. Blue, red, yellow, and black pieces of glass paint a picture of life as it might have been in Joan's time.

This is what I imagine parts of Paris must look like. I close my eyes for a moment, pretending I'm in Notre Dame. Living a tiny part of the dream I've had for so long.

"Wow," says Jett under his breath. He's filming on his phone as we walk.

"Yeah," I whisper, trying to take it all in.

We're the only people inside the chapel. There's a guest book on a carved stand that looks like it's straight out of the set of *Game of Thrones*. I flip through it, skimming the entries. Pages and pages of names, scrawled prayers, and hopes; the whispers of people's secret hearts. How many feet have crossed over these stones in the last six hundred years? The air's charged, like it's holding its breath, waiting for something. Or someone. Like it's missing the girl-saint who stopped inside its walls, her boots muddy, her hair chopped off, her heart full of mystery or madness.

I can't stop touching things. I run my fingers along the cool stone walls, dipping them into the uneven places in the rock. I sit in one of the rickety chairs. I stand on my tiptoes and touch the tapestry fabric. The iron sconces have rounded points on the end, and I press the edge of my finger into one. It almost hurts.

It all feels genuine in the way that history doesn't at the Castle. It's uncomfortable, imperfect, and it makes sense that real lives could've existed in a place like this. Somewhere sacred and strange and utterly out of place in the rush and bustle of an urban college campus.

"They have Mass here every day," Jett says, reading a sign near the back of the chapel. He's stopped filming. "Do you want to stay?"

I shake my head. "The awe of history is good enough for me," I say. "Let's go see her."

Near the front of the church is a statue of Joan of Arc. It's small, like she was, and her pageboy haircut is rendered with painful, awkward accuracy. I'm not tall, but I tower over her. With the exception of the sword at her side and her armor, she looks like an eighth grader going to get her braces adjusted.

I rest my hand on her arm, trying to channel some of her

bravery, spirit, and belief in her own mission. What must it be like to have that sort of clarity in your own life as a teenager? I mean, I have my Big Plan. And my lists. But it's not quite so unswerving as an edict from saints and divine powers.

"She must've been badass to see in battle," says Jett.

"Actually, she never fought in battle," says a voice from the front of the chapel.

A woman wearing an Easter egg–patterned sweatshirt, mom jeans, and a name tag with "Volunteer" on it steps out from a hidden door of what must be the sacristy. "Joan was present at many battles," the woman continues in a tour-guide voice. "But she didn't fight in any herself. It's one of her legends. Like this chapel. We're fairly certain she never set foot in here."

"What do you mean?" I make a face. "This is *the* Joan of Arc chapel."

The woman laughs, like she's heard a thousand other people say the same thing. "It's called that, dear, but it's not true. This chapel is from the southeast of France. Joan was in the north. The windows were put in during the thirties, and the tapestries are reproductions from a rich donor. Everything in here is from somewhere else—the altar is from centuries after Joan, and the statues in the back from a bombed church in Italy—that's why they have no arms."

"You mean it's all a fake?"

I kind of can't breathe, and the dust motes now look tawdry, as does all the other stuff scattered about the chapel.

"It makes people believe," says the woman. She shrugs. "And Joan was real. Those are the important parts."

"But, just to be clear, this chapel really has nothing to do with Joan at all?" My voice has a frantic edge, and I can see Jett biting his bottom lip. I wonder if he found this out already during his research.

The woman tugs at the bottom of her sweatshirt and looks at Joan's statue. "I wish it did. I really do, honey. But it's only a story."

I slump into a chair and bury my head into my hands. Stupid, unasked-for tears fill my eyes. The chapel is really no better than the Castle. A fake, a fraud, an approximation attraction that's playing at being real.

"Would you all like to know more about the history of the chapel?" asks the woman. Her voice sounds worried as she looks at me. "There's real medieval graffiti right over here. . . ."

Jett puts an arm around my shoulders. "We're okay, thanks." His arm is warm, real, and not super-fucking disappointing like everything else. "Let's get out of here. I've got one more surprise."

I swipe my hand across my face and stand up. As we leave, I don't even look at Joan's statue. All my reverence from the moment before is gone. Replaced by the cold, hard facts. Craptastic Reality 1, Mystery of History 0.

Maybe Marquette isn't so great after all.

Jett keeps his arm around me as we walk to the car. A traitorous sob bursts from me as we walk.

"What's up?" His eyebrows come together.

"It's all just so fake and frustrating, and I don't know . . ."

My emotions from last night are still catching up. I'm crying for stupid things like a fridge that can't keep food cold. A job where I'm allowed to serve beer to frat boys but not ride a horse. And the lingering suspicion that my Big Plan is as fake and foolish as a chapel brought stone by stone from France to trick people.

Jett hugs me until I'm done crying.

"Sorry," I say, swiping my hand across my wet eyes and snotty nose because I'm classy like that. "I'm just . . . overwhelmed . . ."

"One more surprise," he says again, a smile tugging at the edge of his eyes. "Promise you'll feel better . . ."

WE DRIVE THROUGH DOWNTOWN, HEADING EAST PAST skyscrapers toward Lake Michigan. It's a bright, breezy spring day, and dozens of sailboats dot the horizon. The metal wings on the Milwaukee Art Museum are closed because it's so windy, making it look like a giant tropical flower that's sleeping. There's something else in the sky too—kites. Hundreds of them soar above Veterans Park, a wide expanse of grass, willow trees, and picnic spots beside the harbor. As we get out of the car, the clanking of sail rigging and the screech of seagulls sound like a nautical symphony.

"What's happening here?" I point to the kites and the crowds of people beneath them.

"Spring Kite Festival." Jett grins. He grabs a blanket and his ratty green backpack from the van. "My grandparents used to live in Milwaukee, and we'd come to this festival every year."

"It's magnificent." My mood lifts as we move through the crowd, rising higher with each gust of wind and dance of the kites.

There's a group from Chicago doing competitive, synchronized kite flying (who knew such a thing was possible?!) to Aerosmith; vendors selling everything from snow cones to vacation packages; and packs of children holding kite strings and gaping at the anarchy of geometry above them. Jett and I find a spot near some trees where a group of teenagers have strung a rainbow of hammocks.

Jett spreads the blanket out and we sit down to eat warm PB&J sandwiches.

"My younger brothers helped me pack these," he says apologetically through a mouthful. "Oh! And my mom told me to tell you that she's excited you're challenging the dominant patriarchal hegemony of the Castle."

Since she teaches Feminist and Gender Studies in addition to anthropology, sentences like this from Jett's mom are like my mom saying, "Kit, mow the grass."

Which I'm clearly not doing, but so it goes.

"Your mom is awesome." I put my sandwich down and lean back on my elbows.

"She is," Jett agrees. "And so are you."

I smile to myself. Jett, like Layla, is the best kind of best friend. Positive, affirming, fierce, and not afraid to push me when I need it. I just hope I'm as good a friend to him as he is to me.

He finishes his sandwich and lies beside me. Our shoulders barely touch as we stare up at the sky. The kites flutter, dip, sway, and soar, a mesmerizing display of canvas and caprice. The wind picks up my hair and wraps me in the smell of Jett's coconut lavender lotion. His mom also insists on all organic, natural products for her kids, so Jett always smells vaguely like a garden and a cookie at the same time.

"This is perfect." I rest my hands on my stomach and close my eyes as the sun warms my face.

"It is," says Jett, shifting around so his head nuzzles between the curve of my neck and shoulder.

Which of course sends my stupid heart racing. But also is a perfectly friendly thing for best friends to do. Right? As far as I can tell he's feeling nothing out of the ordinary from our proximity.

"You should open the letter," says Jett after a few moments of kite watching.

I exhale sharply. "I don't know. After the disappointment of the Joan of Arc chapel being a fake, maybe I don't even want to go there."

"Don't be ridiculous. You have other reasons. C'mon. Open it. I want to see."

He pokes me in the shoulder repeatedly. "C'mon, c'mon, c'mon!"

"So. Annoying!" I say with a laugh. "Okay, fine."

Pulling the letter out of my bag, I take a deep breath. I don't want to spoil our perfect afternoon, but it's better to open it here. With Jett. Because—even if it's a no—I can look at the lake, the city, the kites, and remember that life is full of beauty.

I slide my finger along the envelope and slip out the paper.

"Be brave," says Jett, poking me in the shoulder again.

Please let it be a yes. Please let it be a yes. Please let it be a—

"YES!!!" I shout, startling the family on a blanket beside ours. I sit up quickly, brandishing my letter. "It's a yes!"

"Ahhhhh!" says Jett. He pulls me to my feet in one fluid motion. "It's a yes!"

We jump up and down together for a moment. A few people cheer with us, raising beers. They probably think we just got engaged.

"I'm so happy," I say to Jett as we settle back onto the blanket.

"I'm so happy for you." He bites into an apple. "Does it say anything about financial aid?"

I skim the letter again. "Nope. Just that they're still considering my scholarship application and they'll let me know soon."

"That's okay though. Today is a good day."

"Today is a good day," I agree.

Above us the kites sail through the spring sky, and I can't think of anywhere I'd rather be. Something in me has a sense that this is what the Big Plan is all about. Having the freedom to rest in the sunshine on a beautiful day and look up at the sky with delight. Being in a city that's so big, I can't even imagine all the stories unfolding within it. All of a sudden, I want to move here and go to Marquette so badly it's like an ache. This is the life I want, and dammit, I'll find a way to earn the money I need to make this happen.

IT'S LATE AFTERNOON BY THE TIME JETT DROPS ME OFF AT home. He's going straight to the Castle for his shift. On the way home, I explained the rough outline of the plan I came up with last night, and Jett was perfectly encouraging and curious. As per what an amazing-hot-smart-funny-best-friend-who-I'm-decidedly-not-starting-to-crush-on should be.

"Thank you for today." I open the door, wanting to hug him or something, but feeling uncharacteristically shy.

"Any time. Seriously. And if you go to Marquette, I'll be up there all the time to hang out by the lake with you. You know that, right?"

He smiles at me and I have a sudden vision of us having many more afternoons like the Kite Festival one. Except maybe with more kissing.

"I'd like that," I manage, trying to hide my flushed cheeks.

Jett's already been accepted to a filmmaking program at the school where his parents teach. Between their tuition discount and his academic scholarships, he won't end up paying a cent for college.

Lucky.

"Oh, hey, wait," he says as I open the car door.

He reaches behind the seat, grabs his backpack, and shoves it into my hands. I unzip it: Four more sandwiches, two boxes of granola bars, some oranges, and a chocolate bar as big as my forearm rest inside.

"End-of-the-world supplies?" I ask, trying to smile through my now-redder cheeks.

Jett looks away. "My brothers are zealous sandwich makers. And I just figured you might want them."

He figured I might need these supplies more than he does, is what he doesn't say. Which isn't wrong. But it's the closest we've come to acknowledging the fact that my house is still dark and I eat like I'm not getting a next meal. I want to hand the backpack back to him, but I can't. Throwing away food or passing it up when it's free goes against every survival instinct I have.

"You can give me the bag back tomorrow or whenever we see each other next," says Jett. "Since we don't have school this week, it's not a big deal."

This food is a huge deal. But I'm not going to cry about it.

Not until he's pulled away at least.

"Thanks," I say at last. I'll leave Mom some of the food on the table as a peace offering.

There's a moment of uncomfortable silence. Jett runs his hands through his hair. "Is there anything I can do to help with phase one of the plan?" he says at last.

I think for a moment. "Maybe you can be our official film-maker?"

"I could totally do that!" Excitement fills his voice. "I'm thinking we do a bit of backstory, then film the training sessions, and then interview people at the Castle." A gleam lights Jett's eyes. I can practically see his brain boiling over with ideas.

"I love it," I say. "I'll let you know more when we have a few more people recruited."

"This is going to be amazing," says Jett. "Talk to you later!"

"Have fun in the Dark Ages!"

"As you wish, m'lady," says Jett with an over-the-top smol-dery-Westley-from-*The Princess Bride*-type stare.

Stupid sexy, funny best friend.

As Jett drives off, the sound of banging and hammering rings out behind the house. That sound can only mean that Chris is in his blacksmithing shed, working on something. The grass is shorter now, like it's had a shaggy haircut, and our nonmotorized push mower leans against the garage. Bless him; he mowed the lawn for me.

Taking out two of the sandwiches as a thank-you gift, I go

around the house. The shed door is open, and Chris stands behind a homemade wooden table, wrapping wire around a long metal pole. His hair sits on top of his head in a messy man bun, and he's got headphones on.

The nice thing about doing blacksmithing as a hobby is that it's mostly electricity-free, and you can use recycled materials. Chris's thing is being a sustainable metalworker, so he goes around town picking up scrap steel and aluminum and bending, twisting, and forcing it into the shape of medieval armor. It's decidedly niche but also pays well among certain Renaissance Faire types on eBay.

"How's it going?" I say, tapping him on the shoulder. He jumps about a foot and there's a rattle as he drops the metal pole.

"Jesus, Kit. Warn a guy next time." He smiles and takes off his headphones. There's sweat on his upper lip, and even on this breezy spring day, it's boiling in the shed. He nods toward the pile of silver rings at the end of the table. "Five thousand down, just fifteen thousand more to go."

"Are you making chain mail for an elephant?" I unwrap one of the sandwiches and hold it out to him. He takes a bite without using his hands since they're covered in giant gloves.

"It's for a knee-length shirt," he says through a mouthful of peanut butter. "I'm doing all the rings at once. It's a rush order for an event out in California. Hoping to get a bunch of it done before work tonight."

Making chain mail is a tedious process. You have to wind a

length of wire around a long pole, snip it off with wire cutters into small rings, tighten the rings with pliers as you attach them to each other, and then fashion it all together into a shirt.

"Can I help?"

"A hundred fifty links to a row." Chris nods toward a pair of pliers and some gloves as he devours both sandwiches.

Pulling on the gloves, I start pinching the rings together into a long line.

"Thanks for mowing the grass. Mom would've killed me if it wasn't done."

"No need to thank me. Thank you for taking my shift last night. What did you do today?"

I tell him about going to Milwaukee with Jett, leaving out the disappointment of the Joan of Arc chapel being fake but lingering on kites and my MU acceptance.

He drops his pliers. "Kit! Way to bury the lede!"

"What?" I try to make my voice sound like I don't know what he's talking about, but I can't stop the smile that spreads over my face.

"You got in! That's wonderful news!" He punches my shoulder lightly. "How do you feel about it?"

I punch him back. "Ugh. I'm super excited. And super worried about how we're going to pay for it if I don't get some of those scholarships. And super nervous. And super positive that I need to make more money this summer to save up. And super—"

"When do you find out about scholarships?"

I take a steadying breath, trying to calm the anxiety that creeps through my chest as I think about Marquette. "They didn't say for sure, but it should be soon."

Chris takes up his pliers again. "You'll figure it out. You always do."

"Speaking of figuring things out, how did the talk with Len go?" I keep pinching rings together, my hands already aching.

Chris makes a dismissive noise, not looking up. "I don't think you're going to get fired. But Len's pissed and he says you need to go talk to him before your next shift."

At least that's not for a few more days.

I sigh. I'd almost forgotten about the stress of the Castle during today's perfect afternoon. "I'll work it out with him. But I'm angry too. I did a good job yesterday! And the crowd loved it. I should be able to fight as a Knight. I'd go through the Squire training and everything. I just want the chance."

"I know you do. But I don't see how we can make it work."

"Ahhhh, but I have a plan."

Chris side eyes me. "A Kit Sweetly Official Plan?"

"You know it. And I need your help. Do you think you could train me and a few other people next week? It's spring break, so we have lots of time."

"Train you as Knights? In a week?" Chris shakes out his hand and begins on another row. "It takes a lot longer than a week for us current Knights to learn a new routine. And most of us have been doing this for years."

"You don't have to teach us everything," I say quickly. "But we need to show Len and the Corporate folks that we can fight. And ride. And use a lance to catch rings."

"Who do you have in mind for it?"

I shrug. "Me, Layla, and whoever else wants a chance. I'm going to ask around at the Castle and see. I bet there's a ton of people just waiting to throw off the dominant patriarchal hegemony."

Jett's mom's words feel clunky in my mouth, but I like the authority they lend to my mission.

Chris doesn't even blink at my twenty-dollar words. "What's the end goal? Some kind of tournament? You going to tie up the other Knights and take their places?"

"Yes to the tournament, and I'm hoping you can help with the other Knights. Convince them to let us have a chance. We don't need to take their places, we just want to fight alongside them."

"You're really serious about this?"

"Serious as the threat of plague in seventeenth-century Venice."

Chris wipes sweat off his forehead and grins. "I'll help you. Though you know not all the other Knights are as cringingly dude-bro as Dalton. Some of them are actually nice guys."

Although he's not good friends with the Blue or Yellow Knights, Chris has been buddies with the Purple Knight, a laid-back Black guy named Austin, for a long time. In fact, Layla, Jett, and I spent the better part of last summer with

Chris, Austin, and a few other Castle folks at Austin's family's lake house.

"I know," I admit. "But that doesn't mean the other Knights besides you and Austin will be happy to give us a chance."

"True. And you're right that you deserve a chance. It was good to see you out there, and you really did kill it. It was all I could do to not yell 'That's my kid sister!'"

"You're adorable. Have you seen the video?"

I pull out my phone and we watch it together. It's now up to fifty thousand views. Chris claps when I knock out the Green Knight.

"It's my favorite moment ever. Totally badass. And you should've heard how mad Dalton was after the show. But do you really think you can make it go viral?"

I bite my bottom lip. "Maybe? I really think that with Layla's and Jett's help we have a chance. And if we do that, then maybe the Castle will feel enough pressure to let me be a Knight this summer. And then I can make enough money to save for Marquette and help Mom out."

"Don't worry about Mom," says Chris. "I've got it handled on the home front."

I arch an eyebrow at him. "You know she's not been paying the mortgage, right?"

Chris drops the pliers again. "What're you talking about?"

"I saw a notice last night. Third warning or something. She owes almost four thousand dollars."

"Impossible. She uses her checks from the office job for that. And I give her money for it every month."

"I'm not sure why she's behind. I just know what I saw."

A worried look crosses Chris's face. "I'll talk to her. I'm sure it's just a mistake."

"Let me know what you find out."

He nods, thinking. It could be no big deal, or it could be a huge deal. We both know this. Although Mom's been better lately, her impulse buys have landed us in financial trouble before. The month after my dad left, she spent three months of tips on a spontaneous trip for all of us to Cancún. We didn't end up going because there was no money left to pay for hotels and food when we got there, so she ended up losing all the money she'd paid for airfare.

We work in silence until my phone buzzes.

Layla: Ready for me to pick you up?

Kit: Give me half an hour.

I say goodbye to Chris, who's closing up shop so he can get ready for his shift tonight, and hurry inside. I dump the contents of Jett's backpack out on the table and hope Mom will find the food. Then I take a freezing-cold shower, throw some clothes and my homework into Jett's backpack, and wait outside for Layla.

12

AYLA PULLS UP EXACTLY THIRTY MINUTES LATER. HER purple Jeep is sparkly clean like it's just been washed and she's got the top down and the doors off.

When I get in the car she's practically vibrating with excitement. "Kit, Kit, Kit, Kit, Kit!"

"What's up with you?" I say, giggling at Layla's infectious energy. Even though I'm still worried about Mom, unpaid bills, and everything else in between, it's impossible not to smile when Layla's like this. "Too many Red Bulls?"

"Ha! Not even. Look at that!" She points to a sheet of paper on the dashboard.

I texted Layla my whole plan last night. She's typed it up and printed it out, so we now have a master copy. I pick up the sheet and read over the plan again.

## KIT'S PLAN FOR THE CASTLE

- **PHASE 1:** Make my video viral + connect a website, merchandise, history lessons to it. Somehow? Get Layla's help with this. Also, submit plan to Castle contest and push on it with online pressure.

- **PHASE 2:** Convince others to join me. Get Chris to help me train them as Knights!

- **PHASE 3:** Set up a tournament with current Knights so new Knights can show off skills.

- **PHASE 4:** When Castle execs are here, run the tournament and SHOW them what a good idea this is and how many people it can bring in.

"This looks great," I say. "But why are you literally vibrating with excitement?"

"Phase One has started!" Layla shoves her iPad at me. It's open to a website—www.thegirlknight.com—that declares in bold letters: THE GIRL KNIGHT WILL FIGHT ANOTHER DAY!

My face stares back at me in cartoon form, and then the video of my fight is below it.

"Read that." Layla jabs a finger at the text below the video.

"Last night, the one and only Girl Knight, KIT SWEETLY, fought a brave battle against the medieval notion that only men should fight at the Castle! What kind of message does that send to our kids? Folks, we live in the day of female American Ninja Warriors and women generals. Surely we can reflect this in the Castle's arena!

"We know there weren't many female fighters in the Middle Ages—though there were some!—but at the risk of being anachronistic, we implore you: Sign our petition! Tell the Castle it's time for a change. LET KIT FIGHT!"

Layla beams at me. "We've gotten almost a thousand signatures already. And it's really taking off. I'm going to make T-shirts and posters. You need to come up with some good stuff about badass medieval women for us to put on the site."

I'm stunned. Like in a good way, but also in an ice cream–headache kind of way. Because my vague notion of phase 1 now looks so shiny and professional.

"I love this. You're the best! And perhaps the fastest. I can't believe you've done this already."

Layla's creativity is legendary, and she's always leaping into projects. It gives me whiplash sometimes, but in the best possible way.

"We're going to change things, trust me. I can't wait to start training!" exclaims Layla.

"Even though you won't be here in a few months?"

My heart aches at the thought of not seeing Layla every day, but I push that thought way down.

With a wave to Chris, who's dressed in his Knight's gear and leaving the house, Layla backs out of my driveway. "I don't necessarily want to fight. But I want the chance to consider it as an option. That's what this is all about."

Absolutely.

"I'm not even sure I still have a job," I admit as I buckle my seat belt. Layla floors it and flings us around a corner.

"Worry about that tomorrow," she says. "Tonight, we have work to do!"

As we drive, I fill her in on Jett's contribution to the plan. We both agree that a documentary-style film about our journey to knighthood will help things tremendously.

Before long we're turning into her driveway. Her house sits at the end of a tree-lined corridor, and you can't even see it from the road. The house itself is a four-story Tudor that looks like it should've been featured on some *Real Housewives of Chicago* show. Horses graze in the field behind her house— that's how Layla got into working at the Castle, through her love of horses. It's only luck that her parents sent her to the public school in my district and not one of the many private schools that kids who live in houses like hers go to.

She parks in the driveway, which is so wide it could probably hold a private plane, and we go around the back. Her yard is terraced—the outdoor pool and cabana are closest to the house, then the tennis and basketball courts, and then the gardens, lawn, and fields below it. She grew up here, so the sheer opulence of the place doesn't faze her. But I still gawk every time I visit. Even after nearly a decade of friendship.

When I first met Layla, we were both in third grade. I lived in a mobile home in the middle of a trailer park that had seen better days. The first time I spent the night at her house, I cried when my mom picked me up.

*Mom looked over at me, tears in her eyes too, and handed me a tissue. "You okay, Kit-Kat?"*

*I nodded and wiped my sniffly nose. "I just wish we lived in a place like that."*

*"Me too," Mom had said. "But life is different for everybody. We've got enough."*

I went home that day—at eight years old—and wrote out my first version of the Big Plan. Item number one was "Buy a Nice House."

I left the list on my bed, so my mom could see it. If she did, she never said anything, but a few months later, right around my ninth birthday, my dad inherited some money from his grandfather. My parents used part of that money to buy the split-level house we still live in today. It's not paid off, but the first time I walked into it, I felt like a queen, entering her castle.

"Whatcha thinking about?" says Layla, stopping as she opens the back door.

I hadn't realized that I was staring out over the yard, lost in my memories.

I shrug. "The first time I came here."

Layla laughs. "Oh yeah. That was the sleepover when you first rode a horse, and then we had the roller-skating party in the basement and ate so many Cheetos we almost threw up!"

Layla's basement has an indoor pool, a roller rink, three bedrooms, and a home theater. It's preposterous and miraculous.

"I'd forgotten about the Cheetos," I say, smiling. We've had so many sleepovers, and I've spent most of them in some sort of "stunned poor girl who's slack-jawed at how rich people live" frame of mind.

"Let's go," says Layla. "I've got a good evening planned."

Layla's room is like a mini-apartment. She has a separate sitting area with couches and a big-screen TV; her own bathroom with a waterfall shower and whirlpool tub; and a closet that's as big as my bedroom. Total stereotypical rich girl's room, except it's messy as hell, since she won't let the cleaning staff into it, and she's decorated it with her own art. Dragons, elves, horses, robots, cartoon characters, and caricatures cover the walls and ceiling. In one corner a drop cloth protects the carpet. She's working on a mural that looks like it's out of the pages of a book about Japan.

"Oh my God, this is gorgeous," I say, walking over to the painting. There's a giant swath of cherry blossom trees, mountains, and temples. Pencil outlines of Hokusai-like waves and then kids in jeans and T-shirts who look like people we go to school with are below the trees.

"I'm having fun with that one. Did you see this yet?"

Layla goes to her closet and flicks on the light. A huge mural of Roller Derby girls with manga-style faces fills one wall. "I've

started going to some of the matches lately and had to draw it."
Her fingers linger on a pretty girl with short pink hair.

"Nice," I say, stepping back to admire. Her talent really is
unbelievable, and the years of art lessons have only refined
her style. What will make her famous, however, is her sense of
humor in the art. There are little playful touches throughout
the murals. "When I make a million dollars, I'll hire you to
paint the inside of my house like this."

"I'll do it for free. Anytime." She blows me a kiss.

She's been offering to paint my bedroom for years, but I
think a huge mural might kill my mom. Plus, it means that
Layla would have to see the inside of my house. Which I've
managed to not have her do since my dad left and things got
really tough.

"Movie and phase one?" I ask. "I need to use your Internet
to look up stuff about going viral. Ours at home is acting up
again."

It's a little lie. Not a big deal between friends, right?

Layla nods. "I was thinking *A Knight's Tale*."

"Perfect." I plug my phone in, since it's nearly dead again,
and Layla turns on the movie.

Although we've seen *A Knight's Tale* dozens of times, it's
endlessly impeccable in all its cheesiness.

We sing along to all the songs—like Queen's "We Will
Rock You" at the beginning—which are super anachronistic
and that's why it's funny. The plot is dorky and yet painfully

familiar. Poor peasant Heath Ledger wants to change his stars, so he fakes his way into being a knight. But he's handsome and pretty good at jousting, so he fights, gets a princess—who's both fierce and fickle, like they almost wanted to make her a feminist but couldn't quite get there, and dressed like she's ready for a rave in 1497—and then lo! Heath is knighted for real. Also, it features Chaucer, who spends the movie dressed like he's going to an Ibiza beach festival, and the always sinister glower of Rufus Sewell.

I love it so much, as does Layla.

Basic takeaways here: You can change your stars, ensemble casts are the best, and all of life should be set to as many Queen songs as possible.

As we watch, I skim articles about going viral. According to them, "going viral" generally means your content spreads across the Internet and social media superfast. To be officially viral, it's got to touch millions of people in a few days. Kind of like the Black Death did in medieval Europe, but—thankfully—without the Hieronymus Bosch horror-scape.

"So, according to this, we need like five million views in three days to technically be considered viral," I say to Layla. "Though there is disagreement. Generally, I think if we could get a million views of the video and then really get people talking about it, we'd see some change. I mean, look at this story."

I show her an article about a teen guy who worked at Target.

Somebody thought he was cute, so they took his picture and posted it on Twitter, and by the end of the day he had three hundred thousand new followers. His fame exploded from there.

Layla shrugs. "He's okay, but Internet-sensation hot? I don't think so."

"He got onto *Ellen* for this photo."

She shakes her head. "People are weird. So, how do we make you the next Alex from Target?"

I read another list: "According to this we need to 'have quality content'—done—'know our audience and pair with influencers . . .'"

Layla laughs. "Do we know any influencers who care about the Castle?"

"Eddy Jackson?" I say, thinking about our favorite big tipper. "Maybe some of his friends will tweet something out?"

"Fair point. I'll write him down and see if we can figure out how to contact him. What about others? Know any history professors or famous feminists? Besides Jett's mom, who's not even a little bit famous. Or on Twitter—I already asked. Do you think we can get Roxane Gay to retweet your video?"

"Oh sure, no problem. I'll just call her."

"It could happen," protests Layla. "Might as well try."

"We can try. But what we really need is like an army of a hundred thousand teens in on this. And moms. And Girl Scout troops. And people with little kids. We need them coming to the Castle to cheer us on for the statement it makes. And we need this to be bigger than me. I'm just a white girl from the suburbs. Maybe my privilege makes it easier for me to say this isn't fair, but we need to show people that this is about more than just me doing a man's job. It's about getting rid of gender restrictions altogether."

Layla chews on her pencil for a moment. "Agree. But how to convey that message?"

"Maybe in addition to Jett filming the training, we shoot bios of the other new Knights? Just to help people understand why changes at the Castle matter on both a general level and a personal one."

"That's a good plan. What else do we need to do?"

I skim another article. "It recommends we make interactive content too."

"We can do that," says Layla. She starts furiously clicking away on her laptop. "Open your Twitter for me."

I haven't even looked at my Twitter or Instagram in all this. But when I click on it on my phone, Layla whistles.

"You may only have—" she checks the views on the video, "sixty-five thousand views, but somebody found your social media. Look. They linked it to the video."

My jaw drops. "That can't be real."

In one day, my Twitter has jumped from like three hundred followers (all friends, family, and people at school) to two thousand. And my Instagram is even higher.

Suddenly, I'm feeling a bit unsure about this whole thing. Like overexposed. Or too famous in a not-famous way. I let out a shaky breath.

"Breathe," says Layla, offering me a bottle of water. "This is good and we can use it."

Taking a few sips of water, I calm down.

"You're right," I say. "Okay, let's link these accounts to the website and the petition. And let's also drop a hint about the tournament."

"I'm on it. Did you send your ideas to Corporate yet?"

I swear. "Knew I forgot something. I'll do it now."

As Layla clicks around, linking things to websites and my social media, I pull the crumpled flyer from my pocket. So much depends on the Castle seeing why this could be a good idea. It doesn't matter if we go totally viral if they aren't on board to make it all possible.

I write a long email, explaining why gender restrictions at the Castle are limiting and how we can change things for the better, and then I explain why this is more reflective of the Middle Ages. After all that, I link to my video, website, and the petition. Finally, I propose the tournament as the time for us new Knights to showcase our talent and skills.

With a deep breath and a prayer to the badass ladies of the Middle Ages, I hit Send.

The movie ended a while ago, and while she was waiting for me, Layla has painted a Godzilla monster onto one of her

Kyoto temples. We decide to go get some pizza and stop by the Castle.

"Maybe we can run into Jett," I say. "I've still got his backpack."

"And how did you happen to come by that?" Layla says with a smirk.

I tell her quickly about Jett's and my day in Milwaukee and getting into Marquette. After an appropriate amount of squealing about MU, she shoots me a look.

"And you have no interest in Jett?" she asks as we walk through her house. "None at all?"

I duck my head, smiling. "That thought is not allowed. Not now, not ever. He's a friend. Nothing more."

Layla stops in the entrance hall, that project-to-get-started-on gleam in her eyes. "Uh-huh."

I grab her arm. "Do not—I repeat—do not try to set us up."

A smile flickers across her face. "Of course not! I'd never think of setting you up with someone who's smart, obviously adores you, makes you laugh, and is absolutely gorgeous. Why in the world would I want that for my best friend?"

"Just leave it alone," I beg. "Tell me about your love life. Have you gotten rid of Eric yet?"

"He persists," she says. "But I'm taking your advice. Sort of." A mischievous look crosses her face and she holds up her phone. "He just invited me to the Castle's Ninja after-party tonight, and I think we should go."

Last year, the big bosses at the Castle's parent company mandated that we have "Family Dinner" once a month. It's supposed to be a time for us all to eat, drink, and be merry. No alcohol, no sex with coworkers, just good, honest medieval-style "Castle Family" fun.

Welp.

You can imagine how long that lasted.

Now, Len lets us have one super-top-secret Ninja after-party every month instead of "Family Dinner." The invitations go out half an hour before the event. You can bring outside guests if you're discreet. You can bring booze, but you better have a designated driver. And you're not allowed to post pics on social media.

What happens at Ninja after-party stays there. Unless it doesn't. Which also happens with all the hookups and drama that the party encourages. So far, Corporate hasn't found out about the parties yet. And since Len's band plays at the party, his normally rigid stance on rules bends when he can jam all night on his guitar.

I usually avoid the Ninja after-parties, because what's fouler than your uncle pretending he's hipster Kid Rock? And my dad is a recovering alcoholic, so I don't drink that much, and I have the Big Plan, which could be messed up if someone takes pictures of me drinking.

But this could also be the perfect chance to enact phase two: Convince Others to Join Us!

I glance at my phone. It's after ten now, and the show should be wrapping up soon.

Layla grips my arm. "Please, please, please can we go?"

With a long-suffering sigh, I nod, and she grabs her keys. Together we walk out of her house and into the night.

The only sounds outside Layla's house are the fountain burbling in the gardens, about a million crickets, and classical music from her parents' open window. The house is so big, I had no idea Layla's parents were even home, so it's almost comforting to hear the music and know someone else is here.

But the whole thing is kind of lonely.

As I clamber into Layla's Jeep, I put forward my conditions: "I'll be the designated driver, but no dancing to Len's music—even if you are drunk, you can't do it—and no making out with Eric."

"I promise," says Layla. "I'll drive on the way over. Buckle up." She grins and then backs out of her driveway like she's auditioning for a spot in Formula 1 racing.

Once I've stopped hanging on to the Jeep's roll bars for dear life, I text Jett.

Kit: Phase one is going well! We're going to the Ninja afterparty to recruit people. You going to be there?

I try to keep the desperate note of pleading out of my voice, while trying to ignore the kangaroos that lurch around my stomach when I think about Jett pulling up to the Castle on his motorcycle, in his stupid leather jacket, looking all hot.

And then my mind flicks to an image of the two of us, drinking warm beer out of plastic cups on the roof, snuggled under a blanket beneath the stars.

Goddammit. Kit.

Unbreakable. Rules.

Jett is totally off-limits.

And he doesn't think of you like that. If he did, he'd have given you a hint or clue or something.

While I'm spiraling, he replies.

Jett: Already on my way home, but I'll try to get back there before too long.

I take myself in hand with a third person–style pep talk: You, Kit Sweetly, are the master of your own destiny. You'll change your stars. You'll make it to Marquette, go to law school, make millions of dollars, and buy your mom a house like Layla's.

But you won't make a move on Jett. Not now. Not ever.

Taking a deep breath, I text back.

Kit: No worries. If you're already headed home, no need to come back out. Have a good night!

I shove my phone into my purse after that, not wanting to see his reply.

"Everything okay?" asks Layla. "Jett going to be there?"

"He's already almost home," I say. "So, it's just you and me. Don't abandon me for the sake of Eric."

"Never," says Layla as we pull into the Castle parking lot.

## 13

THE PARKING LOT IS EMPTY EXCEPT FOR STAFF CARS. WE go around the back to the employee entrance. Two busboys in medieval-style vests and linen shirts puff on a joint behind the dumpster. I know them by sight, but I don't know their names.

"Kit!" they say in unison as we approach. One bows to me and flourishes his giant feathered hat. "Welcome, liberator of the fairer sex here at the Castle."

"Oh, for heaven's sake," I say under my breath.

"Told you you're famous," says Layla, poking me in the arm.

Penny, a trans Serving Wench in her early twenties, comes outside at that moment. She's got a pack of Camels in her hand, and her red lipstick and pale skin are flawless under the streetlights. She's Chris's BFF and she's worked with us as long as I can remember.

"Can I get one of those?" I ask.

"Sure you want to do that?" asks Penny as she re-twists her long black hair into a knot at the back of her neck. "A Knight needs to be in top physical condition."

She wrinkles her nose, mimicking one of Len's speeches when he caught Chris, her, and a bunch of the other Knights and Wenches having a poker game and smoking cigars during an after-party.

"Shut up, Wench," I say affectionately.

She grins and holds out the pack. Layla and I both take one and light up using Penny's lighter. I have a rule with cigarettes: Don't smoke them at home or at school, in the car, or at Layla's house. But I crack as soon as I get to work. I grew up hating the smell of smoke, thanks to being the child of smokers, but smoking is practically a rite of passage at the restaurant. The first week I worked here, I came outside during my break for some fresh air. There was a circle of servers sitting on filthy milk crates, puffing on smokes and bitching about their jobs. I stood outside the circle for a few seconds before pulling up my own crate and bumming a cigarette. It was the start of my social smoking habit and an instant in with the Castle staff.

I missed my nightly cigarette last night, and so I take it slow tonight. Nicotine dances through my bloodstream as I inhale deeply, pulling in the smoke and enjoying the burn all the way down. I know this is bad for me, but it's also a part of life at the Castle. Especially among us drudges.

Penny, Layla, and I chat about tonight's show as we smoke—it was a rough one, apparently. Len was in fine form but Princess Jessica kissed the Green Knight on the floor, which makes me worry about whether Chris saw it or not.

Penny sees my look and nods. "Yeah. Chris was there when it happened. Jess made a big show of passing him by to give Green a favor and a kiss. He handled it well, but I wouldn't bet on them not getting into another fight before the party's over."

"Poor Chris," says Layla. "He deserves better."

I've always secretly wished Layla would date my brother. She certainly was all about that when we were kids, but I've not heard her mention it in years.

"He'll find someone better," says Penny, pushing her boobs up higher so they're practically spilling out of her dress. "Even if I have to set him up with someone myself. Also, did he tell you that Len said I could try out to be a Knight if and only if I ride out as a man?"

Layla and I both make noises of disgust.

"Unbelievable!" I say. "That's so unfair."

Penny nods. "Chris told him off for sure, but Len's unrelenting. So, fuck that. Unless of course you can get him to change the rules. I ride as the woman I am or not at all."

"Damn right," says Layla.

"I'm definitely working on it," I say. "Any chance you'd be interested in training with us this week? We're meeting at Layla's house on Monday at two p.m."

"I'm in," says Penny. "Anything to make this place less medieval."

She laughs, but there's a hard, determined glint in her eye as she stomps out her cigarette.

"Feel free to tell others," adds Layla. "The more people we get to join our crusade, the more likely we are to succeed."

"Your crusade?" Penny lifts one perfectly arched eyebrow.

I blush. "Well, maybe not crusade. But we have a plan."

"A four-phase Kit Sweetly plan," Layla adds.

"Ahhhh," says Penny. "I love a good Kit Sweetly plan. You sure it can work?"

"I'm sure we're going to try," I say. "Chris thinks we can be ready before the Corporate folks get here."

"As always, I'm impressed by your initiative, ladies," says Penny with an exaggerated curtsy. "I'm going to try to find Chris and make sure he's behaving himself. See you in there."

We wave to her as she disappears through the Castle door.

"Chris would go out with you," I say to Layla. "You know that, right?"

"He was my eighth-grade crush, Kit." Layla waves her hand through the smoke she's just exhaled. "Much as I love him like a brother, I don't think about him like that. When I move to New York, I'll find someone more serious there."

"Fair enough," I say. "Let's get this after-party over with already."

We both flick out our cigarettes.

"It's going to be fun," Layla says, checking her lipstick in her handheld mirror.

"Your words, not mine." I smooth down my hair and brace myself for what's on the other side of the door.

14

DANCE MUSIC PUMPS OUT OF LOUDSPEAKERS IN THE GREAT Hall. The Castle bar is supposed to be closed, but two bartenders stand behind it, pouring liquor into five-gallon buckets to make punch.

"Are they stealing booze?" I knew people drank at these parties, but I can't imagine Len just giving cocktails away.

"Nah. It's from the bottles everybody brings. If we want to drink, we either have to pay or give a bottle." Layla opens up her bag, revealing three mostly full liquor bottles. One is brown rum, another is raspberry vodka, and the third is a lurid shade of blue. "My parents left these in the cabana after a party last month. They'll never miss them."

As she threads her way over to the bar, a pair of hands grabs me, spins me around, and pulls me into a hug.

Alex, the Castle's resident photographer, squeezes the life out of me. Tonight, their short brown hair is swept to one side, and their rainbow-rimmed glasses stand out brightly against their light brown skin.

"I can't breathe, " I gasp, giving Alex a quick hug back.

Alex started working at the Castle around the time Layla and I did. We've been work buddies for years, but never as good of friends as I know we could've been because Alex is always super busy. They're valedictorian of our senior class, president of two photography clubs (school and city), *and* blocker on our local Roller Derby team (nickname Tyrannosaurus Lex).

Alex grins and drains their cup. "You were a marvel! Sheer poetry on horseback. Let me get you a drink."

They drag me to the bar where Layla's trading the liquor bottles for a jewel-encrusted cup of punch.

Alex pushes a full cup into my hands.

"I'm the driver." I shake my head. "I'll just get a bottle of water."

"Don't be ridiculous," says Alex. "We're celebrating you tonight! Right, folks?"

A group of other Wenches, Pages, and female Castle workers standing by the bar raise their glasses and shout, "THREE CHEERS FOR KIT!"

I look over at Layla, who's chugging her first drink. She smiles and raises her cup. "Go for it! We can always get an

Uber back to my house."

I know I have rules, plans, and I shouldn't. But it's delicious to bask in the praise of my friends. To forget about my worries for a moment and just unwind. Light blue liquor sloshes out of the cup I take from Alex. It smells like something that should be dripping from a car.

I raise my glass: "To a new era at the Castle!"

"Hear! Hear!" Layla and Alex shout.

As we drink, I tell Alex about our training schedule during spring break.

They check their phone for a moment and then smile. "I can make it. And I will. Even if it means moving around a few things."

I snort. Alex is the only person I know who makes more lists than me. Serious evidence we'd be good friends if either of us had any free time.

Layla, Alex, and I clink glasses. We tell a few other people about the training, including Lizzy and Mags, the Wenches I ran into after my first fight as the Red Knight.

"Are you sure Len is cool with this?" asks Mags, glancing up at the stage where Len's band is setting up. Tonight the tips of her hair are fire-engine red, and she's wearing a Ramones tank top, so all her tattoos are on display.

I shrug. "If we can get more guests to the Castle, he'll have to be cool with it."

It's not quite a lie, but it's a far cry from the truth too.

The blue punch goes down smooth, and before I'm done with it, Layla drags me to the dance floor. The electronic dance music has been replaced by Len's shitty band pounding out Pearl Jam, but who cares. As long as Len doesn't stop the performance to yell at me, I'm good. And right now, he's so into channeling early '90s Eddie Vedder, he wouldn't notice me unless I unplugged his guitar.

One cup of punch becomes three somehow, and the dance floor begins to spin. My skin's too tight for my body.

"I'm going to sit down," I call out to Layla.

She's dancing hip to hip with a lovely pink-haired girl who's one of Alex's Roller Derby friends and who looks suspiciously like the painting on Layla's closet wall. Layla's always dated both boys and girls, and I wonder how long she and Ms. Pink Hair have known each other.

The way they move together gives me all sorts of feelings. Including a deep desire to talk to Jett about breaking the Unbreakable Rules.

"I'll be over in a minute," Layla calls.

"You stay here," I say. "She's way prettier than Eric."

"Agreed!" Layla grins and jerks her head toward the back of the Great Hall. "Plus Eric seems pretty busy."

I glance over my shoulder. Eric's wrapped around a girl dressed in a knockoff Daenerys Targaryen dress and platinum wig.

"Superfan!" I shout. "Perfect for him!"

I don't know our very own Mother of Dragons' real name, but she's at the Castle at least three times a week. Sometimes she even poses for pictures with the guests. She's not supposed to do that, and Layla's theory is that she thinks she'll get a job eventually if she keeps showing up. "You sure you're not torn up about losing him?"

Layla rolls her eyes. "I'll heal in time."

The pink-haired girl pulls her closer and they disappear into the crowd. I step away and move toward the back of the room, heading toward the exit. I need air, fast.

I go the long way to avoid Eric's make-out fest and end up winding my way past the display cases that hold weapons and other medieval knickknacks. There's a booth in one corner and Dalton, the Green Knight, calls out from the shadows as I pass.

"Nice work, Sweetly." His voice is rough with alcohol. With the hood of his jacket up, he looks a teeny bit like Strider the Ranger in *The Lord of the Rings*, and an unexpected pang of warmth toward him shoots through me.

For a minute I think he's congratulating me on riding out as the Red Knight, which is so unexpected I stop in my tracks. "Um, thanks. You did a good job too."

"I'm not applauding you," Dalton sneers. "You're worthless as a Knight and that was just a lucky shot."

He stumbles to his feet, drunk and most un-Strider-like. My warm feeling evaporates.

"What do you want?"

"I'm congratulating you for getting the entire Castle in trouble. Thanks to you, we're under review. I heard Len talking with one of the bosses before tonight's show."

"That's bullshit." I refuse to believe it. The alcohol makes my head fuzzy, but even so I can see how ridiculous the idea is. "They wouldn't close us down just because I fought once."

"You're precious." Dalton lurches toward me and I sidestep him. "It's not all about you. Don't you follow the stock market? This place has been going downhill for years. Fewer and fewer people come to our shows. That's why they're desperately pandering for ideas to salvage this dump. Trust me, they're going to close down the whole company within the year. And your little stunt has put us more on Corporate's radar. They're coming here in two weeks—on Friday the thirteenth, of course—to see if we should be shut down immediately. I don't need this job, but I bet your brother doesn't feel the same way."

I lunge at Dalton, but the booze makes me slow, and I trip over my feet and stumble into the wall. "Don't talk about my brother! I'll smash your face this time."

"Such a lady," declares a South Side of Chicago–accented voice behind me.

I spin around. Jessica stands a few feet away, dressed in jeans and a sparkly tank top. She's got two Big Gulp cups of punch in her hands.

"What do you want?" I repeat the question I threw at Dalton moments ago. Apparently drinking too much makes me slow *and* dries up my wit.

Jessica sets the glasses down and mock curtsies. "Nothing more than to see the great Kit Sweetly in action." She can't even keep a straight face as she says it, and Dalton cracks up.

To think that I ever thought this girl was cool. When she and Chris first started dating, she taught me how to do a fishtail braid and we would all watch movies together. I cringe to admit that I looked up to her at one point.

"I never said I was a lady! And you're wrong about this place, Dalton. It won't close. There's too much love for the Castle to shut these doors."

It's hardly a mic drop, but before they can reply, I storm away. Their laughter follows me outside. A warm breeze lifts my hair as I step into a smokers' circle on the lawn behind the Castle. A handful of Serving Wenches, cooks, a few Squires, and some of the other Castle underlings drink from clear plastic cups, laughing and telling filthy jokes. An orange five-gallon cooler sits on a rusted chair, its fading high school track team logo a testament to better times. More Castle staff stand around the door, putting back punch like it's water. I pour a drink from the cooler—electric red with a smell like nail polish remover—and bum a cigarette. Not too many people have noticed me yet, and, needing a moment alone, I step away from the group and smoke at the edge of the parking lot.

I love this little family of weirdos, and it cannot all go away.

It's too perfect. Too magical. Too much mine. We cannot lose the Castle.

I inhale deeply, trying to calm my anger at Dalton, and throw back the cup of punch. It burns its way into my gut, but I don't care. This could be our last Ninja afterparty. Drinking too much, like smoking, comes with the restaurant territory. It's half escape, half desperate grasping at an elusive greater-grander something that's far away from grubby milk crates and crappy shifts. With a belly full of booze, life is dance clubs and beaches on the Mediterranean and—

The roar of a motorcycle cuts into the alcohol-frosted tumble of my thoughts, slicing them in half. The noise grows louder as Jett pulls up on the Triumph, looking cool as goddamn Brad Pitt. He waves at me as he backs the bike into a parking space. My perfidious heart bungee jumps into my stomach, and I take another steadying drag of my smoke.

Sure, I'm glad he's here. Why wouldn't I want my other best friend to hang out with me at a super-wild party when I'm already more than half drunk?

*Steady, Sweetly. You can do this. Be cool.*

It's basically a slow-motion movie star scene as Jett walks toward me in his vintage black leather jacket, jeans, and motorcycle boots. One of the other Serving Wenches wolf whistles, and he grins, his teeth flashing white against the gorgeous brown of his skin. A shock of hair falls into his eyes and he sort of shakes it out. Which would make me gag if anyone else did it, but on him, it looks natural.

"Fancy meeting you here," he says, stopping beside me. He nudges me with his shoulder. "Also, you're staring."

"Just admiring your entrance," I say, in what has to be the world's worst attempt at being cool.

"Really?" There's a note of skepticism in Jett's voice. He reaches for my cup and takes a long swig of the punch. He makes a face as it goes down.

"Really," I say, failing to keep a quaver out of my voice. For fuck's sake. I sound like my junior high self, trying to talk to a cute boy. Ridiculous. I stomp out my cigarette and look away. "You practically had all the Serving Wenches begging for your number."

"Ahhh," he says. "I'm not really into dating Serving Wenches."

There it is. The truth laid bare between us. I'm slowly falling hard for Jett and he's nowhere near into me.

"Of course not," I say, giving him a little shove. "That would be preposterous."

He nods quickly. "Totally. How's phase one going?"

"Done and we're on to phase two. Recruitment! Alex, Penny, Mags, Lizzy, and a few others are in. Can you start filming on Monday?"

"I'm watching my brothers for part of the day since they're off school. But I'll make it work."

He looks at me through what can only be described as

a fringe of eyelashes.

He's so close I can see the eyelash stuck to his cheekbone. I go to brush it off, but my stupid drunk self somehow stumbles into him. And then my arm is around his waist.

He catches me as I fall and helps me stand up. "You okay?"

Our faces are inches apart. All I'd have to do is lean in a little closer. And then we might be kissing.

Or he might run away screaming because I've totally broken an Unbreakable Rule.

The noise of the party and the cheers of the Serving Wenches and cooks break into our bubble.

I pull away hastily. "Totally fine. You had an eyelash on your cheek."

Jett laughs. "Most graceful eyelash removal ever."

"Shut up," I say, finding my footing again. Both literally and in the shifting landscape that is my friendship with Jett. I just have to remember that for him, everything is the same. Nothing is shifting. And he's not into me like that. The thought of us kissing would probably horrify him or something.

I slam the rest of the punch and look away.

"Want to get out of here?" asks Jett.

"Don't you want to go inside?"

"Do you?"

Inside means seeing Dalton and Jessica or running into Len and having him lecture me about my debut as a Knight. My head's starting to hurt, and I can't stomach the idea of more booze. Plus, some part of me knows I need to sort through about a dozen things, starting with the news that the Castle might be closing and ending with the fact that I almost just kissed my best friend.

"Not particularly. Can you take me back to Layla's? I'm spending the night there tonight. You can stay too if you want."

Jett offers me his arm and we walk to his bike. I text Layla to meet us at her house, and Jett hands me the extra helmet he keeps on the back of his seat.

"Hang on," he says as he fires up the bike.

I wrap my arms around his waist and snuggle my head into the hollow between his shoulder blades. Tonight, Jett smells like well-worn leather and lavender soap.

Stupid, sexy best friend.

## 15

THE SUN STABS AT ME AS I ROLL OVER ON SUNDAY morning. Jett and I lie together in a tangle of blankets on the pullout couch in Layla's pool cabana. I'm wearing the pajamas I packed for my sleepover. Jett is shirtless but wearing jeans and socks.

I sit up, and a groan escapes my lips. The blue-and-red punch broke my brain, and I'll never be the same again.

"Good morning." Jett smiles a sweet, sleepy smile as he rolls over to look at me.

I mumble a good morning and go back to contemplating the insides of my eyelids.

The night comes back to me in snatches. We took a ride on Jett's bike; made it back to Layla's; she and her pink-haired friend joined us soon after that; there was dancing, swimming, and then . . .

Oh my God. My eyes fly open and I turn gently onto my side.

"Did I throw up on your motorcycle?"

Jett sits up. I try not to look at his flat stomach or the ridges of his shoulder muscles. How does a guy whose main hobbies include watching documentaries and playing the trumpet get shoulders like that? And what would it feel like to run my fingers over them?

"And my shirt. After we went swimming, you were insistent we should go for a ride."

"But then I barfed."

"Then you barfed," confirms Jett. "And I helped you get to bed."

I bury my face in my hands. Kill me now.

"Is that all you remember?" he asks.

"Did anything else happen?" I say through my fingers.

Please tell me it didn't. Please tell me I didn't make more of a fool of myself.

"That's pretty much it." His voice is tinged with the teeniest bit of something that could be disappointment but is more likely amusement.

That's a small mercy. Thank you, Kit, for not throwing yourself at Jett and ruining everything. "I'm so sorry."

"Don't be," Jett says with an easy smile. "It was a good night."

"Before I barfed on your bike."

Jett smiles. "Before you barfed on my bike."

Please bury me now.

I pull my hand away. "I'll clean it up. Is Layla here?"

"I took care of it already. And she's in the house."

"Alone?"

Jett shrugs. "I doubt it."

I'm certain I would remember this, but I have to ask. "Did we do . . . anything else? Like things that would go against the Unbreakable Rules?"

Jett pauses before he speaks, as if he's trying to decide how to answer. Finally he says in a goofy British accent: "I can assure you, my lady, our virginities—and our vows—are still well intact."

I have to laugh. It's a line from a seventeenth-century comedy we did in last year's drama finals. I know for a fact that neither of us is a virgin. I lost mine in the world's most awkward hookup at theater camp sophomore year. Jett lost his last summer to some out-of-town friend of a friend at Austin's lake house.

"That's a relief," I say. "Not that I wouldn't do that . . . well, I wouldn't with you. Because of the Unbreakable Rules. And because you're not into Serving Wenches. And, well, it's you. And I'm me. But it's a relief . . . that we didn't . . . you know . . . while I was so drunk . . ."

He quirks an eyebrow at me, letting me dig myself deeper

into the hole of my own words.

I'm clearly not helping this at all.

Stop. Talking. Kit.

"Let's go get pancakes," says Jett. "I'll run home and get a shirt. You get cleaned up, and then we'll go for breakfast. Everything else can wait."

Ahhh, Jett. My breakfast food bestie.

I catch a glimpse of myself in the mirror hanging by the cabana door and nearly scream. I look like a costume that should be at the bottom of a Halloween bargain bin. Half my hair is plastered to my head and the rest stands up like a cloud. All my makeup's run down my face, like a melting clown, and my breath. Oh boy. My breath is roadkill bad.

"You're asking me to breakfast, when I look like this?"

Jett tilts his head. "Do you look different than usual? I couldn't tell."

"Beastly man!" I grab a tasseled pillow from the floor and fling it at his head.

He dodges and steps closer to me. Even through my own stink, his coconut and lavender smell envelops me. "As your best friend, it's my job to tell you that you're beautiful every day. No amount of barf can change that."

"Ugh," I say, covering my stinky mouth. "Just give me a breath mint and get out of here already. I need to shower."

Jett grins. "So, that's a yes to pancakes?"

"Yes," I say as I unwrap the red-and-white mint Jett hands

me. He steals them by the handful from the candy bowls at the Castle, so his pockets are always full. Kind of exactly like my grandmother. I pop the mint in my mouth. "Wait, no. Rain check. I've got to get home soon and talk to my mom."

I need her to un-ground me so I can train at Layla's this week. And I'd like to ask her why she's not been paying the mortgage.

"Okay," says Jett, shrugging. "Text me if you want to talk about your documentary later."

"Will do. And thanks for taking care of me last night." I offer him my most grateful smile. "You're seriously the best guy a girl could have."

"Best guy friend," he corrects gently. He offers me another mint and then he's out the door.

There it is. The sound of me being put solidly and forever in the friend zone.

Outside, his motorcycle roars to life. I peek out the curtains as Jett races down the driveway. A little bit of my barf and a huge piece of my heart goes with him.

WHEN I FINALLY STUMBLE INTO THE HOUSE, LAYLA'S MADE COF-fee and is sitting at the breakfast nook table with her laptop open.

"You're up to over three hundred thousand views in two days," she says in lieu of a greeting.

"Are you serious?" I plop down into one of the fancy ergonomic chairs and try not to stare at the sun streaming in through the bay windows.

"Dead serious. Do you know how big a deal that is?" Layla dips a piece of bagel into her coffee and pops it into her mouth. She swings the screen around and points to the comments.

I read a few and then shrug, too tired and hungover to process them right now. My breath's better thanks to the breath mint, but everything else still hurts. I unscrew the lid from a bottle of French vanilla creamer and take a long swig from it. It goes down sickly sweet, but since there's not a bathtub of frosting to drown myself in, this will have to work.

"Gross," says Layla, taking the creamer away and pushing black coffee and a piece of whole wheat toast toward me. "Eat that."

"Where's your pink-haired friend?"

"Maura? She left right after you and Jett went to bed." Layla waggles her eyebrows at me, as if that will make details of my night emerge from my mouth.

I refuse to take the bait. "Are you going to see her again?"

"Maybe. We had fun," she says. "But it's not serious."

"Jett knows all about that."

"Uh-oh," says Layla. She closes her computer. "That bad?"

"He told me he's not into Serving Wenches. Which I'm taking worse than I thought I would." I slurp some black coffee and nibble a bite of toast.

"He'll come around," she says. "You feeling okay about phases one and two?"

"I'm not feeling good about anything right now. Maybe once my brain stops ping-ponging around my skull, I'll be capable of opinions again."

"Poor baby drinker," murmurs Layla. She gets an ice pack out of the freezer and plops it on the top of my head. After I finish my coffee and drink a bunch of water, she turns on the TV. I curl up on the couch beside her with a mumbled "Thank you."

I don't wake up until she nudges me. My head's resting on a plump, satiny pillow, and there's a line of drool soaked into it.

Ugh. I'm awesome.

"It's three p.m.," says Layla. She's dressed in her work clothes. "I texted your mom earlier, pretending to be you, and told her we were still doing homework and you'd get a ride home with me. But she pretty much yelled at me through the phone. So, I think you better get home now."

"You are the best. Friend. Ever. What do you see in me?"

Layla laughs. "Get moving, Wench."

"I love you too."

## 16

Mom's not even home to yell at me because she's on another double shift, and I end up sleeping the rest of Sunday away in my dark house. At some point, Chris brought me a Gatorade, which I took after a long soliloquy about how he was the best brother ever. I expected an argument from Mom when she got home from work, but she just planted a sleepy kiss on my forehead and un-grounded me, saying she was too tired to keep up my punishment or even argue about it any longer. I didn't have enough brain power to confront her about the mortgage, and all of us went to bed exhausted and ready for the new week to be better.

By Monday morning—the first day of spring break—I'm among the living again and super excited about the first training session with the other Knight-hopefuls. Our electricity is also on, so I take a scalding-hot shower and microwave water for instant oatmeal. Thank you, gods of modern technology.

"Ready to go?" Chris asks around noon. He's on spring break too this week, though he was up early to drive a few Uber pickups before we start training.

I close my own laptop and smile. I've been checking all the viral strains of the Girl Knight campaign, and so far it's going great. There are more than four hundred thousand views for the video, and it's been shared almost as many times on social media. No major news outlets have picked it up yet, and I've still not heard anything from the Castle, but hopefully that will change as the workweek gets underway.

"I'm ready," I say, grabbing my purse and Jett's backpack. "I just need to get some food."

Opening the fridge, I peer inside. Mom must've gone grocery shopping, because there's milk, cheese, some fruit, and pasta in there. The Cooler of Doom is still under the table though. I shoot it a dirty look.

"Forget it," says Chris. "I picked this up for you on the way."

He tosses a sub sandwich toward me. I catch it using my Knight-like reflexes. "Turkey and Muenster, good job," I say, reading the wrapping.

"Just looking out for you," he says, sitting down at the kitchen table across from me. He unwraps his own sandwich. "I figured we should start day one of training with some food in our bellies."

As we eat, he goes over his plans for the day and the routines we're going to learn. It's a lot, but we might just be able to pull this off.

Penny, Alex, Mags, and Lizzy are at Layla's by 2:00 p.m. Jett's there too with the fancy video camera he got for his last birthday. I'm not sure if I should give them a pep talk or what, but Layla pokes me hard in the back as we all stand in her barn, each of us gripping one of the practice swords Chris has smuggled out of the Castle for us.

"Say something," she hisses. "You're the fearless leader here. Tell them the plan."

Okay. Pep talk it is.

"Hi, everyone!" I call out over the sounds of their conversations. I step up onto a rectangular bale of hay. "Thanks for coming out today."

Alex whistles and Penny calls out, "Anytime, Kit!"

A horse whinnies in a nearby paddock and Layla runs her hand along its face, soothing it.

I grin, feeling more confident. "I know we have a lot of work to do, but I'm certain we can be ready. Today's Monday, the second. We're planning on taking over the tournament on Friday, April thirteenth, when the Corporate folks are in town. We'll try to get together here to train a bit every day. If you can make it, great. If not, practice on your own."

Lizzy raises her hand. "Are we going to be able to use the other Knights' gear?"

I give Chris a look. We're still figuring out this piece of things.

"We'll have it taken care of by then," he says smoothly. "Kit and Layla are working on bringing attention to this cause. All you need to do is work hard and be ready by the thirteenth."

Mags salutes Chris. "Understood. And will do. Can we get started though? I've got to be back home by three thirty."

And thus begins the day in my life that is basically one big Knights' training montage. Layla even plays Queen's *Greatest Hits* through the stable's speakers, so we can joust just like the dudes in *A Knight's Tale*. Chris spends the first hour teaching everyone except Layla and me how to stay on a horse. Layla's long-suffering horses are beyond patient, and eventually Penny, Lizzy, Alex, and Mags have the basics down and are no longer gripping the reins with expressions of terror plastered on their faces. After that, we work on swinging swords and fake falling, and then Chris leads us through round after round of trying to catch rings with lances and other knightly games. It's all stuff I've practiced with Chris before, but it's so much more fun with a big group of friends.

Jett films it all, adding in commentary here and there along with heaps of laughs and cheers.

"Bravo!" Chris calls out from the sidelines encouragingly, even as Alex falls off their horse (again) and Mags misses all the rings she's trying to capture. We've got a long way to go.

After a few hours, we're bruised, battered, and a tiny bit

better at jousting and fake fighting. We've seen the show so many times that memorizing the moves is relatively easy. But applying them in the arena? I'm not so sure about that.

Once everyone leaves—with a promise to be back here tomorrow at the same time—Layla and I walk up to the house. It's blissfully cool inside, and I get us two bottles of fancy water out of the fridge.

"So, you know how you said you didn't want me to give you any money?" Layla sits down at the kitchen table and opens her laptop.

"I still don't want that." I plop down next to her. "I can figure out all that money stuff alone."

"Sure you can," says Layla. "Just like you know CPR?"

"Shut up."

"Tell me it's not the same thing."

"It's totally not the same thing. That was years ago. I was just a kid!"

"It wasn't that long ago and you're still that same kid."

Two years ago, Layla, Chris, and I went to an ice-skating rink where Olympic figure skaters train. I was fifteen, and fresh off CPR classes at school. Needless to say, I was feeling super confident in my lifesaving abilities. It was a family skate day, and the ice was busy with kids, parents, and couples. Somehow I ended up in the fast-skate lane. I was wobbling my way toward the edges when a teen girl wearing a fuzzy pink hat crashed into this mom who was tentatively making her way off the ice with a toddler. The mom flopped backward, hitting her head on the ice. She fell right at my feet and passed out. I dropped to my knees.

I could do something about this!

I KNEW CPR!

I checked the woman's pulse. I reassured the toddler. I had things under control.

Layla and Chris skated up to me.

"Oh my God, Kit!" said Layla. "What happened? Is she okay?"

Chris looked around, trying to see where the closest exit was. "I'm going to get some help. Stay here."

"NO!" I shouted. "Don't go get anyone. I KNOW CPR!"

Layla and Chris looked at each other. Their feet were moving before the look was done.

"We need help over here!" shouted Layla as she raced toward the exit.

"Don't move her, Kit!" Chris called over his shoulder.

Of course I didn't move her. I held the toddler's hand as a medic helped the now-awake and dazed woman to her feet. My cheeks were brighter than my red jacket as I handed the child off to a staff member.

"You know CPR?" muttered Chris as we left the rink and got into his car. "What were you thinking?"

I was thinking that I could save someone. That I could do it on my own. That I didn't need anyone else.

Which of course was ridiculous.

Beside him in the front seat, Layla cracked up.

"Let us never mention this again." I crawled into the back seat and pulled my scarf up to my nose.

Much to my undying shame, the CPR incident still comes up with regularity.

"Hey, Earth to Kit," says Layla, poking me in my very bruised arm. "Did you hear anything I just said?"

"Nope." I shake my head and take an apple out of the fruit bowl in the middle of the table. "I was lost in memories of my 'I know CPR' shame."

Layla laughs and points to the screen of her laptop. "Okay, so as part of phase one, we made some swag to sell. I printed T-shirts and stickers, and I put ads on your site. Plus, we're charging people to use your content when they write articles about you."

"What does all that mean?" I ask through a bite of apple.

"It means that you're making money. You've already generated more than a thousand dollars in revenue."

"You're shitting me." The apple falls from my hand. "It's only been a few days."

Layla shakes her head. "The Internet is a mighty capitalist tool. Look."

She walks me through numbers, profits, and a bunch of other things I don't fully understand. But what it all boils down to is that I now have money coming in. And I can use it for school or to help Mom catch up on the mortgage.

Save the day or follow my dreams?

I'd like to say I was heroic enough to not struggle with the choice, but that's a lie.

"When can you get me this money?" I ask Layla.

"You can have it within a week if you'd like," she says. "Going to put it toward Marquette?"

"Something like that," I reply.

17

WE TRAIN HARD ON TUESDAY AND WEDNESDAY. BY Thursday morning, I'm painfully sore from all the falling, hitting, riding, and practice, but I think we're getting better. Each of us is good at some part of knighthood, and Chris has been helping choreograph a very basic routine that can work for the tournament. Jett's got a few hours of video, which he's working on editing for the next few days. He's promised to keep the David Attenborough–style voice-over to a minimum, but I'm betting he won't be able to help himself.

After I arrive home from practice on Thursday, I find Mom sitting at the kitchen table. She's got a stack of bills beside her computer and stares at the screen with a dismayed expression.

"Hey Kit-Kat," she says. "How was school?"

I shoot her a look. "It's spring break, Mom. I've been at Layla's most of this week."

Chris and I both agree it's best not to tell Mom about the training and my goals for knighthood. At least not until we're sure it will work. No reason to worry her unnecessarily.

"Ahh, that's right. Spring break. Sorry." She lets out a tired sigh. "I've been working as much overtime as the office and the diner will let me. I lost track of the days."

"What's all this?" I ask, sitting down next to her.

"Bills. Always so many bills."

"Can I help with anything?" I really want to ask her more about the unpaid mortgage, and what that means for us. Like, will we have a place to live at this time next month? But I did some googling, and even if we default on that loan, we would have months before the bank took the house.

"You're doing enough already," she says, squeezing my hand. "We just have a lot of unexpected expenses lately."

I take a deep breath for bravery. It's no good to be trying to inspire change at the Castle if I can't figure out what's going on with my own mom.

"Speaking of that . . . I saw the late notice on the mortgage. What's going on, Mom?"

She runs a hand across her eyes. "You saw that?"

I nod.

She sighs. "I was trying to keep it from you. So you didn't

have to worry about it on top of college applications and finishing your senior year."

"Why aren't you paying it?"

"How would you feel if we didn't live here anymore?"

I look around the house that's been my home since I was a kid. It's everything to me. Family. Home. The place I finally felt secure.

"I suppose it could be okay," I lie. Trying to keep my voice steady. "If we had somewhere else to go. And I guess this would be a lot of space for you if Chris and I were away at school."

"Exactly my thought," Mom says. "Downsizing has been my goal since your father left. To that end, I hired a lawyer to officially get the divorce from your father going. But, in order to pay the legal fees, I've had to skip a few mortgage payments. But maybe it's serendipitous. A smaller place could be a really good thing. I know I'd like less house to take care of. And you and Chris won't have to worry about helping out around here so much."

"Won't you miss living here?"

"Sure," Mom says. "But when the divorce finalizes, that means we're free of your dad, and your financial aid should be higher because it'll pull from my income only. Plus, I want you and Chris to have your own lives. I want you to get out of here. See the world. Figure out who you are and what you want without worrying about me. And who knows, maybe getting rid of this place will help me move on to new things. I still have dreams too, you know."

Of course I knew that on some abstract level, but it's strange to think about my mom with dreams that don't involve Chris and me.

But I don't say all that. "What do you want to do?"

Mom bites her bottom lip for a moment. "I always wanted to be a writer. And go to Asia. And go to college. I had you and Chris so young, I never got to do any of those things. But now, I'm thinking that since my baby girl is leaving the house, it's time for me to try some new things."

She points to a book of travel essays under the bills. "This is about a woman who left home after a brutal divorce. And now she lives all over the world, making friends, trying out new things, and really taking a slow approach to travel."

I flip the book over and skim the back copy. "Please don't leave us just yet. I'm not sure I can make it through my freshman year without you around."

Mom smiles at me, her tired, worn-out smile looking a bit less run down. "Of course not. It'll take me a year to save enough money for my plans, but getting this house off our hands will be a huge first step."

I take a deep breath. I guess I'd never thought about this house not being ours. Or about Mom not being in it. But everything she says makes sense. And if she does this, then maybe I can use the money from my promotion to knighthood just for school. "If this is what you really want, go for it," I say. "Have you told Chris?"

"Not yet, but I will soon. And your father should be coming around in the next few days. He's supposed to bring me the papers to finalize things."

"What changed his mind?"

Mom shrugs. "Not sure. But I'm so glad he did."

"Me too, Mom."

AFTER MY TALK WITH MOM, I HEAD BACK TO MY ROOM. There's still a pile of homework to do, but I can't face it. It's still spring break for the next three days, and some part of me feels like I better spend as much time as possible relaxing in my room before this house is no longer ours.

My phone dings that I've got a new email, and I pop it open.

It's from the Castle email address where I sent my idea for the contest.

My heart goes zooming around my chest. This could be good or bad. Depending on what they think. Steeling myself, I click on it.

Ms. Sweetly,

Thank you for your refreshing suggestion about how to change things at the Castle. Although we appreciate your idea, we don't feel that this sort of radical change really fits with the Castle branding. As such, we'll have to pass on your idea at this time.

We do appreciate all your hard work at the Castle and without Wenches like you, we couldn't do what we do.

Best,

The Castle Committee for Guest Engagement.

I read it again. And then again.

Oh no. No, no, no, no.

I feel like I've just been shoved off a very tall building. One I was so excited to get to the top of, and then *whoosh*. All the air is gone from my lungs and I'm tumbling head over heels toward the ground.

How could they say no?

I gnaw on a fingernail as I read the email again.

Everything I was working for depended on the Castle committee saying yes. And for them to send such a perfunctory "nope" and then try to compliment me for wenching?

Infuriating. And not how this story is supposed to go!

Especially not now that I've told everyone we're riding in the show a week from tomorrow.

How am I going to tell them we have to cancel? That all their hard work is for nothing? That the Castle doesn't really care about them, but hey, "thanks for wenching!"

I don't know where to hurl my anger, so I pick up a book and fling it at the wall.

It tumbles into a sword, which somehow manages to both

clatter to the ground and knock over like half the photos on my dresser.

"GAHHHHH!" I scream, giving voice to the maelstrom of feelings inside me. This is so fucking wrong. And my friends are going to be so upset.

And it's all my fault.

"You okay in there, Kit?" Mom pops her head in through my doorway.

I take a deep breath. "I'm fine. Just frustrated by a math problem. It's no big deal."

She gives me a disbelieving look, but lets it go. "Okay, I'm headed to the bank. Please try not to Hulk-smash the house while I'm gone."

I laugh at that. Mom's a die-hard Marvel fan.

"I'll keep it together," I tell her. "Good luck at the bank."

"Thanks, Kit-Kat. See you later."

Once she's gone, I read the Castle email again. Some of my anger has dissipated, and I see now that this doesn't have to be the end of everything. What my friends and I are doing has momentum already. It doesn't need the Castle's blessing.

"Ask forgiveness, not permission," I say as I move the email to my Deleted folder. If this does all blow up spectacularly, I'll take the blame. But in the meantime, I don't want to dash my friends' hopes. And I certainly don't want to end the dialogue with Corporate on the note of "great job wenching."

Rather than write back, I'm going to show them how

wrong they are. We'll have the tournament. We'll kick ass as Knights. And we'll fill every seat in that house. How's that for a reply? Sometimes the fake sword *is* mightier than the pen.

That just leaves the problem of what to tell my friends. If I tell them the truth, some of them might walk away from the tournament. Or they might be mad that we've proceeded this far only to have things fall apart.

Maybe I just don't tell them and try to figure out a solution between now and next Friday.

Deciding that if anyone asks, I'll just say: If we can fill the seats, then who's to argue with that?

Sounds good. Though a seed of guilt stirs in my stomach at the thought of lying to my friends. But a little lie is better than the ugly truth in this case.

Once the email is deleted, I upload two videos of our training sessions to the Girl Knight website. One is us actually doing some things right, and then one's all bloopers and Alex, Mags, and Lizzy cracking up as they try to stay on their horses while wearing armor. Orders are pouring in for T-shirts and stickers, and we're getting lots of people taking our interactive quizzes.

The Girl Knight and her band of other Knights will ride at the Castle next Friday. We will fill all the seats. And even if Corporate doesn't like the idea now, they'll be hard-pressed to argue with our popularity and our skills.

At least that's what I hope.

18

I RIDE TO WORK WITH LAYLA ON FRIDAY NIGHT. SOMEHOW A
week has already passed since I took Chris's place as the
Red Knight last Friday. I wasn't scheduled for any shifts
during the week, and although I've been grateful to avoid Len,
I'm in desperate need of some cash.

Today's training session was the toughest yet for all of us.
I'm glad I had some training before, but I feel for the others.
Chris drilled us on hand-to-hand fighting for over two hours.
Alex and Penny managed to stay on their horses and catch
all the rings with the lances we'd made out of garden rakes.
And Lizzy brought cupcakes to celebrate the fact that my
video is up to half a million views. Our other videos are also
picking up steam, and we've had some coverage from online
news outlets.

"How you doing?" asks Layla as we walk toward Len's office.

I've still not told her about the Castle group rejecting my ideas, and anxiety about that makes it feel like there's an electric current under my skin. I let out a deep breath. Best to stick to the safe sources of anxiety that she knows all about. At least until I have a better plan in place.

"I'm dreading talking to Len," I admit. "This could all fall apart if he fires me tonight. What will I tell the others then?"

"You've got this, Sweetly. You're the famous Girl Knight. No man can get you down."

"Damn right," I say.

It comes out way more bravely than I feel. Which is fine. Faking it is what we do at the Castle.

Layla gives my elbow a squeeze. "Good luck."

"If you don't see me in fifteen minutes, send help."

"Half a million views and counting," says Layla bracingly. "You've got leverage."

I think of the comments from my website as I walk into the room. Most of them are from girls all over the country. A few people have even posted videos of their daughters dressed up in knight costumes doing their own Éowyn "I am no man" moments.

The girl who inspired all that is not afraid of facing her boss, even if he also happens to be her uncle.

My confidence wavers as I push open the door to Len's office.

"Well, if it isn't 'the Girl Knight.'" Len's voice drips sarcasm like my mom's car leaks oil. "Take a seat." Len strolls to the printer and picks up a piece of paper.

I clear my throat and sit down. Plunging ahead before he can start a tirade seems like a solid move. "You're mad at me. I get that. But if I could—"

"I'm not mad," says Len. "Actually I want to thank you."

"You're joking." My voice is wary.

"What do you think this is?" He drops the piece of paper on the table in front of me.

Lists of names in neat columns line the page. "It looks like next week's bookings?"

"Exactly. Do you see how many are there?"

"A lot?"

"Three times our normal. It seems you've really tapped into the feminist zeitgeist."

"Female empowerment and gender equality are human rights, not 'zeitgeist.'" I swig some coffee and make a face at him.

"Whatever. Semantics." Len grabs the paper and points to a column on the far side. "All the Girl Scout troops in the greater Chicago area are coming to the Castle in the next month."

"That's great!" I still can't believe he's not yelling. "But I heard the Castle is closing."

"Nope. I needed an idea to bring more people in, and you've delivered one. Do you know that every time someone likes or shares your video, Corporate gets an email?"

I smile to myself at Layla's brilliance. But if my idea is bringing people in, why did Corporate say no? Has Len not heard about that and he's just seeing the numbers of guests add up? The Castle is a big enough company that they may not have talked to each other about this yet.

"So, they're getting lots of emails?"

"They've gotten more than a half million emails and they keep coming in. . . ." Len sits back and folds his hands over his stomach. "It's a brilliant stunt you pulled."

"Does this mean I get to fight again?"

Len barks out a laugh. "Don't be ridiculous. Company policy isn't going to change."

"Despite me single-handedly bringing in all this business?" I lean forward and grip the edge of his desk.

"Be glad you're not getting fired."

The worry I've been carrying around like armor lightens a bit. I fall back in the chair. "It's not fair that you won't let me fight. I put on a good show out there!" I can't keep the bitterness from my voice.

I don't tell him that I've already started training a handful of other Knights. And that we're going through with things, no matter what he says. If he'd bothered to watch the videos on my website, he'd know that. It's not my job to do his research for him.

The preshow trumpet sounds, signaling to us that it's time

to begin the grand medieval game all over again. We both stand up.

"Maybe you can be a Queen someday," says Len, settling his crown on his head. "Just imagine, Kit. When I retire, all this will be yours." He gestures grandly at his run-down office, taking in the chipped paint on the walls and the dingy tapestries covering the cinder blocks.

"Thanks but no. I've got other plans. Are we done?" I stand up. "I've got a long night of wenching ahead of me."

"One more thing," says Len. "Did you see this?"

He turns his computer screen around. On it is a video of a local newscaster interviewing members of a kids' show featuring animatronic dragons. They're all theater types, and I lean closer to the screen, searching for familiar faces from the Castle. The reporter walks through a set, dwarfed by pink and blue dragons.

I spot my dad immediately. He wears a regrettable green bandanna that's about as rock-and-roll as my Wench's uniform. His electric guitar—one that once belonged to his and Len's dad—is strapped over his chest. He plays a few riffs as the newscaster looks on in feigned delight.

I guess the church thing didn't work out. Maybe this is why he agreed to the divorce with Mom. Because he needs the money from the sale of the house.

"Oh my god." I sink back into the chair, half-mortified that my dad still thinks he's rock-and-roll and half-relieved that he's still alive. "I thought he pawned that guitar."

"Me too," says Len. A scowl crosses his face. I wouldn't want to be in the same zip code when Len finally confronts my dad about stealing the guitar from his living room.

"Are you going to his show?" I ask, looking again at the dates the dragon show is in town.

"Not even if you paid me," says Len. He takes a small copper flask out from his desk drawer and takes a long sip. "But if you see him hanging around here, let me know. I don't want him bothering you and Chris."

It's an unusually paternal sentiment that brings tears to my eyes. Which is way more emotion than I can deal with before a double shift.

"Whatever you say, boss." I knock my paper coffee cup against his flask. Now's not the time to tell him about my conversation with Mom and the divorce. And that's none of his business anyway.

He starts to say more, but I stand up and hurry out the door before we can discuss my fame, my father, or my feelings any further.

**M**Y SECTION IS FULL TONIGHT. BETWEEN THE FRAT BOYS demanding more pitchers of beer while ogling my cleavage and the soccer moms asking for gluten-free versions of everything, I've been pretty much jogging since the first trumpet blast. I'm working in the Red Knight's cheering section as usual, and every time Chris strikes a blow or wins a favor, I holler along with my customers. He throws a rose into our section and shoots me a grin as he rides away.

All of me wishes I was out there riding with him and the other Knights, not hauling a bin of turkey scraps up slippery concrete stairs. I pause in the hallway between the arena and the kitchen, trying to catch my breath. Sweat soaks my armpits, leaving half-moons on my dress.

Eddy Jackson and four of his buddies—two enormous

linebacker types and two very fit-looking women—are in my section again tonight. They're sitting in the front row, right beside the arena floor. As I'm bringing them a plate of turkey legs (their fourth serving since dinner started), Eddy holds his phone up and shines the light on my face.

"I knew it! You're Kit Sweetly! The Girl Knight!"

I blink in the glare from the phone but shoot him a wry smile. "In the flesh. Though tonight I'm just a Serving Wench."

"You all need to see her video!" says Eddy, pulling it up on his phone. "This is the girl I was telling you about." His friends lean in closer, watching as I vanquish Dalton (all of them groan as my mace makes contact) and then deliver my "I am no man!" line.

"Why aren't you out there tonight?" asks one of the women. Her long dark hair is twisted into a high ponytail, and she looks vaguely familiar. "I'd love to see something other than dudes beating each other up when Eddy drags us here."

"You know you love the food!" Eddy teases, raising his mug of ale at her and grinning.

The woman rolls her eyes. "That's got to be it."

He laughs and reaches for another turkey leg. "I love the food. Makes me feel alive to eat turkey legs in a communal setting. Like I'm part of something greater. Some Viking shit or something."

I blink, trying not to laugh. Absolutely nothing comes to mind in reply to that statement. The food at the Castle is mass-produced and it hasn't changed in like a decade. But to each their own.

"Ignore this barbarian," says the woman. She slaps Eddy's shoulder affectionately. There's a loud cheer from the section as Chris almost unhorses the Blue Knight.

I cheer with them, watching Chris move through the on-ground fighting routine he's been teaching us all week. He's slower than usual, and his steps are off. Like he's distracted. I must've been mirroring him because I feel a hand on my shoulder as I mimic a sword thrust.

"When are you out there again?" Eddy calls over the noise.

I shake my head and lean in close enough so he can hear me. "Sadly, that fight the other night might be my one and only."

"They're not going to let you fight again?"

"Company policy is that only cis men can be Knights." I make a face. "The other night I snuck in and took my brother's place." I point toward Chris.

"That's some bullshit," says the dark-haired woman beside him.

"Tell me about it," I reply. "Especially since reservations are up by like two hundred percent thanks to me. I've got an online petition going around and my video's gotten a lot of attention. My friends and I are training, and we're determined to stage our own tournament next Friday."

A tournament that's already been vetoed by Corporate.

Not that my friends know that yet. Or that I'm going to tell them anytime soon.

"Do you think it'll really change things?" Eddy asks.

"I'm hoping it'll at least make things more fair. We want to remove gender restrictions for all the jobs around here. And I want to work as a Knight so I can pay for school."

"Well, I'm on your side," says the woman. "What was that website?"

Eddy clicks around on his phone. "I'll send it to you. Here, Kit, take a selfie with us."

He holds out his phone and I lean in. The other people in his group lean in too, and all of us smile.

"That's great," says Eddy. "Uploading to Twitter now with your video and tagging you all."

"Thanks for your support," I say. "Hope you can make it next Friday."

"You know we wouldn't miss it!" says Eddy. "*Whoa*, shit! Watch out!"

In the arena, Chris's horse veers wildly toward us. For a moment it looks like he's about to run it into the mesh surrounding the crowd. But he pulls up at the last minute.

I shoot him a look. Our eyes meet.

"Are you okay?" I mouth.

He nods slightly, then smiles and waves to the crowd.

I'll have to talk to him after the show, but that's still a long way off.

"Need anything else before I go get more beer?" I ask Eddy and his friends as I pick up the empty pitchers in front of them.

They shake their heads, but the dark-haired woman puts a hand on my arm.

"I'm Bettina Vasquez with *Good Morning, Chicago!* I love stories like this, and I'd be happy to have you on the show sometime." She hands me her card.

Ahhh, that's why she looks familiar.

"I'd love that." I tuck the card into my pocket. "I'll email you."

She waves to me as I trudge up the concrete stairs away from their party.

I'm on my way back to the kitchen, wiping sweat from my forehead with what I thought was a clean napkin, when I see Jett. He's reading something on his phone and carrying his backpack.

He's not seen me yet, and I'd love for him not to see me covered in this mess of a wenching dress. For a moment, I con-template ducking behind the curtain that separates the arena from the hallway, but that's the coward's way out. Besides, he told me I'm beautiful all the time. And I'm not trying to impress him.

Yeah. Right.

I swipe at the globule of turkey grease running down the bridge of my nose and clear my throat. "Not staying for the fanfare?" I blurt out as Jett passes me.

It's a stupid thing to say, but it works. Jett stops walking and looks up from his phone. The fanfare is the part at the end of the show where he and the other musicians play a trumpeting end to the tournament.

He shoots me an easy smile. "Hey, friend. I'm ducking out early because my little brothers are sick, and the sitter can't reach my parents."

He shrugs. Such a good big brother.

I almost make a joke about barfing, but mercifully restrain myself. "That's right," I say, remembering a snippet of last night's text conversation. "They're downtown seeing *Hamilton*, right?"

"Lucky them," mutters Jett, making a face. "Next time they get tickets, you and I are tagging along somehow, some way."

"I second that plan."

His eyes crinkle at the edges as he smiles at me. "How's your night going?"

Sweet lady knights who've come before me. Please, grant me the strength not to kiss this boy. Right here. Right now. "All good here. Eddy Jackson's in my section with his buddies. They all just shared my video on their Twitter accounts."

"Love that guy," says Jett. "There's your influencer part of the plan in motion."

"Indeed. Hey, want to get late-night-after-show breakfast once you check in at home?"

Jett nods. "And you can tell me what Len said. And how you managed not to get fired."

"Achhhh! You won't believe it!" I say, grabbing his shirt-sleeve playfully, like I always do. This time, though, when my hand brushes his wrist, something inside me lurches in the space between my ribs and my spine. I imagine it's how Harry Potter must've felt when he touched that first Portkey.

I drop my hand, and Jett's eyes find mine.

"That bad?" he asks, making an unreadable face. He looks a little stunned, like he's just gotten Portkeyed too.

Before I can reply, a thunderous, terrified scream—the sound of more than a hundred people yelling in shock all at once—swells from the arena behind us.

## 20

JETT AND I BOTH DASH TOWARD THE NEAREST DOOR. There's not supposed to be a scream-worthy moment this late in the show. This is the wrap-up. Time for cheers and more beers. Almost time to trumpet the exit of the King.

But that's not what we're hearing.

The crowd is on its feet, and I can't see much as we push back into the arena. Murmurs, concerned voices, and the sounds of little kids crying fill the air.

"I better get my money back," says someone waspishly as we pass. "If this show doesn't go on, I'm leaving a nasty review."

I send a death glare over my shoulder, but I can't make out who said it. There are people standing on the concrete stairs, trying to get a better view.

"Excuse me, pardon us, Castle staff coming through," Jett says as we weave around the crowds.

We're three steps from the edge of the arena when I understand what's happened.

"Oh no," I whisper in a strangled voice.

A riderless horse stands in front of my section. It wears the colors of the Red Knight. But I can't see Chris anywhere.

In the front row, Bettina grips Eddy's arm, both of them peering into the arena. One of the frat boys next to us looks down at the arena, his beer halfway to his mouth.

"Is he dead, bro?" he asks the guy standing next to him.

"Is who dead?" Jett asks, spinning toward the frat dude. "What happened?"

The frat boys point toward the arena right as the riderless horse moves aside.

Now we have a clear view.

The Red Knight lies on his back. Not moving. Completely still. His helmet is in the dirt a few feet away and his leg is twisted underneath him.

A scream tears out of my throat. My feet somehow move down the last three stairs, and I'm at the front of the arena.

From here, I can see the blood soaking Chris's white undershirt. His forehead is slick with it. He still doesn't move, but there's a flurry of activity in the arena that some part of my brain processes: A group of Castle medics runs out onto the pitch, their boots throwing up sand. Chris's horse whinnies nervously. The Red Squire catches the horse's reins and runs a hand over its flanks. The Green, Blue, and Yellow Knights huddle together at the far end of the arena. The Purple Knight, Chris's friend Austin, has thrown off his helmet and is running across the arena toward Chris.

From two sections over, I catch sight of Penny with her hands over her mouth. Layla's pushing her way through the crowds on my left, calling out my name.

"Help me, Jett!" I scream as I tear at the netting that separates the guests from the arena. It tangles around my hands maddeningly, as if it can sense how frantic I am to get to Chris. I can't let my brother die three feet away from me while I'm snarled like a fish in some cheap netting.

Eddy and Jett are by my side at once. Both of them lift the netting, freeing me. I clamber over the low wall and land in the sand of the arena. Jett's a second behind me, but I'm already running toward Chris. Pushing my way into the circle of medics, I kneel in the filthy sand beside him. My hands fly to the wound on his head, trying to stop the blood.

"Don't touch him," snaps one of the medics. "That cut is deep."

"What happened?" I insist. "Why isn't he moving? Somebody help him!"

"Back up," says one of the medics, as he pushes my hands away and gently holds gauze over the wound. "He's unconscious and he's likely broken something after that fall."

"This is my brother," I hiss through gritted teeth. "I'm not going anywhere."

Out of the corner of my eye, I see Len yelling orders. A line of Pages carrying heraldic banners runs onto the field. They surround Chris, me, and the medics, blocking us from the crowd's view.

The medics gently lift Chris onto a stretcher. I step back. Jett's right behind me. For a moment, I lean into his chest. Grateful for his presence and his solidness. We follow the medics out of the arena.

Len's voice comes over the loudspeaker once we clear the doors: "Just a little spill, folks. Let the show go on!"

*Let the show go on?*

As I climb into the back of the ambulance with Chris, I'm seriously tempted to run back into the Castle and murder Len. So much for his protective paternal feelings.

21

ENNY, LAYLA, ALEX, MAGS, AND AUSTIN ARRIVE AT ST.
Thomas Hospital as soon as their shifts end. Jett fol-
lowed the ambulance here, and now he sits in one of the waiting room chairs. His left leg bounces and he keeps looking
between his phone and me, like he's unsure how to best help.
A few of the other Squires and Wenches cluster at one end
of the waiting room, pouring coffee and getting stuff from
the vending machines. Len sent a sympathetic text but said
he can't make it over until later. Chris's ex, Princess Jessica,
wipes tears from her eyes and gives me a small wave. I shoot
her a poisonous look. Everyone's still in their Castle uniforms,
and a middle-aged couple keeps glancing at us curiously.

As we all gather, I'm reminded of the fact that sick people
in the Middle Ages flocked to saints' shrines, like St. Thomas

Becket's in the Canterbury Cathedral. Although we're in a hospital named after that saint, I'm incredibly grateful we're not living in the age of medieval medicine, with its focus on the humors, examining urine for answers to everything, and its barber surgeons who—

"Kit," says Layla, planting herself in the middle of the track I've been pacing through the waiting room and pulling me into a hug. I sink into her, letting all the anxiety and fear for Chris that's been building up in me lighten for just a moment.

"Any word yet?" Worry makes deep lines in her face. "Is he okay?"

My voice is shaky when I reply. "He's still in surgery. The doctor said he broke at least two ribs, fractured his arm, and needs stitches on his head."

"Where's your mom?" Penny asks, sizing up the waiting room. She adds her arms to Layla's, holding me up. I take a deep breath.

"She hasn't returned my calls yet, so her phone must be off. I could call the diner—"

"Or I could go pick her up," Jett replies, standing up quickly. He sounds relieved to be doing something to help. "I have to get home soon to relieve the sitter, but I can drop your mom off first."

I nod, wiping my leaking eyes on the Castle napkin I find in my pocket. "Tell her it's urgent."

I'm hoping it's not urgent, and that Chris will be back to

his old self any moment now, but my mom should be here.

"Be back soon," says Jett, giving me a small, sad smile as he leaves.

I follow Layla to a row of chairs and sink down next to her. Alex, Penny, and Mags sit beside us.

"You hanging in there, Girl Knight?" Alex asks. "Anything we can do to help?"

They hand me a cup of coffee, which I accept with a grateful smile.

"You're doing enough by being here, thank you all."

"He's going to be okay," says Penny. She squeezes my knee. "He's a tough old thing. Did he ever tell you about that time we tried snowboarding in Colorado?"

She then launches into a hilarious story about her, Chris, and some other friends failing miserably at snowboarding during the spring break trip they took a few years ago. I've heard it before, but I hang on her every word. Loving the picture of Chris she paints and deeply appreciating the distraction.

After the story is over, Penny gets up. "I'm going to go change clothes and find a sandwich or something, but text me if you get any more news."

Alex and Mags go with her, promising to bring us back provisions.

Layla raises her eyebrows once we're alone again. "So did something happen between you and Jett? Something you've not told me about? Because it's super weird between the two of you."

"Don't be ridiculous. He's just worried for Chris."

"Are you sure there's no secret date plans?" She pokes me lightly and I have to smile. In the midst of all this stress, this is exactly the lightness I need.

"Well, we were going to go for pancakes before all this, so that's pretty exciting."

Layla's eyebrows shoot up. "Pancakes? Is that some bizarre code for realizing your true feelings for each other?"

A laugh bursts out of me. "No. Dork. It's a code for breakfast. Of the griddled, hotcake variety. Nothing more. Nothing less."

"Uh-huh." Layla doesn't look convinced. But she doesn't push it. "I'll leave you be for now, but something is odd with him. Trust me, I can tell."

"Let's move on," I say, stretching my neck. I'm exhausted all of a sudden and acutely aware of how badly I stink of grease and beer. "Do you still have our emergency kits in your car?"

The emergency kits came about our freshman year, after I got my period unexpectedly while wearing white shorts. I'd changed into a pair of leggings Layla had in her bag, and the crisis was averted, but after that, we'd started keeping an emergency change of clothes and toiletries in our lockers and Layla's car.

"Right here," says Layla, holding up a plastic shopping

bag and my backpack, which she must've retrieved from the employee lockers. A pair of my jeans and a T-shirt poke out of the top of the shopping bag.

"Love you. Thanks." I take both gratefully.

"Go change." She shoos me away with her hand and makes a face. "I've got something to show you when you smell less like a medieval frat house."

When I come back from the bathroom, Layla's staring at her phone with a smug smile on her face.

"What's up?" I pull on a fuzzy blue cardigan and sit down beside her. I scrubbed my face under the cold water, and my cheeks still sting. Most of my makeup is gone, but I don't care.

"Look at your website! Thanks to Eddy and his buddies tweeting the video out, you're now trending. Several news outlets have picked up the story." Layla holds out her phone. "And you just hit eight hundred thousand views of the video. I can't wait to check the income streams from all this when I get home tonight!"

I scoff. "Apparently, all my fame is just bringing more dollars into the Castle's coffers." Quickly, I explain to her about Len's spreadsheets and the "feminist zeitgeist" he thinks he's cashing in on. "But I'm still determined to have the tournament next week. We've been working too hard to not do it. Plus, Chris would want us to keep going. "

"It's going to be epic," says Layla. "Though you'll have to train us more if Chris is out of commission."

I should tell her that the Castle has already rejected my idea. I shouldn't keep something like that from my best friend in the world. The words are on the tip of my tongue, right as Layla's phone rings.

"Hi, Maura," she says. "I'll be over here if you need me," she mouths, pointing to the far corner of the room. I wave to her and chug some of my coffee.

As I scroll through Twitter on my phone, strategies for training the others fill my head. We'll have to really map out the entire routine. And figure out how to get uniforms and gear. And convince the other Knights to let us fight, something that I was counting on Chris to help with. Maybe I can talk to Austin about it later.

Even as all these thoughts tumble through my mind, some other part of me wonders: *How can I even be thinking of fighting again when Chris is lying in a hospital bed, knocked out? Why would I risk any of us getting hurt for the sake of a silly, fake tournament?*

But it's not that silly, is it? It's serious, and adventurous, and something both Chris and I love. Which is why it's not fair that only he gets a chance to do it. Although the Castle has formally rejected my idea, I can't give up now. There are literally thousands of people excited about the changes we want to make. And getting rid of these arbitrary gender restrictions is the right thing. And it could have an impact far beyond me or Chris or any of the rest of us.

Digging through my dirty clothes, I find Bettina's card in my pocket.

I shoot off a quick email:

Hi, Bettina,

Great to meet you tonight, and tell Eddy thanks again for tweeting out my video and helping me into the arena. My brother is still in surgery, but I'm hoping he'll be okay.

I'm writing to take you up on your offer to be on *Good Morning, Chicago!* I'd love to talk about what we're doing at the Castle and why it matters. What day would be a good one for you?

Thanks so much,

Kit Sweetly

Her reply comes back before I finish my coffee.

Hi, Kit,

I was just thinking about you, and I'm so glad you reached out. How does Monday morning sound? I'll send a car for you so you don't have to fight traffic. Send me your address and please have a parent sign the attached parental consent form. See you on Monday morning, and all my best to your brother. Eddy and I are rooting for him!

Warmest regards,

Bettina

Before I can really process her email, Mom rushes into the waiting room.

**22**

MOM'S FINGERS DIG INTO MY BACK AS SHE HUGS ME.

"What happened?" She glances around the lobby. A fat glob of syrup stains her yellow uniform and she smells like cigarettes. Her voice strains as she looks around, as if she might find Chris out here somewhere, among all the Castle staff. "Is he okay?"

I hug her, clinging like I haven't in a very, very long time. "I don't know," I whisper.

Something about being held by my mother breaks me. I desperately want Chris to be fine, but I don't know if he will be. Fear hollows out my insides like someone scooping the guts out of a Halloween pumpkin.

We hold each other, standing together in the middle of the waiting room.

"He'll be okay." I say, trying to reassure myself as well. I rub Mom's back as she cries.

"Kit?" Jett's voice touches the edge of our circle, bringing me out of the moment with Mom. He's holding a Styrofoam takeout container. "I've got to go home. But I'll check on you later. Once I get my siblings sorted out."

"You don't have to do that," I say, shaking my head.

Mom gives my arm a squeeze and heads over to the nurse's station.

Jett thrusts the takeout container toward me. I open it and a laugh spills out of me as I take in the gooey, gloopy stack of food.

"Pancakes?" My stomach rumbles.

"I picked them up from your mom's diner because we missed our late-night after-work breakfast. Plus, my mother always says feed a cold, but breakfast a worry."

"Thank you," I say. I throw my arms around him. He stands aloof for a moment and then leans into me. I don't care what rules I'm breaking for the moment. It's good to hold Jett.

He pulls away first and rummages in his pocket. He pulls a plastic fork out and hands it to me. "See you soon."

Before I can say anything else, he plants a quick kiss on my cheek and turns away.

I hold my hand to my cheek, a smile finding its way to my lips. Layla walks in at that moment and shoots a look toward Jett's retreating back. I shrug, still grinning.

"Kit. Chris is awake. C'mon." My mom grips my hand, and I grip my pancakes, and together we stride down the hallway toward Chris's room.

As it turns out, they won't let you keep takeout containers of pancakes in the ICU. So, I have to leave them in the nurses' station fridge. Mom goes into Chris's room first, but I linger by the fridge, still holding the container. Delighted Chris is awake. Unsure I want to see him all banged up and injured.

Being a Knight was supposed to be fun. Something Chris and I practiced together. Everything at the Castle is scripted, sorted, and planned in advance. People aren't supposed to get hurt.

So what happened tonight? How did Chris injure himself so spectacularly?

As I stand there, hand on the fridge door, our first training session comes back to me.

Chris was seventeen and had moved up the ranks to top Squire. He was still in high school, but his tryouts for the Knight position were coming up. He needed someone to practice with, and I was the only one available and willing to help. I was almost fifteen and had just been hired at the Castle. I spent every minute that I wasn't handing out cheesy souvenirs watching the Knights.

Every day for the month before his tryouts, Chris and I would get the bus over to the Castle after school and watch the Knights' mock fights. Chris would record them with a phone he'd borrowed from his girlfriend, and then we'd practice the moves back at home after school.

Every weekend, the clang of blunted metal practice swords would ring out throughout our house.

"Outside!" Mom would roar. Dad usually wouldn't look up from whatever bottle he was trying to find the bottom of.

Chris and I would then take our battle down the stairs and into the yard, dancing across the turf like Westley and Inigo Montoya in *The Princess Bride*.

At first it was about trying to sword fight gracefully and avoid each other's blows. Then, we'd work on the skill exercises. We didn't have our own horses (shocker, I know), so we'd hang a set of rings from a low-hanging tree branch and ride our bikes up the driveway with long sticks in hand. It was remarkably stupid and incredibly fun.

"Hold that lance!" Chris had shouted during one of our first training sessions. "You're meant for more than wenching, sister of mine! RIDE!"

When we graduated from our short driveway, we moved to a city park down the road. There was a long trail that ran beside a pond filled with suburban runoff, electric-green lily pads, and cattails. Midway down the path, right in the center of a narrow isthmus where the path crossed the pond, Chris had hung five rings in a row from an overhanging willow branch. He argued that putting the rings on this narrow strip of asphalt between the ponds would force us to stay balanced, just as if we were on real horses.

It was my turn first.

"Ride!" I whispered to myself, balancing my feet on the bike pedals.

I gripped the end of a garden rake that was standing in for today's lance, and I pedaled. The trees and playground equipment raced past, smears of green and yellow. Kids' laughter filled my ears, and I imagined they were roars from a crowd at the Castle.

As I approached the rings, I adjusted the garden-rake-turned-lance (exactly like the ones we're using to train at Layla's) in my right hand. As real knights had done in the Middle Ages, I angled it across my body.

My left hand gripped the handlebars, steering.

"GO KIT!" Chris yelled from the sidelines.

One ring, swish.

Two rings, swish.

The rings rattled down the garden rake's pole and landed on my wrist like bangles. A wide grin split my face. One more left.

I was almost to the last ring, balanced perfectly in the middle of the isthmus, when the wind shifted. The ring wavered, and I adjusted the garden rake accordingly. It was a matter of the briefest bit of timing. Maybe a butterfly flapped its wings in South America and that threw me off. Maybe there was a stone on the path. To this day, I don't know. But whatever it was, it disrupted my fragile balance. My hand slipped; the pole dropped from my grip. With a clatter it fell onto the path, bounced sort-of sideways, and somehow wedged itself in the spokes of my bike. The front of the bike tipped forward, rocketing me off the seat.

"Ahhhhhhhhhhhh!" I screamed as I tumbled into the pond.

Rocks scraped my arm as I fell, and I landed in the sludge deep within the cattails. Mud splashed up into my face, and one of my slip-on sneakers came off in the muck. Water rose up to my waist.

"KIT?!" Chris crashed through the reeds, looking for me.

"I'm fine," I called. I reached into the mud, looking for my sneaker, but it was long gone.

Chris appeared at the edge of the bank, parting the cattails to gape at me. "Are you hurt? I'm so sorry. I shouldn't have insisted we practice on the isthmus."

I started to reply, but—no joke—at that moment, a frog leaped off its lily pad and landed on my head.

Brave Kit, sitting in the mud, with a frog on her head.

Laughter bubbled out of me, and I reached for Chris's hand.

"I'm fine," I managed to get out through gasps of laughter. "Not your fault at all."

He pulled me up the bank and we collapsed on the ground,

both of us laughing too much to speak. A mother pushing a stroller called out to us, "Are you two okay over there?" She shot us a look like she suspected we were smoking pot or something.

"Totally fine," Chris had called out, waving her down the path.

"But, m'lady," I added, "we fear the garden rake may never be the same!"

Giggles overtook us again, and when we were finally done laughing, we lay on the grass, looking up at the spring sky.

"Still want to keep training?" Chris asked as he handed me a water bottle. I used it to wash some of the mud from my face and hands.

"Ha! Of course. I'm going to be a Knight. Even if it kills me."

"At this rate it very well might," muttered Chris.

I punched him lightly in the arm, and we retrieved our bikes. As we ambled home, we talked about sword moves and new plans for training.

But now, despite all that training, being a Knight could've killed Chris. Was it worth it?

I still want to say yes, but first I want to see Chris. Shoving the pancakes from Jett into the nurses' fridge, I walk down the hall to see what shape the Red Knight is in.

"THE GOOD NEWS IS, HIS BACK'S NOT BROKEN," SAYS A SKINNY doctor in neon-green running shoes as I slip into Chris's room. He looks at the chart he's holding and makes a cryptic doctorish noise.

Chris lies in the bed, wearing a light blue hospital gown. Bandages poke out from beneath the gown, and his right arm is in a cast. A bandage wraps around his forehead, covering the nasty cut on his head. His long hair is smushed beneath it. His eyes are closed, his breathing shallow.

He looks like a caricature of an accident victim. Someone who's so injured, it's almost cartoonish. Except it's not. And this is real life.

"What's the bad news?" I say, walking over to Mom and putting an arm around her waist. She stands beside the bed, gripping the bedrail so tightly her knuckles stick out like pebbles beneath her skin.

The doctor looks at both of us. He sucks on his teeth for a moment and puts Chris's chart down. "The bad news is, your insurance isn't the greatest. And X-rays and those surgeries we did to set the bones in his arm are expensive."

"How can you discuss money at a time like this?" The question escapes my lips before I can stop it. I glare at the doctor, knowing it's not his fault, but taking my frustration and worry out on him.

The doctor shrugs, holding up his hands. "I wouldn't if I could help it, but it's hospital policy. We have to inform you of costs and insurance information."

"We'll figure it out," says Mom. She bites on her bottom lip.

"What sort of recovery are we facing?"

The doctor drones on. Telling us about physical therapy, what sorts of exercises Chris will need to do, and how his knee is seriously messed up (my words, not his).

I brush a piece of hair from Chris's cheek. "What about riding? When will he be able to ride a horse again?"

The doctor gives me a flabbergasted look. "Were you not listening? Your brother has a broken arm, torn ligaments in his knee, fractured ribs, and his head is in bad shape. He'll be on painkillers for a few days, and then we'll recommend physical therapy. It'll be a long time before he gets on a horse again."

There's a noise from the bed, and Chris groans in his sleep. The pain medicine the doctors have given him must be working, because a smile crosses his face as his eyes flutter open.

"Hey, Kit," he says. "How'd the garden rake come out?"

I swipe at the tear leaking from my eye as I give him a weak smile. "It didn't stand a chance."

"Mr. Sweetly," says the doctor, coming over to the bed and shining a light in Chris's eyes. "You're very lucky. We'd like to keep you here for a few days to keep an eye on your vitals and make sure everything is setting properly."

Chris nods his head, half listening. Soon, he's snoring again. Mom follows the doctor into the hallway, peppering him with questions. I pull up a plastic chair so it's right beside the bed and take Chris's hand. The machines by the bed beep like video games from the '80s. I yawn, suddenly exhausted.

My fear is still a cold lump in my belly, but at least now Chris has a direction and plan for recovery. I can deal with a plan.

"You can get through this." My voice is just a whisper. I squeeze his hand as I say it. "I know the Red Knight will ride again."

**23**

I'M NOT SURE WHEN I FALL ASLEEP OR WHEN MOM COMES back, but a cheerful nurse buzzes in early on Saturday morning, opening the curtains and shooing us out so she can check Chris's vitals and give him a sponge bath. A piece of paper covered in numbers falls to the floor as Mom stands up. I get a look at it before Mom snatches it away. "Estimate for Hospital Services" is emblazoned across the top, and at the bottom there's a big circle around a double-digit number with too many zeros after it.

I want to puke thinking about how we're going to get that much money.

Still waking up, Mom and I stumble into the hallway and walk toward the waiting room. I clutch my backpack to my chest. All the other Castle staff are gone, but I hope someone told them Chris was awake.

"Coffee?" I ask.

Mom's bun has come undone and dark circles ring her eyes. She nods and stretches, reaching toward the ceiling like she's doing yoga.

"Be back soon."

Shouldering my backpack, I make my way to the bank of elevators. The door opens with a *ding*. Despite the early hour, it's crowded with several nurses in scrubs, a woman in a bathrobe, and two sleepy-looking middle schoolers carrying Styrofoam takeout boxes. A gray-haired woman in a pink sweatshirt and rhinestone-covered baseball hat wrinkles her nose when I step into the elevator. She moves to the far back corner, putting as much distance between her shiny self and my rumpled one as possible. My last shower was yesterday morning before training and work. I'm sure I smell fairly medieval right now.

I give up on making my hair behave sometime between the third floor and the lobby. When the doors *ding* open, the nurses and kids shuffle out.

"You look exhausted," says the old woman in pink as she walks past me. "My husband's been in here for two weeks. Best to pace yourself, dear."

Much to my surprise, she gives me a small, sympathetic pat on the arm.

I smile to myself, buoyed for a moment by the small compassion of a stranger.

The cafeteria is at the end of another long hall. It's crowded with doctors in white coats, men and women in green scrubs, families getting breakfast, and an enormously pregnant woman who's moving up and down the cafeteria line, looking like she can't decide between Jell-O and crying.

I fill two cups of coffee and move into the checkout line.

"Four fifty-six," says the teenage girl behind the register. She looks almost my age, and I wonder for a moment why she's not in school. What sort of shit does life have to throw your way to end up cashiering in the hospital before six o'clock in the morning? Then I remember this is my spring break week and it's Saturday, and her presence there makes more sense.

Smiling at her in an attempt to pass on a little bit of the elevator woman's kindness, I pull a crumpled five-dollar bill out of my pocket and hand it to the girl. Since I missed out on last night's tips, it's the last of my cash.

My stomach grumbles as the smell of bacon rises from the person's plate behind me. I'll only have change left after the coffees, but at least there are still the pancakes I left in the nurses' fridge.

Thank you, Jett, for always showing up. With pancakes. And for generally just being a miracle of a human.

I'm about to take the receipt from the girl when I freeze.

"What's he doing here?" I mutter, peering toward the ketchup station in the dining area.

My dad's hair is still long, but it's now almost fully gray. He wears a faded flannel and dark blue jeans.

God help me, he's brought Len's electric guitar and has it out. In the middle of the hospital cafeteria. Face-palm.

Oblivious to the looks he's getting, he strums a few riffs lightly, looking completely out of place. Fury chases embarrassment as I watch him. I want to go over and dump my coffee on his head. I also want to skulk out of the place, ignoring him completely.

How did he know Chris was here? We haven't seen him since he left. Does he think he can just come back into our lives and pretend like everything is okay?

"Miss?" The cashier knocks on the counter like she's banging on a door. "You have to move on. It's breakfast rush. You can't just stand there."

I come back to myself and shake my head. I'll ignore him for now and get coffee to Mom. Maybe he'll be gone when I come back for lunch.

Trying to hide behind a group of med students in scrubs, I make it to the door. But, like Orpheus, I'm betrayed by my treacherous heart. I turn, and my dad's eyes meet mine.

"Kit-Kat!" he calls out, waving to me.

I sigh. Sometimes the only way out is through. Taking a long sip from my coffee, I wave back and walk toward his table. At first I think he's going to hug me, but then he stands up and gives me another weird little wave. Then he changes his mind and opens his arms.

"Fancy meeting you here," he says. His voice is strained, like he's trying too hard.

I pull out a chair and sit down, neatly sidestepping his hug. "What are you doing here, Lars?"

His eyebrows go up at my use of his first name, but he doesn't say anything. Up close I can see all the gray in his stubble and the deep circles under his eyes. He looks rough. Like the last few years have been hard, despite the glossy church advertisements that have somehow airbrushed his face into a smooth, youthful picture.

"Len called me last night, asking about the guitar. I didn't tell him I was going to bring it by the Castle. I was there for the whole show, sitting in the Green Knight's section."

"And you didn't even say hello?"

"I talked to Chris before the show," he says, picking up a coffee stirrer and twisting it in his hands. "He didn't want to talk, but I wanted to apologize. Which he took badly."

Maybe that's why Chris was distracted enough to fall off his horse and get so injured.

"He's furious at you. As he should be since you stole all his money for college."

Lars shakes his head. "I wish I could make up for the college fund I . . . um . . . borrowed from. But I don't have the money anymore."

I gape at that. "Borrowed?"

He has the good grace to look embarrassed at least. When his heroin habit ran through all his and Mom's savings, he drained the college funds Mom started for us when we were kids. Somehow, she'd kept them hidden from him. She had thousands of dollars of cash stuffed into jars and hidden in an old box of diapers in the attic. But he found them. And wiped them out entirely. The party he must've had from that money took him halfway across the country and into who knows what sorts of sleaziness.

"I'm clean now," he says, taking off his jacket and pulling up his sleeves. Where before there had been long track marks, like overgrown roads running down his arm, there are now just knotted skin and thick scars. "I left the church because of a fight with the other guys, but I'm still clean."

I mostly believe him.

"Good for you," I snarl. The words come out fiercer than I'd expected, but I don't regret them. "But we don't want anything from you."

"I went by the house the other night and saw how it is. And it's probably my fault that Chris fell last night. He was so worked up about our fight."

"Don't give yourself so much credit." I grab a handful of creamers out of the metal basket on the table and begin dumping them into my coffee. When I'm done with that, I tip the sugar container over and let a white river of sweetness pour in.

I make eye contact with my dad as I do so, as if I'm daring

him to lecture me on sweets. He looks like he wants to say something but shakes his head. I stop pouring the sugar and stir.

"I know I messed up, Kit-Kat," he says. He runs a hand through his hair and shifts his eyes to the side. For one moment, he's the dad who used to take me out to breakfast and who taught me to ride a bike. He's the dad who whisked Chris and me off to "adventures" every Sunday so Mom could sleep in. He's the dad who sang us songs and made up riddles for us to solve.

"Don't call me that," I say softly.

Chris needs me to be strong. Mom needs me to be strong. Neither of them need to know Dad is here. And the last thing I need is to get emotional about my dumpster fire father.

I take a sip of the coffee. Sweet Baby Jesus. It's like drinking cake.

"Courtney then," he says. "It's a more grown-up name for sure."

"Just Kit." My voice is forceful, and I look away from him.

Silence stretches between us. I should get up and deliver Mom her coffee. I should yell at my dad. Instead, I just drink more coffee, waiting for him to say something else.

"I'm going to sit here until Len comes," he finally says. "I called him and told him I'd be here. To return the guitar. He wanted to meet in a public place."

"So he doesn't kill you," I mutter. "Smart man."

"Yeah. How's school going? You looked perfectly in charge at the Castle last night."

He must've seen me delivering turkey legs and beers.

"I'm a Wench, Lars. Nothing to be 'perfectly in charge' of there."

"I meant in your video. The one where you rode out as a Knight."

Something in me stumbles. I can't believe he saw that. Did he feel proud of me while he watched? I push the thoughts way down. Nothing but pain waits for me there.

"You don't get to ask me about school. And you don't get to ask me about that video. My life is pretty much off the table for your opinions."

"I'm sorry, Kit. I didn't mean for it to go this way." He strums a note when he says it, making the doctor at the next table look up from the chart he's reading.

Why can't my dad be like that guy? Professional, competent, and put together. Someone who goes forth into the world every day to save lives and help people, not play some hokey soundtrack for a robot dragon show. Literally, a tape recorder could do his job.

Almost as if he's reading my mind, he pulls a newspaper clipping from his pocket. "My show's in town and doing really well." He points to the top of the page, where his face is barely visible above the wing of a baby dragon. "That's Lillyheimer, and that's Starzy." He points to pictures of each dragon.

The coffee is perking me up and anger rushes in, knocking over nostalgia and sadness like dominos. "I'm not a child anymore, Lars. And I don't care about your robot dragons. Chris is in the hospital, most likely because of you. Mom is broke because you took everything from her. So, forgive me if I don't want to sit here, shooting the shit about the kids' show you're doing."

He looks stunned for a minute and then holds up his hands. "Fair, fair. You can be angry. I understand that."

His trying to rationalize and empathize with my anger makes me want to pelt him with creamers. I take a steadying breath. "I'm leaving." I scowl as I grab both coffees. "Don't come up to Chris's room and don't bother Mom. Unless you're ready to sign the divorce papers already."

He pulls a folded pile of papers out of his inside jacket pocket. "I've got them right here. Tell her I'm down here. And Len has my phone number, in case you want to chat someday. But you don't have to call. Tell Chris I'm sorry. And that I love him."

He sounds so much like that dad I used to know. The dad I loved once. The dad who was my friend and hero, who I'd gift with handfuls of flowers and funny drawings.

"Goddamn you, Lars. You don't get to just come back and pretend like things are fine between us. I thought you knew that by now." My voice is thick with unshed tears.

"I love you too, Kit," he calls as I walk away.

I don't turn around this time. He loves the idea of the child I was. And I love the notion of the father he was before he left.

But all that's gone now.

**24**

MOM REACHES GRATEFULLY FOR THE COFFEE WHEN I get back to the room. Chris is awake, and a breakfast tray sits on a table over his lap.

"Morning, Girl Knight," he says with a lopsided smile. "I guess you'll have to take my place for good now."

Mom shoots me a look. "Don't even think about it. I'll break your legs myself to keep you out of that arena. In fact, I'm voting that both of you get jobs at the library effective immediately."

Chris and I both laugh. "Message received, though I think that you'll find Kit's in quite high demand lately. Show her."

Mom narrows her eyes. "What've you done now?"

I finish my coffee, sucking up the sweet, crystalline sludge from the bottom. "Well . . . remember when I fought in Chris's place last week? After that, Layla and I made this website, and it's pretty much gone viral. . . ."

I open my phone and press Play on the video. Mom holds her coffee in both hands as she watches. One hand flies to her mouth as I whip off my helmet, but she keeps smiling as the video finishes.

I can't help myself as I let out a little cheer.

"Read the comments," Chris says. He takes a small sip of apple juice and makes a face. He looks at me and nods toward the coffee. "Anything left in there?"

Mom hands him her coffee, her eyes not leaving the screen. She scrolls down, reading the comments.

Chris takes a sip and makes a face. "Too bitter," he moans, handing it back. He tries to eat more toast, but his eyes get droopy as he sits there, and he's soon back asleep. Mom holds a finger to her lips as she reads.

"Kit, there are thousands of comments here," she says. Wonder fills her voice.

"I know," I say. "And that means Corporate is getting tons of emails."

"But you can't fight," says Mom. "What happens if you get hurt?" She nods toward Chris.

"I won't get hurt. I promise."

She shakes her head again. "You can't guarantee that."

I take another peek at Chris. He's still asleep. I lean toward Mom and whisper the thing that I've told no one, ever. "I'm better than him. I won't get hurt."

Mom gives me a wry smile. "Confidence is good, but arrogance will break a leg."

I've heard her say it a hundred times, but the meaning is so much clearer now that Chris lies in bed, with his body pinned together.

"We'll see what happens," I say, and smile at her. "The Castle probably won't even let me fight."

Is this a lie or the truth? This is the land of pure moral grayness, as it's hard to tell, since it's true they won't let me fight. But it's false because I'm absolutely going out there again.

"But you're going to try, aren't you?" Her eyes meet mine.

"I'm going to try. The gender restrictions at the Castle are awful. And me, Layla, Penny, and a few others are really getting better at the Knight routines. We have a chance to make things fair."

"Kit—" Mom takes a deep breath. I imagine she's regretting all those times she read me books about the women's movement. But her reply surprises me. "Okay, fine. I'm proud of you. I really am. And I think what you're doing is incredibly cool. Just promise me you'll be careful. We can't afford another five-thousand-dollar deductible. And my heart can't handle seeing another one of my children in the hospital."

I go over to her and wrap my arms around her. "Thanks, Mom. And I'll be careful. And, um, speaking of all this. Could you sign something for me?"

"What is it?" The tone of her voice is wary.

"Just a permission slip for me to be on the news."

"Kit!"

Her voice wakes Chris.

"What's going on?" he says, dazedly.

"Nothing. Go back to sleep," I say softly.

"Kit," my mom hisses more quietly once Chris is asleep again. "You're going on the news?"

Quickly I tell her about Eddy and Bettina, and then I show her the email I got last night. "It's on Monday, so we have to reply soon."

"Well, thank goodness tomorrow's Sunday so you have time to get your homework done. And they're picking you up," says Mom. "Which is perfect, since I have to work a morning shift and don't want to fight traffic. But you're going to miss the first day after spring break, and that won't look good."

"Mom. I'm like a month away from graduation. Missing one day will be fine. And this exposure could be what actually makes Len and the Castle listen to us!"

"Doing this will make Len mad *and* it will help you?"

Mom and Len have what you might call a complicated relationship. One mostly based on mutual dislike.

"Yes to both."

"Fine," she says with a smile. "You can do it. Give me that form."

She signs it digitally, which I guess in retrospect I could've done. But it feels good to be honest with someone about this whole thing.

"Thanks, Mom," I say. "You're the best."

She gives me a small hug. "Oh, by the way, did you see your father downstairs? He was supposed to bring the signed divorce papers by the house last night, but I told him we were here. He texted to say he'd bring them over sometime around this time."

"He was there when I left," I admit. "But I'm not sure he's still there. He didn't look great."

Mom swears and grabs her purse. "Sit with Chris until I get back?"

"I'll be here," I say, grabbing the remote and changing the channel from baseball replays to a show on the History Channel about the Knights Templar.

Mom blows me a kiss as she hurries out the door.

25

OT LONG AFTER THAT, I'M READING ON MY PHONE AS I walk through the lobby doors toward the bus stop. Dad was long gone (of course, he was), and Mom has sent me home to get her fresh clothes and do some laundry. The air is warm and hints at the summer yet to come. Part of me wants to see if I can find Dad, lurking somewhere around the hospital, but I don't. Why pour salt in that wound? Plus, Mom will sort out how to get the divorce papers from him. Somehow.

Layla's sent me fourteen texts since yesterday. I write her back, telling her all about Chris's injuries and recovery plan.

Her reply comes in immediately.

Layla: So, remember how I was supposed to check on the website clicks and money coming in after Eddy and co boosted it?

Kit: Yes . . .

Layla: You're up to a million hits and we've made three thousand dollars so far.

Kit: SHUT UP!

Layla: Not even lying. I'll go over it with you later. Are you working tonight?

Kit: Nope. I've got to catch up on homework for the next few days. My next shift is on Wednesday.

Layla: Okay, I'm off tonight too. Text me if you want to hang out.

She texts a smiley face back, and I'm about to put my phone away, but Jett's face appears on my screen.

"How's Chris?" Jett asks when I pick up.

"Awake, alive, and telling me I should take his place as the Red Knight."

"Glad to hear it," says Jett. I can practically hear him grinning. "Can I come get you? My mom is making fancy grilled cheese."

The bus pulls up as he says it, but it's already crowded. It belches stinky smoke, and somehow the thought of riding the bus to my empty house, with its cooler full of melting ice and disgusting food, is just too much for me right now.

"I could eat grilled cheese."

"Be there soon," says Jett.

He pulls up in his mom's minivan fifteen minutes later and honks twice, and I open the passenger door. "Thanks for the ride," I say, pulling the door closed behind me. "Nice wheels."

"Dad's taking the bike out, so I got stuck with the van again."

"Well, I appreciate the chance not to barf on your bike. Again."

A pained look crosses his face. "You have a terrible sense of humor," he says, and smiles. "You know that, right?"

"That's what friends are for." I laugh.

Which is apparently our new motto, and a great big fat lie.

JETT'S MOM LOOKS NOTHING LIKE MINE. WHEREAS MY MOM looks tired and crumpled, like a tissue that's been used up and thrown away, Jett's mom is still glamorous. She was a model before she went to college, and she's tall and thin, and her hair always looks like she's just come from a Brazilian blowout. Even when she's wearing a T-shirt, jeans, and a cardigan with holes in the elbows.

She sits at their kitchen counter, a cup of tea in one hand and a book in the other.

"Hello, Kit," she says as I walk in. She puts her book down and comes over to kiss me on both my cheeks, which makes her that much more glamorous and European. "I hope you are hungry." She gestures to a plate piled high with grilled cheeses. White cheese flecked with herbs and peppers oozes out of them.

My stomach rumbles, reminding me I've not had more than coffee and cold pancakes today.

Jett takes my backpack and puts it on the living room couch.

"Be right back," he says, taking the stairs two at a time. From upstairs there's the thump of a kid jumping out of a bunk bed and then a bunch of feet pounding around.

Jett's mom glances upstairs and smiles. She looks just like Jett when she does that. "'Let's have lots of kids,' I said to my husband. 'I want a houseful of naughty boys.'"

"Be careful what you wish for?" I say, smiling back.

"Always," she says. "Come here. I want you to see this."

I sit down next to her and she pushes the book she's reading toward me. It's as large as a coffee-table book and ragged at the edges. Pieces of paper are shoved into it, and they stick out of the top, bottom, and side. I open it and run my fingers over the handwritten Russian words. Kids in red and blue bell-shaped coats, Easter eggs, farm animals, and many other drawings cover the pages.

"What is this?"

"It's a book of stories," says Jett's mom. She pushes her glasses up her nose and runs her hand over a page, caressing it lovingly. "In Russia, when I was growing up, there were not very many books. My mother would take me to the booksellers near Gorky Park. We would read what was there and then pass them on; but there were more kids who wanted to read than there were books. So we would share. My mother, like so many others, would copy stories into books like this. We'd pass these books around and draw pictures in them. This one came to me via a friend in Europe. Her mother gave it to her. I'm going to document it as part of a larger project I'm working on."

"It's so pretty." I turn another page. "What's this story about?"

"That is a fairy tale, about two children who find a house made of plums—"

"'Hansel and Gretel'?"

"Something like that," says Jett's mom. She reads a few lines in Russian, the words lilting off her tongue. When she stops, I turn another page.

"Is it hard to be away from your family?" I say as I look at all the handwritten stories and pictures.

Jett doesn't talk about the Russian side of his family. All I know is his mother went to Australia on a student visa and met his dad there, and they moved to America before Jett was born.

"There are not many of them left," she says, wrapping both hands around her cup of tea. "My mother died when I was your age, and my father passed away when I was a university student."

"I'm sorry," I whisper, kicking myself for bringing up bad memories.

"It's nothing to be sorry over," says Jett's mom with a sad smile. "They were wonderful people, but it was their time."

Silence stretches between us, and I turn another page.

Upstairs, more footsteps pound around.

"What's your project about?" I ask as I come to a particularly beautiful page. Colorful statues resting on the top of spectacular onion-domed buildings look on as children ride winged horses through the snow.

Jett's mom takes a sip of tea. "I'm still figuring that out, but I know I want to use books like this to talk about how sometimes things aren't ideal, but you find a way; you get creative, and you have a network of people to help you."

It's a little bit like what I've learned from my time as the Girl Knight. Which is—of course—way less important than people bonding together to share literature and stories in an authoritarian culture where such things are tightly regulated. But still. Take the lessons where you can.

Before I can ask any more questions, two of Jett's younger brothers race down the stairs and swarm the plate of grilled cheese.

"Hi, Kit!" shouts Feliks, an energetic third grader with a gap where his front teeth should be.

Jett's other brother, Marc, a fourth grader, doesn't look up from the book he's reading as he sits down at the table.

I wave and take the oozy half of grilled cheese Feliks offers me. Jett's mom hands out napkins, while Feliks and Marc eat apple slices and burp the alphabet.

"Charming family I have, I know," says Jett, coming down the stairs holding his youngest brother, two-year-old Aarav, who's clearly just woken up from a nap. His curly dark hair is plastered to his forehead and he hides his face on Jett's shoulder when I wave to him.

Jett hands Aarav to his mom, who's wisely covered her book of stories with a plastic bag. The baby nuzzles into his mom, and she sings to him softly in Russian while she hands out juice boxes.

Jett grabs a plate. "We're eating outside," he calls out as he jumps into the scramble for grilled cheese. He emerges with two full triangles and one half-eaten one.

"Sorry," he says, appraising the half-eaten one.

"No worries," I say, through a mouthful of sandwich. I grab two cups of lemonade and follow him outside.

When he closes the sliding door behind me, the noise of the house recedes. We sit side by side at a picnic table. It's suddenly, awkwardly, hugely not quiet in the way that it can be only in the suburbs on a weekend in the spring. Meaning there are lawn mowers going, some music from a garage down the way, and the shouts of kids playing down the street.

Jett doesn't say anything.

I don't say anything.

I take a bite of grilled cheese, savoring its buttery, melty goodness.

"So, you're not allowed to ask me about how the *Girl Knight and Friends* documentary is going. Because it's top secret for now," Jett finally says through a mouthful of sandwich.

"Chris might never ride again," I blurt out at the same moment. My voice is thick with snot and unshed tears.

"Oh, Kit." Jett pulls me into a side hug. "I'm sorry."

"I mean, not riding isn't the worst thing ever. I know that. But I'm so angry. Do you know why he was so distracted and fell?"

Before I can stop myself, the story about meeting my dad, and him trying to apologize to Chris, and what he said to me comes out in a rush.

Jett sits there for a moment, processing things.

I wipe my eyes with the back of my hand. For a moment, it's on the tip of my tongue to tell him about everything else— the Castle saying no and how I'm lying to everyone; the tournament I've somehow got to make work so I can become a Knight and pay for college; my mom's money troubles; the divorce; Chris's hospital bills—but I just stay quiet.

"What're you going to do?"

I shrug. "I'm not going to see him again. I don't want him in my life."

"What do you want from him?" Jett drops his arm from my shoulder, like he's just realized it's there.

I take a shaky breath. I've been asking myself the same question all day.

"What I want is a dad who does more than pop into our lives when it's convenient for him."

"I'm sorry," says Jett. "I think I lucked out in the dad department, so I can only imagine how hard this is for you."

His dad is at the library right now, but he's the best kind of dad. Interested, reliable, funny. Comes to kids' soccer games and does stuff like offer to take Jett on trips to India, so Jett can fulfill his dream of volunteering at schools there. I would be lucky to have a dad half as good as Jett's.

"It's okay." I finish my grilled cheese. "I think the trick with my dad is to not let the past overwhelm me too much. Keep looking ahead. He's been gone so long, it's not hard to imagine a future without him."

"That's a good plan." Jett nods and stands up. "Want me to drive you home?"

I take his offered hand and get up too. "Can you drop me off at the Castle so I can pick up Chris's car? I've got to go to the laundromat. Our washer's broken again."

My hand stays in Jett's for a moment, but then he drops it like it's crawling with medieval vermin. He looks like he wants to say more. Or hug me again. But we settle for a silence that's clammy and uncomfortable in a wet-bathing-suit-when-you-get-out-of-the-pool kind of way.

**26**

I'M ALMOST RELIEVED WHEN JETT DROPS ME OFF AT THE Castle. Almost. But I'm also a little bit sad, because it's starting to feel like there's so much we need to say to each other. But there's not much I can do about that. At least not right now.

I fish Chris's key from under his right tire and pray his ancient Volvo will start. He locks the door as a formality, since both back windows are covered in clear plastic and duct tape. Mercifully, the car starts on the first try, and I manage to stall out only twice on the way home. As I pull into my driveway, I half expect to hear Chris hammering away in the blacksmith shop out back.

But no. Birds sing and cars race by on the freeway, making a low, steady hum in the background, but my house is quiet.

It's so quiet, it almost feels like a funeral home with its empty stillness. I move through the house, opening drapes, clicking on light switches, and gathering laundry. I take the last few bills out of the jar on the table, hoping it will be enough for all the loads. Then I head downstairs to Chris's room.

Since Chris's room is in the lower half of our split-level, only small slivers of afternoon light make it through his grimy windows. I flick the light on, looking for dirty laundry to gather up. My eyes land on a LEGO model of the Sears Tower (well, now the Willis Tower, but it'll always be the Sears Tower to us here in Chicago) on top of Chris's bookshelf. I haven't been in his room in a while, and I didn't realize he still had this.

I pick it up carefully, blowing the dust off it.

It's something I bought for him a few years ago, after he and I took the train into downtown without telling Mom. As we walked the concrete corridors of Michigan Avenue, Chris brimmed with plans for the buildings he would design.

"Mine will be as tall as these," he gushed, pointing up at the skyscrapers. "But I want them to look like the gorgeous buildings in Singapore or Dubai. To achieve that, I'll have to . . ."

He went on and on, sharing his dreams and plans.

We went to the top of the Sears Tower and the Hancock Building. The views of Lake Michigan captivated me, but Chris was fascinated by how the buildings were held together. He told me—in exacting and excruciating detail—about the type of steel used, how long it took to construct each building, how much concrete was required, how many feet of wiring the buildings contained, and much, much more that can only be filed under the category of "shit Chris cares about and Kit spaces out on."

But I knew he loved it. And that his dream was as tall as those buildings piercing the sky. So, I saved up money from babysitting jobs and my first shifts at the Castle and bought him this LEGO Sears Tower building set. Clearly, he was too old for LEGOs, but that didn't matter.

"It's so you can have something to look at when you forget what you want out of life," I said, handing it to him.

He laughed and began building immediately, like he used to on the rare occasions when he got LEGOs as a kid.

A few hours later, it was built, and he hugged me. "It's perfect, Kit. Thanks."

Now, it gathers dust on his shelf. Forgotten, pushed aside. Like so many other dreams.

A lump rises in my throat as I start to put it back, knowing there's nothing I can do to help him this time.

But, no. That's not thinking like the Girl Knight. The Girl Knight takes action. I carry the LEGO Sears Tower upstairs and set it by my bag. If—and admittedly, this is a very big if—I can manage not to break it, then Chris can see it while he recovers in the hospital. Maybe it will inspire him to pursue a new dream.

Or maybe it will just be some dumb LEGO, but it's worth a shot.

When I get to my room, I raise my blinds and flop onto the bed. Above my bed, my poster with "KIT'S BIG PLAN" mocks me with its assertion that the world can be ordered, that it's tidy and plannable.

But life isn't like that, is it?

There are accidents, and mistakes, and brothers who fall off horses, and absent dads who reappear. And boys who should be kissed, no matter that it's not a smart idea or against the rules.

As I stare up at the bullet points on the poster board, I feel them closing in around me. They were supposed to be ordering points. Compasses to move me forward. But now they feel more like bars, holding me back.

Have I trapped myself behind all the walls of my own plan?

But another voice whispers somewhere inside me, my mother's voice: "Kit, if you don't have a plan, life will just sweep you along in its current. That's what happened to me. I got swept away and never found my footing. You can chart your own course and steer your own way."

I'm not even sure what the way looks like anymore, and so I stand up and rip down the poster with "KIT'S BIG PLAN" written on it.

I can't quite bring myself to throw it away, but I don't want it staring at me either. Shoving it under my bed, I leave my room.

There are things to do. Tomorrow I can revise my big plan. Today I need to do the laundry, visit Chris, and do my homework.

I gather the laundry and the Sears Tower and head back out to the Volvo. A weary Lady Knight, leaving home again, for another day of questing with the most ordinary of dragons.

**27**

THE WASH BASKET LAUNDROMAT GLOWS LIKE A BEACON in the gloom of the afternoon. Rain falls in a steady, soft patter as I run from Chris's car to the entrance. There's only one other guy inside, a huge, bearded dude. He looks like the Mountain from *Game of Thrones*'s overgrown son. He takes up two chairs and the edge of a third. Part of me knows I should be sketched out, being all alone in here with him, but mostly I'm just tired. And needing to get back to the hospital with clean clothes for Mom.

I prop the door open and haul my hamper, two trash bags full of towels, and then a few bags of Mom's and Chris's laundry through the door. The bell jingles as I walk in, and the dude looks up from the copy of *Powerlifting Elite* he's reading.

"Need some help?" he calls out. He starts to stand, but I shake my head.

"I've got it." I lug the hamper toward the nearest machine and go back for the bags.

All the dryers are full, humming away with what I can only presume is an avalanche of laundry from the Mountain Jr.

I fill washers one through ten and then trudge to the industrial washers at the back, stuffing a bunch of towels into one and then filling the other with the remaining laundry. As I cram the last few washcloths in and get the cycle started, I imagine how the Girl Knight would stand up to someone like the Mountain. She'd have to be fast. And get the first strike in and then dart away. Strategy, like higher ground or using natural elements, would—

*Oh, lady knights, help me.*

The Mountain Jr.'s got a knife.

I freeze behind the washers, clutching my container of cheap laundry detergent to my chest as well as my phone. The enormous man holds a knife as long as my arm. It's triangle-shaped and looks like it's from one of those kitchen sets that people used to sell door-to-door. From here the metal looks dull, but the point is sharp. Surreptitiously, I click Video and then Record on my phone, in case the police need evidence or something when they find my body. The man doesn't look at me as he rests the knife on top of the small table beside him.

My heart plays a wild burst of fanfare. I try not to panic.

Is the Girl Knight going to end up dead in a laundromat? If it comes down to it, will I be able to defend myself with this flimsy blue jug of laundry soap?

Held in suspension by the two thoughts, I stand there. The guy doesn't look at me as he rummages around in his backpack. I calculate the number of steps to the door.

He makes a satisfied noise as he pulls a block of white cheese from his bag.

A. Block. Of. Cheese.

Who brings a block of cheese to a laundromat?

I burst out laughing.

The dude looks up and smiles sheepishly. He carves a neat little piece of cheese from the side of the block and holds it out. "Want some?"

I shake my head, trying to still my racing heart. "I . . . um . . . just ate a bunch of grilled cheese. Thanks."

He smiles and goes back to carving off blocks of cheese and reading his powerlifting magazine. I go back to my chair and slump into it. Once my fingers have stopped shaking, I open the Layla-Alex-Mags-Lizzy-Jett-Penny text chain I've had going since we started training together.

Kit to the Knights for Days Group Text: Y'all. OMG. I'm at the laundromat with the Mountain Jr., and he's eating cheese with a carving knife. WTF???

I send them the video. Replies come back a few moments later.

Jett: Um . . .

Layla: OMG. Who does that?

Alex: I'm dying. You okay?

Kit: Alive, but so bored. Laundry is going, so I have time to kill. (And watch this guy eat cheese.)

Jett: Do your homework.

Kit: Thanks, Mom, but it's only Saturday. I'll get it done tomorrow. Plus, I left it at home. I think I'm gonna practice some Knight moves, just to throw the cheese-eater off.

Jett: 😂 😂 😂 Don't do anything until I get there. I'll bring my video camera and film it for the sake of the documentary.

Layla: I'm on my way too. Which laundromat are you at?

Kit: The Wash Basket by my house.

Mags: Knight training at the laundromat? I'm in.

Alex: Me too. Though I've only got a few hours before I have to work.

Penny: I'm going to the hospital to visit Chris, so I can't make it. But send me videos!

Lizzy: Boo! I'm at my grandma's in Wisconsin. Can't make it. Send me pics too!

My washers are done, and the Mountain Jr. is loading his laundry into his car by the time Jett, Layla, Alex, and Mags arrive. Jett has his camera, and Layla carries an armful of pool noodles.

"Safer than practice swords," she says with a smile. "And less likely to get the police called on us."

"You're a genius," I say, holding the door open for her.

Once we've switched my laundry over to dryers and Alex has handed out granola bars because they're the friend who always shows up with snacks, I explain to them the training setup I've been planning.

"Okay, so I think we need to work on both our ground routines and some of the jousting." I point to the bank of washers running through the middle of the laundromat. "We can pretend that's the tilt, and then we can come at each other across it with the pool noodles."

"Please tell me we get to use those laundry carts as horses," says Mags with a wicked grin. She points to the two metal carts sitting near our chairs. They're the kind with four small wheels, a large metal basket, and then two poles with a third across the top for hanging laundry. Decidedly meant for low-impact situations, not jousting.

"We're absolutely using those." I return her grin. "Want to start with the jousting or the floor routine?"

Alex grabs a green pool noodle. "Floor routine. En garde, Girl Knight!"

I grab a pink pool noodle. Darting around the Wash Basket, Alex and I go through the steps Chris taught us. Forward, back, forward again. I lunge into Alex's guard, and then they do a forward roll out of the way. On the other side of the laundromat, Layla and Mags spar in a similar routine using blue pool noodles. Jett films it all, sometimes on one side of the room and sometimes on the other. He even climbs onto the bank of washers to get a bird's-eye view of the action.

After nearly twenty minutes of ground fighting, we're all panting and our pool noodles dangle limply from our hands. Alex hands out water bottles, and we slump together on the hard plastic chairs, catching our breath.

"That was amazing," Jett exclaims as he reviews the footage. "I think you're all getting much better!"

"We better be," says Layla. "The tournament is less than a week away. We've got to be flawless."

"I'm so stoked," says Mags. "I invited my boyfriend and my parents. I think Lizzy told me her grandma and a few of her cousins are coming."

"Yeah, my parents will be there too," adds Alex. "They haven't been to the Castle in a few years, but as soon as I told them I was fighting, they bought tickets."

Just hearing my friends speak of the tournament sends a flutter of butterflies into my throat. I should correct them. Tell them this is far from a sure thing. But they all look so happy going over the moves and talking about the costumes. I don't want to take that from them. Plus, I can still figure this out. There's got to be a way to convince Len to let us fight.

"So, um, did you know jousting is the official sport of Maryland?" I say, changing the subject in what's got to be the least subtle way possible. "Yeah. Since the 1960s. Apparently it was huge in colonial times and they still have tournaments. Both men and women—they call them Knights and Maids—ride out."

Alex rolls their eyes at the "Knights and Maids" bit, but otherwise everyone is startled by my revelation.

"That's a fairly amazing fun fact," says Jett. "I don't even think our state has an official sport."

"I've been doing research for the interview on Monday," I admit. "In case I get asked a bunch of questions about jousting."

"What's happening Monday?" asks Mags, shooting me a look. "You going to tell someone at school this?"

Shit. I'd forgotten that I've not yet told them about going on *Good Morning, Chicago!* Layla's eyebrows are practically in her hair, and I feel especially bad about not telling her. Quickly, I explain what's happening and how I met Bettina.

"That's going to be epic," says Alex. "I wish I could stay home and watch. But I can't because I've got a photography club meeting and a math test in the morning."

"You have a test the day after spring break?" I rack my brain trying to figure out what math class they might be talking about, since we have a ton of the same classes.

"*We* have a test," says Jett. "Remember that math homework I keep nagging you about?"

I groan. A memory of our calc teacher saying something about a test rises in my mind. "I'm gonna miss it. I have to do this news segment."

"She'll let you make it up," says Layla. "Don't even worry

about it. We'll tell her what you're doing."

"You all are the best, you know that, right?" I smile gratefully at my circle of friends.

"We are," says Alex. They pick up an unbent pool noodle from the pile. "Now, enough talking. We've still got the place to ourselves. Let's joust. Mags, will you push me?"

Alex rolls one of the laundry carts to the far end of the laundromat and climbs in. Layla gets into the other. I push her to the opposite end of the bank of washers. Both Layla and Alex kneel in the carts, pool noodles out.

"READY, SET, JOUST!" Jett yells. His camera's on and he balances on a chair as he films.

I push Layla's cart hard, running behind it and trying to steer so she's close enough to hit Alex over the washers but not so close we crash into them. She holds one of the cart's poles to steady herself and balances the pool noodle with the other.

They're closer, closer, closer. And *crash!*

Well, okay. Not *crash*. Because pool noodles sound more like Rice Krispies crackling than lances shattering when they hit each other.

But still, we make contact.

"AGAIN!" Alex shouts, grinning. Their cart is at the far end of the room now.

"One more time, then it's my turn," Mags says, as she turns the cart around. "You're heavier than you look."

Alex turns around and bops Mags with their pool noodle.

"Agreed, my fair Knight."

Mags grabs a nearby noodle and whacks Alex with it. While they have a spontaneous sword–pool noodle fight, Layla trades places with me in the cart.

"It's super fun, Kit; you've got to try it."

I take the yellow pool noodle from her and climb in. The metal of the basket digs into my knees, so I end up squatting. Alex and Mags get back to their starting position.

"READY, SET, JOUST!" Jett shouts.

Layla thrusts the cart along the side of the washers. I can feel every wiggle of the squeaky wheel on the front left side of the cart. Alex looms closer, their pool noodle brandished. I lean forward ever so slightly, ready to knock the noodle out of their hands.

Almost to them. Almost. Almost . . .

"Ahhhhh!" I yell, right as we make contact. I manage to knock the noodle out of Alex's hand, but somehow, I'm pitched too far forward. Startled by my scream, Layla loses her grip on the cart and it slams into the washers. I fly out and land on my belly across two of them.

"Kit!" Jett yells, putting his camera down as he runs toward me. "Are you okay?"

I roll over trying to catch my breath. "I'm okay," I say through the laughter bubbling up inside me. Tears stream down my face. "That was so fun. Let's do it again."

Layla punches me lightly on the arm. "Don't scare me like

that. After Chris's injury, I'm not sure I can handle seeing another Sweetly flying through the air."

I wipe my eyes, suddenly a little less amused. "Fair point. But I'm fine. You want another turn?"

With a grin, Layla climbs back into the basket and Mags takes Alex's place.

We joust for another ten rounds before a tired-looking mother comes in with her two toddlers, shooting us dirty looks.

Still laughing, my friends and I load my laundry into bags. Layla and Jett gather all the pool noodles—stuffing a bunch of the broken ones into a trash can, which is sure to baffle someone when they come in to do laundry later.

"Good luck with the interview," Layla says, giving me a hug as we leave. "Call me the minute it's done."

"I'll be watching," says Jett. "Just imagine you're talking to me, so you're not nervous."

I wave to him, Layla, Alex, and Mags. I'm not sure I deserve friends as good as these, especially since I'm still lying to them. But, damn, I'm grateful to have them.

28

CHRIS IS AWAKE WHEN I GET TO THE HOSPITAL ON SATUR-day night. Mom heads to the bathroom to shower as soon as I hand her a bundle of clean clothes.

"I have a problem," I announce when the bathroom door clicks shut behind Mom and the water turns on.

Chris raises an eyebrow and struggles to sit up. "What is the problem?"

"Don't move, you lout," I say affectionately as I arrange the pillows behind his head and lift the bed. "Your bones are broken."

"But never my spirit," he rasps weakly. He grins and some of part of the worry nesting inside me settles.

It's a line from the Red Knight's script at the Castle. Something we've practiced a hundred times. If Chris can make jokes, maybe all this isn't so bad after all.

"One problem of many is that I don't know how I'll do this without you. Who's going to convince the other current Knights to help us?" I pull the giant, pleather-covered arm-chair over to the side of his bed.

"We'll figure that out." Chris gives me a crooked smile. "How has the Knight squad been managing without me? What phase of the plan are you at?"

"Phase three, I think?" I exhale sharply. Then, in a rush, I tell Chris everything about our training in the laundromat, meeting Eddy, and going on the news with Bettina.

"Viking Eddy!" says Chris, with another smile. "Did you know he once paid a server to bring him twenty turkey legs and he ate all of them during the course of one show?"

"He had twelve when I waited on him last."

Chris shakes his head. "That guy. He's a legend among the Knights. Even Dalton likes him. We have a board in the Knights' locker room that has a collection of his greatest feats."

"You have a board? What is it, like classic locker room stuff? Tell me you don't do that patriarchal nastiness."

"Nah," says Chris, blushing. "It's record holders like Eddy Jackson—most turkey legs eaten in one sitting. And then peo-ple to watch out for, like Viviane, this rich, middle-aged lady who would do creepy stuff like throw panties into the arena. She's the record holder for kissing the most Knights. She'd sneak up on us during a photo."

"*Ewwww*. That's harassment and not okay for anyone to do. Ever."

"Exactly," says Chris. "She's been banned from the Castle, but we get lots of people who do similar stuff."

My blood steams to think about it. Chris sees the look on my face and nods.

"Yeah, I'm hoping that the changes you're making will help with things like that too. But back to our board. It's not all bad. Like I said, Eddy's on there. And then there's Owen, this little kid who came to every show for an entire month, as part of his Make-A-Wish program." Chris's voice trails off and I can't bring myself to ask what happened to Owen.

"That's a lot of ground to cover on one board."

Chris yawns as he nods. "I'll show you when you're a Knight."

"Hey, I brought you something." I pull the still-intact-through-some-miracle LEGO Sears Tower from my bag.

Chris reaches out for it, his eyebrows raised in surprise. "You're so weird. What did you bring this for?"

"It's a reminder of your dreams, stupid. Remember you want to be an architect?"

"Your eloquence is dazzling," says Chris, smiling. "But thank you. I'd almost forgotten about this."

"It's here to remind you that you can do other stuff, you know, after the Castle. Even if you don't get to ride again."

"I know that," says Chris softly. He sets the LEGO tower on the bedside table again. "So, it seems like things are going well with the Knights and you're going on the news. But something else is wrong. I can tell. Spill. What's the problem?"

The truth is on the tip of my tongue, but saying it out loud is hard. Even harder than I thought. What if Chris tells Penny? And she tells the others? What if they all just back out because the Castle said no? But this is Chris. He'll keep my secret.

I exhale sharply. "Well, I'm lying to my friends and also I have no idea how to set up this tournament that's not supposed to happen." I give him the broad-strokes version of how the Castle rejected my idea. His eyes widen as he realizes just how deeply I've dug the hole for myself.

Before Chris can reply, a nurse bustles in to give him his pain meds, and Mom comes out of the bathroom, toweling off her hair.

"So, we have to take Chris home tonight," says Mom, holding up her phone.

"Tonight?" My voice is too loud for the small room, and the nurse shoots me a look. "Why? He's still barely put back together."

A desperate look crosses Mom's face. "I've been on the phone with the insurance company all day, and they've just sent me an email about costs and coverage. We can't afford to linger. With our terrible insurance, a stay like this costs hundreds of dollars a day. And with the huge deductible, we're just going deeper into debt the longer Chris stays here."

She looks at the nurse, as if there were an answer there.

"I know, honey," says the nurse, checking the machines

that monitor Chris's heartbeat and vitals. "It's a broken system. Wish there was something I could do for you all."

"Let Chris stay another night," I say as the nurse leaves. "My website is making money. Not much, but enough to pay the deductible at least so far. We can use it to let him stay one more night."

"Kit, no," says Chris. "That's your money for college. Go clean out my account. Or just let me go home. I'm fine. Really." He tries to swing his legs around the bed, but collapses into Mom's arms before he can fully stand up.

"Rest, you ridiculous man," I say, smiling at them both. I'm so happy I can help out, I could do a cartwheel. Right there in the hospital room. "I'll get the money. Mom, you make the arrangements. I'm sure I'll get a scholarship; and, I'll have plenty of time to make up the rest of the money from working this summer."

"Are you okay going home alone? I'll stay until the morning, but I have to get back to work tomorrow." A frown of worry crosses Mom's forehead. I can almost hear her counting up the number of shifts she's missed and worrying about what her boss will say.

As I hug Chris goodbye, he whispers to me. "You have to tell the others, Kit. They'll help you think of something, but they should know."

I know he's right, but that doesn't mean telling them is going to be any easier.

29

I SPEND SUNDAY DOING HOMEWORK AND WATCHING THE views of my video grow (over a million!). Mom comes home around dinnertime and we eat ramen and look through an apartment-rental website, trying to find a new place to live once our house is sold. I fall asleep to dreams of fighting, telling lies, and driving a cart through a laundromat that turns into a labyrinth.

As promised, a car pulls up outside my house at 4:30 a.m. on Monday morning. Except it's not a car. It's more like a baby Batmobile, with its shiny chrome and sleek lines. My reflection and the first hints of sunrise blink back at me from the mirrored windows. One unrolls as I approach. I clutch my coffee and try to comb the bedhead out of my hair.

"Kit Sweetly?" asks a bright-eyed young woman with flawless

brown skin, perfect hair, and an expensive-looking blouse.

I nod and cover a huge yawn with my hand. I was up late texting with Layla, who is perhaps more excited than I am about this morning show appearance. I still didn't manage to tell her the truth about the tournament, but that's because I'm hoping today's news appearance will convince Corporate to let us fight. When we finally said good night, it was after one o'clock in the morning. I barely heard my alarm go off half an hour ago. Mom was already up, and now she stands at the door.

The Batmobile door opens and the lovely, put-together woman gestures me inside. "I'm Isabel. Junior production assistant for Channel 6. I'll get you downtown and to the set."

"Hi." Waving to Mom, I settle into a posh leather seat beside Isabel. "Thanks for picking me up."

"Bettina was very clear that you'd need a ride," she says. "Is that what you're wearing on the air?" She looks down at my jean jacket, faded red-and-white polka-dotted sundress and less-than-clean blue canvas sneakers—really the nicest things I could muster without asking Layla for something.

"Erm, no. This is just my Minnie Mouse costume," I joke, trying to smile.

Isabel smiles a tiny bit. "It's cute, but you look very girl-ish. . . . I was under the impression you're famous for doing something only boys do?"

I quirk an eyebrow at her. It's far too early for feminism lessons, but I can't just let that assumption alone. "I can wear dresses and still do things like fight as a Knight. That's kind of the point."

"True," says Isabel, with a wry smile. She gestures to her outfit. "I guess it's easy to forget that in this job where I have to dress like talk-show Barbie every day."

I laugh. She's funnier than I'd have expected someone with a perfect updo to be. Which shows again how appearance can wrongly skew expectations. "So, what do I do on the show?" I ask as I take a long sip of coffee.

"You're going to be Bettina's first guest. She'll ask you a series of questions and then roll your video . . ."

She keeps talking about the upcoming show, and I space out a bit. My coffee hasn't taken hold, and I'm fighting to stay awake. The driver steers us onto the highway, and we head into the city, merging into the early-morning traffic. As suburban houses, parks, stores, and billboards race past in a blur, I suddenly have the strongest feeling that I'm a guest in someone else's life.

I mean, a little more than a week ago—was it really only a week from this past Friday?—I fought in Chris's place. Now, I'm rolling toward Chicago in a car with its own minibar so I can be on TV.

What. Even. Is. My. Life?

And how does this all fit in with being the Girl Knight?

I snap a picture of myself in the car and text it to the Knights group text.

Kit: ✌ Fingers crossed I don't barf.

Most of them are still asleep, but I feel better knowing they're rooting for me.

Finishing my coffee, I lean my head against the window. Surely talking to people on camera is easier than riding a horse while wearing pounds of armor and carrying a lance?

Right?

BETTINA LOOKS EVEN MORE BEAUTIFUL THIS MORNING THAN she did at the Castle. Her skin glows beneath the lights, and her hair looks like it's never been out of place in her life. She wears a tailored white-and-blue dress that sort of shimmers as she moves. Next to her, I look like a scabby teenager who's fled a picnic hosted by a gang of fashion school rejects. Or something like that.

But she smiles when she sees me, putting me more at ease than I've felt since the car pulled up at my house.

"Kit!" She kisses both my cheeks and beams at me. "It's so good to see you again."

A witty reply isn't forthcoming, so I just smile back. "Thanks. I'm really excited to be here!"

And I am. Now that I'm actually here and people from hair and makeup surround me, a fizz of excitement rises. This is a HUGE part of phase three—getting the word out there—

and I can't wait for other people to hear about what we want to change at the Castle. Of course, this exposure means Len could see it, but it's not like I didn't warn him I was going to do something to change his mind. Plus, my friends are counting on me.

Ooof. That gives me a sick feeling in my stomach. They're counting on me and I'm lying to them.

Before I can reflect on my missteps as a friend or what I'm going to say, the lights go on, the music for *Good Morning, Chicago!* fills the studio, and Bettina smiles for the camera.

"Sit up straight," she hisses through her teeth as she holds her smile.

I sit up as straight as I can, shoving all negative thoughts away and remembering the times my grandma would poke me in the back with her cane and yell at me for slouching. A producer counts us down.

Three, two, one . . .

And, showtime!

"Good morning, Chicago!" says Bettina enthusiastically. "We're so glad you've joined us. This morning, I'm having coffee with a very special teenager. Folks, I'd like you to meet Kit Sweetly, Chicago's very own Girl Knight!"

The camera turns to me, and I give a little wave. Inside, my stomach churns, the coffee I just finished a slurry.

Please don't barf, please don't barf, please don't barf.

"Hello, Bettina, hello, Chicago!" I manage to get out. My

voice sounds strained. Like I'm choking on something.

"Kit, why don't you tell us what it's like to work at the Castle?"

I shift a bit in my chair, and then smile. "Well, I've been working there for almost three years. We're kind of like a family. A great big medieval-modern family. Actually, a whole lot of my real family works there. My uncle is my boss. My brother is—or was—a Knight there. Or maybe he still is? He's in the hospital right now. And my two best friends work there. And all the other Wenches, Squires, Pages, Knights, and Royalty are really close."

Bettina makes a funny little noise and wrinkles her nose. "Did you say *wenches*?" The word sounds like something that gives you food poisoning when she says it.

I grin. "Yep. That's my official title. Really, I'm a server. Though I'm hoping for a promotion to Knight soon."

"Speaking of that." Bettina smoothly transitions as a producer holds up six fingers for time. "You're doing more than hoping, aren't you? Folks, just last week, Kit fought in her brother's place and gave the crowd a real show! Let's take a look at her clip."

She turns to the large video screen behind us, and my YouTube video comes on. It's been edited so it's a montage of me riding, fighting the Green Knight, and then whipping off my helmet and making my declaration.

When it's done, Bettina claps. "Well, that certainly was

invigorating. As you can see, folks at home, Kit's video has been watched and shared more than a million times. She's even got a website, right?"

"That's right," I say. "It's www.thegirlknight.com. You can sign my petition to tell the Castle to get rid of gender restrictions for knighthood and other jobs. Right now, it's company policy that only cis men can be Knights, and that's absurd. People across the gender spectrum are now astronauts, soldiers, presidents, and more. To say only men can ride a horse at a dinner theater? C'mon."

Bettina gives me a knowing look. "We're almost out of time, but I wanted to ask you, Kit, what are you trying to prove with all this?"

I shift in my chair. *"Erm* . . . Well, at first, I didn't think I was going to be able to change or prove anything—I was just helping my brother out. But, as I was fighting, I realized I liked it. I wanted to show kids they can do anything, regardless of gender identity. So, yes, it might be symbolic. But what better way to smash the patriarchy than with a lance and sword?"

Bettina laughs, a lilting, gentle sound that's refined and warm. "Indeed. One small step for women, one giant step for Wenches."

That strikes me as so funny, I give a bark of laughter. Then immediately cover my mouth as the awkward noise rings out around the TV studio. To fill that space, I plunge ahead.

"So, yes, Bettina, and all of Chicagoland, if you want to

see more of the Girl Knight and my friends, because there are quite a few of us who've been training—you can check out some of those training videos on our website—you should definitely reserve seats at the Castle this Friday night. We're having a tournament at the seven thirty show, and it's going to be something totally new and totally amazing!"

"You heard it here first," says Bettina to the camera. "Thanks again to Kit Sweetly for joining us, and stay tuned, folks. After the break, we learn all about how to make French pastries for breakfast. Yum!"

As the lights fade, Bettina turns to me. "That went great! You're a natural."

"I wouldn't say that, but thank you. Hope you can make it to the Castle on Friday."

"Oh, sweetie, I'm headed to New York then, but good luck! Keep on smashing through those walls. You're going to do great things."

She shakes my hand and then makeup people swarm around her. Isabel, the assistant from earlier, comes up to my chair. "Time to move it. Next segment starts in three minutes. Do you want to stay for the rest of the show?"

I really, really do want to stay, but I also need to get home. I'm nowhere near ready for the calc test I'll have to make up, and I need to study, though Mom's letting me miss the whole day of school because we weren't sure how long I'd be in the studio.

"I can't. Can you get me home? I think we can beat rush hour if we hurry."

"Not likely," says Isabel. "I have to stay here until the end of the show, but I'll radio the driver to meet you out front. You were great out there!"

"Thank you!" I call out as she strides away, talking into her walkie-talkie.

I hustle out of my chair as Bettina moves away from me and into a stage that's set up like a kitchen.

As I'm walking out the door, Isabel hurries back to me. "Hey, Kit. My six-year-old niece just saw the clip before school. Can you leave some tickets for us up front for Friday's seven thirty show?"

"Absolutely! What name should I put it under?"

Isabel smiles at me, dropping her super-serious work face for just a moment. "Put it under Sofia, Future Girl Knight in Training."

"I'd like nothing better. Tell Sofia my friends and I will see her Friday."

Isabel waves as she walks away, and I have to pinch myself as I take the elevator down to street level.

What we're trying to do feels much more real now that I've announced the plan to the greater Chicagoland area. If only I could figure out how to actually pull the tournament off. Or tell my friends that things aren't going quite as smoothly as they seem.

If this was a small hole to start, by going on the news I've just dug myself the foundation of a house. Or maybe something grimmer that will bury me when it all collapses.

I've got to make this tournament happen. Despite what Corporate or Len says, we've got to fight.

I write out a text message to the group chat.

Kit: Hey, all! News segment went great. I think we're going to get a lot of people to the Castle from it.

I send that, then type out a quick message after it.

Kit: I've got to talk to you all about something else though . . .

My fingers hover over Send as the driver pulls up.

I delete the second message once I'm in the car.

It's only Monday. I've got the better part of a week to figure this out. No reason to worry my friends too soon, right?

The car pulls away from the TV studio, headed into a snarl of morning traffic that's almost as thick as the knot of worry and dread in my stomach.

WHEN I FINALLY GET HOME, THE SUN IS FULLY UP, AND there are a bunch of messages on my phone. Layla, Layla, Layla, Jett, Mom, Chris, and Len.

Oh, saints and lady knights help me. If Len's already seen the clip, I'm in trouble.

But, I'll deal with that later. First things first: breakfast.

Something in the kitchen smells. Bad. Like rotting eggs on a sardine sandwich that's been left in a gym locker for too long. I sniff around for a minute, and then I see the Cooler of Doom by the back door. It's open just a crack and the smell coming from it should be illegal. I slam it shut, open the back sliding-door, and drag the cooler onto the deck. File under "to be dealt with later." Part of me, the girl-who's-kinda-Internet-famous-and-is-making-money-from-her-website part, wants to chuck the cooler out. But the other part of me, the more sensible, hungrier, my-mother's-daughter part, can't do that. When you've had nothing for a long time, it's hard to get rid of anything. That's why you see run-down houses with tires, old swing sets, broken down appliances, and cars piled out front. Not because people are too lazy to get rid of them, but because they know what it is to be desperately poor and needing to cling to every last scrap of things they have. Rusted and nasty though they may be.

In the Middle Ages people didn't throw much of anything away either because they had so little. Everything was used, reused, and then used again. Especially for peasants, but even for kings and queens. Certainly some of them had diamonds and jewels to spare, but clothing was expensive, and things got reused. We live in a time when Duchess Kate can't even wear the same dress twice without incurring the scorn of the tabloids. Imagine what they would have said about Queen Elizabeth the First's pit stains or lead-eaten skin.

Before the impulse to daydream all day about everything medieval totally hijacks me, I start another pot of coffee, make some toast, and go online. Jett's already posted my video from *Good Morning, Chicago!* on our website, and it's getting lots of likes and comments. One of those comments is from user KingLenTheBold.

I roll my eyes, willing myself to read his take on my interview.

"KingLenTheBold: There is no surprise at the castle on Friday. Come for a normal show. Can't wait to see you there!"

Annoyed at Len's attempt to save face, I consider replying. Doing so is basically a declaration of war with Len. Which should go over great with him. But maybe he's still not heard from Corporate about the whole thing. Plus, I don't want people thinking I was lying about Friday. Ironic though that is, since I'm totally lying about Friday.

I shoot off a reply before I have time to talk myself out of it.

"Girl Knight: Don't be so modest, Len! The surprise is going to be incredible! See you all there! xo, Kit!"

I could sit here, reading comments all day and replying, but that can't be healthy. Somehow, I force myself to close my laptop. My toast pops up, and I slather cream cheese and jelly on it. It's been so long since we had food like this in the house, I lick the spoon clean. My pile of homework stares at me. If I leave now, I could just barely make it to school in time for the calc test. I don't want to, but it's the right thing to do. But apparently, I'm making a habit of not doing the right thing lately. So, instead of homework and school, I watch some TV and then take a short nap on the couch. An hour later, Jett calls.

The phone is in my hand and I start to pick up, but I let it ring and ring until voicemail takes it. I want to talk to him. Desperately. But I also can't add whatever I'm feeling for Jett right now to the soup of feelings inside me. And his voice would be just the thing to tip me over the edge and make me confess everything.

I text back.

Kit: Leaving the house to get Chris. Talk to you tonight?

We're getting together for training tonight at Layla's.

Jett: You were great this morning! See you tonight. 😉

What?

Is this a friend kissy face? Or a hey-let-me-be-your-boy-friend one? Or a mistake?

My heart rate speeds up, helped by the enormous cup of coffee I'm chugging. I'm nosediving into the worst kind of teen-girl-wonders-does-he-really-mean-it spiral when two more texts come in in rapid succession.

Jett: 😕😕😕😬😬 Sorry! Meant to send this. 🙂

Okay.

Glad that's cleared up. Stupid texting.

I send a smiley face back and then put my phone into my backpack. It's not even 9:00 a.m., and I've nearly had three heart attacks already.

CHRIS IS DRESSED AND WAITING FOR ME IN A WHEELCHAIR WHEN I get to the hospital. He slow claps as I walk into the room.

"Well, you did it," he says with a wry smile.

"Did what?" I ask, trying to sound nonchalant as I gather up his clothes and the LEGO Sears Tower and put them into the grocery bag I brought.

Chris reaches for the bag and rests it gingerly on his lap. "You broke the secret code of the Castle on national TV."

"Oh please." I roll my eyes. "Nobody is going to care about that little interview. Maybe it will bring a few more people in, but that's it."

"You're going to get fired for real, Kit."

I very well might. But it was worth it. If going on the news is what it takes to get my friends and me into the arena, I'd do it all over again.

"I doubt that."

Chris shakes his head. "You didn't hear Len's call to Mom."

At that I drop onto the bed. "Shit. Len called Mom?"

"I could hear it through the phone. He's pissed. Saying you've gone too far and there's nothing he can do to stop what's going to happen."

"He's bluffing. I'll talk to him during my next shift on Wednesday."

Chris nods, looking tired. "We'll see. I'll try to come in with you to help talk to him. I've got to get my shifts sorted out anyway."

"You'll do no such thing," I say, as I wheel Chris out of the room. We stop at the nurse's desk so he can sign some papers, and then I push him out to the car. On the way home, he leans against the window, eyes closed, clutching his ribs. He looks so tired, and a little bit broken. And I'm not sure how the Girl Knight can fix that.

THE LAST TIME I SAW CHRIS LOOKING THAT WORN-OUT WAS the morning Dad left the first time. We were twelve and fourteen. By then, Chris and I were used to the fights, but this one felt different. It had more texture than the usual ones over stupid things like how to load the dishwasher or Mom not paying enough attention to Dad. This fight had sharp edges. It was barbed like a harpoon, and as they went through the house yelling at each other and throwing things, I could almost feel their relationship shredding with each new insult.

"Get in the car!" Dad shouted at Chris and me once Mom had stormed out of the house, headed to yet another shift at her crappy job.

"Where are we going?" I grabbed the bag I always kept packed because I once saw this show about a mom and dad getting divorced, and the mom took the kids without any warning and they had none of their stuff. My bag was stuffed with snacks, clothes, books, and a few photos.

"Just get in the car," said Dad, yanking my arm and pulling me roughly toward the door. He wasn't normally a hitting dad. But I could smell the alcohol on his breath.

"We're not going anywhere with you," said Chris, grabbing Dad's hand. He pried it loose from my arm, and I shook off Dad's grip. Chris was in the trenches of the teenage years, and his thin face had a smattering of acne spread across it like freckles. But he'd grown a lot in the last few months, and he stood as tall as Dad.

"GET. IN. THE. CAR." Dad's eyes were bloodshot.

"Make us," said Chris. "You're drunk and will probably kill us all."

"Plus, we don't want to go with you anywhere," I added. Chris and I had talked about this at length, and both of us agreed that staying with Mom was the better choice.

"I'll be goddamned if my children are going to tell me what I can and can't do," said Dad. He opened the door. "If I leave, I'm not coming back."

"Fine with us," said Chris.

"You're a shitty kid, you know that?" said Dad, stumbling up to Chris. "After all I did for you? This is how you treat me?"

It was a tired refrain. Something Dad said to Chris every time he got blazing drunk.

Chris shoved Dad away. When Dad found his footing, he stumbled back at Chris. Without thinking, I put myself between them.

Meaning I took the full brunt of the fist Dad swung in Chris's direction.

It knocked me down, my cheek stinging powerfully. Tears rose into my eyes.

Dad looked stunned. "Kit-Kat," he said, his voice just a whisper. He knelt down beside me and reached out a hand for my face. I shoved it away.

"I'm so sorry, Kit. That wasn't meant for you. You got in the way."

"You shouldn't be trying to punch Chris, either," I growled through my tears. Sobs broke my voice into clumsy chunks.

Chris grabbed the back of Dad's shirt and pulled him away from me. "Get out of here. Now."

I scrambled to my feet and stood beside Chris. "Yeah, get out. We don't want you here."

Dad's face fell. "Fine," he said. All the fight drained from him. "But never say I didn't try to give you a better life."

When his car had pulled out of the driveway and gone swerving down the street, Chris turned without a word and went to the freezer. He brought me a half-eaten bag of frozen peas. I pushed it to my cheek and let the cold seep in, hoping it could numb all the way to my heart. Chris sat down on the bottom step of the split-level staircase and let out a shaky breath. I slumped down beside him and leaned into his shoulder.

"It's going to be okay," he said to me. "We've got each other."

Exhaustion, sadness, and the remains of his anger played across his face, like cloud shadows shifting across the ground on a windy day.

I nodded, as tears ran down my face. At least we had each other.

A few days later, Dad came back. And this time he stuck around for more than three years. None of us ever mentioned that fight again. But when I look back on it, I can see the man

Chris became in the boy he was.

But now I know he's worried because he can't work any longer. And what's Mom going to do? And how can we find Dad so the divorce can go through? And everything else in between. Reaching over, I squeeze his shoulder.

"It's going to be okay," I say softly. "We've got each other."

He shoots me a tired, grateful smile.

DESPITE THE DOCTOR'S WORRY THAT CHRIS'S KNEE IS MESSED up, he makes it from the car to the front door without too much trouble.

I help him hobble up the front stairs, and then we're standing on the landing.

"Upstairs or down?" I point at his room on the lower level and the kitchen and other rooms upstairs. "I made you a bed on the couch if you want to be closer to the fridge."

"Let's go up," said Chris.

Our feet move over the spot where we sat together on the stairs so many years ago. With each step, Chris winces. I help him to the couch and get him settled. I hand him the remote, and he flicks on the TV, scrolling through the channels until he lands on reruns of *The Venture Bros.* I laugh along with him for a few minutes, grateful that he doesn't want to talk about work or his injuries or my TV appearance.

I don't remember when I fell asleep, but suddenly, my phone alarm is going off, and it's 3:30 p.m.

I've slept through the better part of the day.

Shit, shit, shit. I've got to be at training in half an hour. The TV is still on, but Chris is asleep on the couch. I jump off, grabbing my phone, so I can text Mom to get Chris's medicine.

"Kit?" Chris calls from the living room. "You leaving, Sis?" Pain medication makes his voice drowsy.

"Just going to Layla's. I'll be back with dinner and your meds in a few hours."

"Fight well, Girl Knight," he says in a drowsy voice.

"As always," I reply with a smile.

EVERYONE'S ALREADY THERE BY THE TIME I GET TO LAYla's house. Alex and Layla are on horses, galloping around the paddock and shouting medieval insults at each other. Penny and Mags (whose hair is purple at the ends today) practice a set of on-ground sword-fighting moves. Mags is surprisingly light on her feet, and she keeps jumping out of the way of Penny's jabs like she's skipping rope. Near the barn, Lizzy's working on a complex slide-out-of-the-saddle-and-roll-to-your-feet move, with the help of Layla's oldest, most patient horse. Jett films it all, standing to the side in his leather jacket.

"Hey," I say, punching him lightly on the arm. Because that's easier than giving him a hug like I want to do. "How goes the documentary?"

He lowers the camera and smiles at me. "It's mostly done.

I edited in the news report today during free period. Now, I just have to add in the tournament footage from this Friday and we'll be set."

I stare at my shoes, trying not to hear the excited shouts and laughter of my fellow Knights.

I have to tell him.

"Yeah . . . about that tournament. I'm not so sure it's going to happen."

Jett's eyebrows quirk. "What're you talking about? You just told everyone in Chicago to come. I thought you had permission for all this?"

"Sort of? Kind of not really?" As I did with Chris, I explain to Jett what the Castle people said about our tournament not being "on brand."

"Well that's ridiculous," says Jett. "Of course it would be 'on brand.' They just don't want to change anything. What does everybody else say about this?" He gestures to the others who are still training.

"I haven't told them yet," I admit in an oh-so-small voice. "I keep thinking I'm going to figure out something to make it all work, but if I tell them before I figure it out, then they're going to be pissed and maybe stop training."

"They're going to be pissed that you're lying to them."

"I know," I snap too loudly. Lizzy looks up from a particularly hard fall and waves. I wave back and then lower my voice so it won't carry. "I know. But I can't figure out what to do.

I keep thinking if I don't tell them, then we'll be all ready and it'll somehow all come together on Friday."

Jett shakes his head and says in a soft voice, "That's not fair to them or you. It's too much for you to worry about and too much to expect from them. They're your friends, Kit. Tell them."

"Tell us what?" asks Layla as she leads her horse toward us. "Tell us you know the rest of the routines Chris started? Because we've got the first part of the show down, but after about twenty minutes, we're just doing the same things over and over."

"Yes, that's it," I say quickly. "We'll go over the rest of the routine today and then talk about how we're going to make it happen on Friday. Can you see if everyone can do one last training session on Thursday afternoon?"

Layla nods and rides off to ask the others.

I can feel Jett shooting daggers into my back behind me.

"What?" I spin around.

"You have to tell them."

"I will. But we've got so much more to work on, there's no sense in dashing their hopes yet. If I can't figure out something by Thursday's training session, I'll tell them then. I promise."

"Pinkie swear?" asks Jett with a hint of a smile playing across his face. He holds out his pinkie.

I loop mine through his. "Pinkie swear." My heart races a bit as our hands linger together.

"Kit! C'mon!" yells Alex. "Get over here and teach me how to knock you out with this mace." They hold a kid's Skip-It that's been attached to a toilet plunger. It's hardly a medieval weapon, but it's better than a pool noodle.

"See you," I say to Jett as I extricate my pinkie from his and join the other Knights.

By the time we're done training, it's after six, but we've got the better part of a full routine down. Everyone promises to stop by after school on Thursday for one more run-through of the routine and then a check-in about how we'll get costumes. Penny tells us that she, Austin, and Chris have been working with the other Knights to make it happen, but they'll have everything finalized by Thursday.

"See you all at the Castle for Wednesday's shift," I call out as we head back to our cars.

"Sure you can't join us?" Layla says. She's headed for tacos with Mags, Lizzy, and Alex. "We miss you, Kit." She slings an arm across my shoulder.

"Silly thing," I say. "I've just been busy with Chris getting hurt and the interview. I'd love to join you, but I've really, really got to catch up on homework tonight. I'm going in early to make up that calc test."

Layla gives me a hug. "See you at school tomorrow!" Then, she and the others pile into her Jeep.

Jett walks me to Chris's car. "The test is easy, you'll do fine. But can I do anything to help with the other stuff?"

"I mean, if you can figure out a brilliant way for me to tell everyone the truth and also actually make this tournament happen?"

Jett gives me a rueful smile. "I have complete confidence in you. But call me if you need to brainstorm."

"You're my favorite," I say with a smile as we say goodbye.

"You're my favorite too," he says back.

We linger there for a moment outside Chris's car. So close. But I'm not brave enough to lunge across the invisible barrier between us—which is made up of the words of our Unbreakable Rules—and kiss him.

32

TUESDAY IS A BLUR OF SCHOOLWORK. BY WEDNESDAY—TWO
days before we're supposed to ride out and fight—I'm still no
closer to figuring out a solution to actually hosting this tournament. But Chris and Austin have talked to the other Knights,
and all of them except for Dalton have agreed to let us take
their places for the 7:30 show.

"Kit! Don't you have to be at work?" Chris calls to me from
the living room. It's almost four and I'm already running late
because I had to stay after school for more catchup from Monday, since every teacher I have decided to give an exam on the
Monday after spring break, and I somehow managed to forget
about those tests.

"I'm on my way," I yell back, as I head into my bedroom.
I shimmy out of my school clothes and into my Wench's

uniform. Gross. I missed it when I went to the laundromat, so it's still crusted with food from my last shift.

"It'll do," I mutter, as I pin up my hair and then douse myself in fruit-smelling body spray. I'm sure the smell of roasted meat and horses will cover up my stink anyway.

"I'll see you later," I call as I grab my bag and keys. "Mom will be home by nine and there's food in the fridge."

Chris wanted to go into work with me today, but he's much more couch-bound than he thought he would be.

I stop midway down the steps and pound back up to the kitchen. Grabbing an apple, some peanut butter, and a handful of cheese sticks, I dump them on the couch next to Chris.

"Nice touch," he says, quirking a half smile. "You're really a domestic goddess, you know that, right?"

"Just eat it."

Chris struggles to his feet. "I gotta pee anyway, so I can get something to eat."

There's nothing more I can do to help Chris, and he's got to move on his own sooner or later. "Just don't fall off anything, okay?"

"Aye, aye," he says. "Maybe you can convince Len to let you ride tonight in my place."

"Ha, fat chance! I'm just hoping he doesn't kill me. Or fire me."

The thought of talking to Len has been giving me nightmares, but I don't tell Chris that.

Chris shoots me a knowing look and then laughs. Or tries to laugh. A noise escapes his throat and then he clutches his ribs.

"Give 'em hell, Girl Knight." He raises an arm and cheers weakly. "Restore honor to our family's name!"

I GET TO WORK FIVE MINUTES BEFORE MY SHIFT STARTS. IT'S all I can do to run down the service hallway toward the Wench section board. As I move past clumps of Pages, Squires, and other servers, I hear the odd shout-out or grumble about me being on the news. But I don't have time to listen to them. I've got to get to my section, get the bread baskets filled, get—

"Why isn't my name on here?" I hit the wall with the flat of my palm, which hurts more than it should.

Two line cooks shoot me smug looks as they pass.

"Looks like the Girl Knight is having a bad day," snickers one of them. He has *Foie Gras* tattooed across his knuckles like an aspirational slogan.

"Shut up," I mutter.

The other one, a pimply thing who's buddies with Eric Taylor, scoffs. "Things are never going to change around here. Don't know why you're even trying."

"You're the worst. Go away." I make a face at them both.

They laugh as they walk away, and I swear under my breath.

Running my finger down the line of servers and sections again, I scan each one, looking for my name.

Mags, Beth, Penny: Red Knight Section.

Madison, Nina: Blue Knight section.

Lizzy, Megan: Purple Knight section. . . .

But no Kit.

Not anywhere on the board.

I check the schedule posted next to the board. There's my name, slotted for tonight's shift. But I don't have any tables?

"What the hell?" I check the names again.

"Sorry about that, sweetie," says Penny, coming up behind me with a tray full of empty water pitchers. She gives me a one-armed hug. "I had you in the Red Knight's section as usual, but Len pulled you out of rotation. Said you have to go see him before shift starts."

"Am I fired?"

Penny shakes her head. "No idea. But everyone's seen the news clip and the website by now. Dalton's pretty pissy about it, but you know we all have your back."

"Thanks, Penny," I mumble.

"Can't wait for Friday," she says. "We're going to put on such an amazing show."

"It's going to be great." My voice is full of false confidence. I even manage to wink conspiratorially at her. "Now, I'm off to see what fresh hell Len has in mind for me."

Penny opens her pack of Camels and takes out the cigarette

that's turned upside down. She offers it to me. "For after you talk to him," she says with a smile. "I'm betting you'll need it."

"Not your lucky one." I push it back. "Besides, I owe you like ten packs by now."

"Just take it," she says. "Lords and Ladies know you need the luck more than I do right now."

"Fair point," I say, slipping the cigarette behind my ear. "See you soon, Wench."

"Good luck!" she calls out. She readjusts her tray and hurries toward her section.

I wave to her and begin the long, circuitous walk to Len's office.

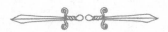

"SO, HERE WE ARE AGAIN," SAYS LEN AS I ENTER HIS OFFICE. "But this time, Kit, I don't think I can shield you from Corporate. Why in the world did you go on the news?"

I stride to his desk, willing myself to calmly sit in the chair across from him. "I had an opportunity and I took it! The Castle needs to change to stay relevant. Also, I want to fight as a Knight. Permanently."

Len makes a noise. "You're hilarious."

"I'm serious. Why don't you let me fight as the Red Knight tonight? I know all of Chris's moves, and it would show everyone how committed you are to gender equality, and it would get people all fired up for Friday's tournament."

"Friday's tournament?" Len arches an eyebrow at me. "You still think that's happening?"

"C'mon, Len. I'm the best choice to fill in while Chris is hurt, and it also proves the Castle is really progressive. I've got a bunch of other non-male Knights who are ready too, and we can put on a great show!"

The whole conversation feels like déjà vu, but the stakes are higher tonight. Now that Chris is hurt, my friends are expecting to fight, and half of Chicago knows my name and what I hope to accomplish here. Len shakes his head and picks up his crown.

"Not going to happen. A Squire will fight tonight in Chris's place."

"That's bullshit, Len! And you know it!"

"Yes! Kit, dammit. That's how it goes sometimes. And I'm sorry you don't think it's fair, but that's how it was in medieval times, and that's how it goes here."

"Not for long," I mutter darkly. "You just wait. There are going to be changes around here."

"You're hardly in the position to make changes," says Len. "Effective immediately, you've been demoted from Wench to lower stable hand. Your new job is to take out all the horses' straw and wood shavings for the night."

Lower stable hand is one of the worst jobs in the Castle. Think backbreaking labor meets intolerable stench meets minimum wage. Usually it's reserved for entry-level applicants, but every now and again, Len saves it as a special job for someone who's really in trouble. Lucky me.

"Only for one night?" I resign myself to getting through the next eight hours.

"Oh no," says Len. "Welcome to your new role at the Castle. Certified Shit Shoveler. I don't want you anywhere near the arena until our Corporate visit on Friday is over. If you—and your friends, because I know you're not alone in this—can manage to keep your heads down, then maybe I'll let you Wench again. But if you don't, I'm firing you all."

Every part of me wants to tell Len to shove it, but I still need this job. At least for the summer, so I can have some money for college this fall. And I don't want to screw my friends over even more.

"Fine. I'll do it until Friday. I won't mention the Knight stuff again, but you better let Chris fight when he's better."

I don't say anything about the tournament because I'm still not giving up on it completely. Even if Len says no, as long as everyone else is ready to fight, we still have a chance, right?

Len smiles. "Good girl. And that reminds me, tell your brother to come get these forms. We both need to sign them so he can fill them out next time he's here." He holds out several pieces of paper.

"Workers' Compensation forms?" I read the title of the top form out loud. "Does Chris qualify for this?"

"Yep," says Len. "I checked with HR and the hospital. Since Chris wasn't drunk or under the influence of any substances, this is a Workers' Comp case. They should pay for all his bills."

"Well, that's a relief!" I blurt out. And it is. Mom and Chris will be thrilled to know that the Castle will take care of the hospital bills.

"I thought it would be," says Len. He smiles at me. Almost like he's a nice guy. Or that he remembered all of a sudden that we're related. "I'm not trying to punish you and Chris, Kit. I swear. I've just got to think of my own job too. Your little stunt on the news this week has all the Castle managers across the nation talking. Most of them are worried and trying to make sure similar rebellions don't happen at their Castles. So, if we can just get everything back to normal, this should blow over, and my job—and yours and Chris's and all the others you're working with—will be fine."

"You're a prince, Len." I make a face.

"Nope, a King. And your boss. Try to remember that as you're shoveling poop tonight."

"Ugh," I mutter under my breath, as I push the door open to leave.

"What's that, Kit?" he calls out as I leave.

"Nothing, Your Majesty," I yell over my shoulder. "Absolutely nothing!"

As his door closes, I flip him off.

I T'S STILL HALF AN HOUR BEFORE OUR FIRST SHOW. I'M
stuffing my backpack into my locker when Len's voice
comes over the loudspeaker.

"Attention, everyone," he says. "This is your King speaking."

I roll my eyes and slam the locker door.

"If I could have you all gather in the Upper Banquet Hall, I
have an announcement to make. I know it's nearly showtime,
but this won't take long. See you all up there in five minutes."

A very bad feeling settles in my bones as I hear Len's message. Perhaps I can intercept him or somehow lock him in
his office? Does that even work in real life or just movies? Or
maybe I can find Layla and everyone else and tell them the
truth before Len does?

But there's no time. And so I trudge with everyone else

in the Castle into the Upper Banquet Hall. Dread coils in my belly like a rattlesnake about to strike.

The Upper Banquet Hall is usually reserved for Corporate training events, big private parties, or meetings. It's huge, but there are over a hundred of us working tonight, and we're practically elbow to elbow as we crowd into the room.

Wenches, Squires, Knights, the Falconer, the Fool, all the gift shop employees, cooks, and everyone else in between whisper to each other. Layla is waiting for me near the back of the room. I squeeze in beside her.

"Hey, friend," she whispers.

This is going to be awful. I just know it. I try to layer all my apologies and good intentions and the reasons I lied into the hug I give Layla.

"What's this all about?" asks Alex, slipping into the spot beside Layla and me. Jett waves at me from across the room. He's still in street clothes and must be running late tonight.

"I have no idea," I say. Though the sinking feeling in my stomach tells me it can't be good.

"You okay?" Layla asks. She puts her finger under my chin and lifts it up. "You're looking a little green."

"Len demoted me to a lower stable hand," I say through my teeth.

"WHAT?" says Mags. She and Lizzy have pushed their way through the crowd to join us.

"He can't do that," says Penny, standing beside us. She

smells like bubblegum and cigarettes. "You can't let him do that. What was his—"

Len's voice interrupts her righteous indignation.

"Hello, everyone!" he calls out over the dull roar of a hundred people gossiping. "I know we've got a show to do, but I've gathered you here for a quick chat. So, shut up for a few and let me get it over with."

A few people laugh, but even more of them roll their eyes. Layla threads her arm through mine and I lean into her.

"As I'm sure many of you have heard, the Castle's been in the news quite a lot lately. Thanks to the efforts of our very own Kit Sweetly—"

"And her friends!" calls out Layla.

"And her friends," says Len, inclining his head in our direction.

I immediately wish she hadn't said that. Len's now going to know who at least one of my coconspirators is.

Every person in the room turns to look at us. I know now what someone in a dinghy surrounded by sharks feels like.

"Thanks to Kit and her friends," continues Len, "we've gotten a lot of attention. Some of it's been great—we're booked solid for the next few weeks and there's a waiting list for Friday's show. I don't need to tell you what good news this is. But there is something I need to say."

I bite my lip.

"While Corporate appreciates all the new guests, they

want you to know that nothing is changing at the Castle. We're not changing the gender restrictions and they informed me that they told Kit this last week via email."

There's a low murmur throughout the room. Layla drops my arm and all my friends gape at me.

Len holds up a hand. "Be kind to Kit, everyone. We do have her and her friends to thank for all this press. But please let me be clear. The only Knights who are riding out this week— or ever—are going to be male. This is company policy. As Corporate told me in their email, which I'm happy to share with any of you who are interested, anyone who rides out as a Knight who isn't supposed to will lose their jobs. Let me say that again. In case you have big plans for this so-called tournament on Friday. Anyone. Who. Rides. Out. As. A. Knight. Who. Is. Not. A. Current. Knight. Or. Squire. Or. Male. Will. Get. Fired. Full stop. No questions asked. We are here to represent the Middle Ages, not stir things up. That's all. Get back to work."

The room erupts in noise, and my name is bounced around the room like a tennis ball made of whispers.

I bury my face in my hands. Wishing the floor would open up and swallow me. All of my friends are talking at the same time.

Shit.

This is bad.

34

"I CAN'T BELIEVE YOU DIDN'T TELL US ABOUT THIS, KIT!"
Mags hisses. Her arms are crossed so tightly across her
body it looks like she's going to tie herself into a knot.

The room's nearly empty, but a few people have stayed to
listen to what we're talking about.

Jett shoots me a sympathetic look as the crowd carries him
out the opposite door. He points to his backpack, as if he's
saying "I've got to change." I wave to him. He'll find me later.
And besides, he already knew my terrible secret. And he told
me to tell them, so it's not like he could say anything other
than "Told you so" or "Sucks to be you." Not that he would say
such things, but—

"It's not a big deal," Layla starts to say, coming to my
defense and interrupting my spiral. I smile at her, but her eyes

dart away from mine. They're narrowed and her jaw twitches slightly. She might be defending me out of habit, but she's mad too.

"It is a big deal," snaps Penny. "Not just the lying, but also the fact that we're going to get fired if we do this. You all are off to college, but I need this job!"

"Me too," says Mags. "And not all of us are off to college. My plan was to work here through the next year while I look for acting jobs in the city."

"I'm sorry," I say. "I was going to figure out a way to stage the tournament without us getting in trouble. I didn't mean to lie. I just didn't want us to stop training."

"It's super shitty you didn't tell us the truth," says Alex. Their voice has a hard, annoyed edge. "I mean, we would've understood. Or tried to help. Do you know how many other activities I've said no to in the last two weeks in order to make this happen? I've missed so many derby practices, they benched me for the next three games. I know you said we're in this together, but this just feels like you wanted to do this all on your own."

"Yeah," says Lizzy bitterly. "It's the Kit Sweetly show. And the Kit Sweetly plan. And Kit Sweetly on the news."

"That's not fair!" I burst out. "I asked you all to join me. I want you to fight with me! This is about all of us."

"Sure it is," says Penny. "That's why everything's all about 'the Girl Knight' and they only showed your clip on the news."

"I can't help what they showed!" I shout. "And I'm trying to figure out how we can all fight."

Alex runs a hand through their hair. "We just don't like that you lied to us."

"And we're allowed to be a bit mad," says Layla. "Even though we love you, we can be mad."

I let out a frustrated breath. "I just didn't know what to do, okay? I got the email, but then the online campaign picked up steam. And we were having so much fun training. And I thought I'd figure out some way to make it work."

"But you didn't!" Mags snaps.

"I didn't. But we can still do something! Maybe we can ask Len again? Or I can call Bettina back and see if we can all be on the news?"

"I'm out, Kit," says Penny. "You know I adore you, but I'm not going to do this if there's no point."

"I'm out too," Mags adds. "Maybe try not lying to your friends next time before roping them into your schemes."

"Sorry, Kit," says Lizzy. "If they're all not doing it, I can't. I need this job too. At least through the summer."

That leaves Alex and Layla.

I look at both of them. "Please?" It comes out way smaller and squeakier than I intend.

Alex shakes their head and walks out. Their lips are pressed into a thin line, and I can tell they're keeping back all sorts of things they want to say to me.

"Layla? Are you in at least? The two of us can ride out together."

"Call me later," says Layla, shaking her head. "I need some time to think. I can't believe you didn't tell me. At the very least you tell your best friend about things like this. I gotta go, I'm back on admissions tonight."

She leaves without a goodbye and I slump to the ground. Hot tears rise behind my eyes. For a minute, I think about texting Jett to tell him what happened. But he'll hear soon enough, I'm sure.

I drag myself to my feet and trudge away from the roar of the crowd and the anger of my friends, slouching toward what is certain to be a terrible night in the stables.

35

THE HORSE STABLES ARE BEHIND THE CASTLE, FAR ENOUGH away that the animals can't hear the crowd, and the crowd can't smell the horses.

I sit on the concrete stairs at the back of the Castle, smoking the "lucky" cigarette Penny gave me and feeling anything but lucky. My hands shake as I inhale. My anger toward Len and my hollowed-out sadness is finally catching up with me.

It's so incredibly, unspeakably awful that only cis men can fight as Knights. But apparently that's the way it is, and there's nothing I can do about it. I scroll through my phone as I smoke, doing everything but checking the views on my video. Who cares how many people have seen it and loved it? None of that can change what's happening at the Castle.

There's a new email in my inbox. From the Marquette

Scholarship and Financial Aid Office. Maybe the universe will send me just a little bit of good news. Maybe? Is that too much to ask?

With a drag on my smoke, I click on it.

Ms. Sweetly,

Thank you so much for your application for the full-tuition scholarship. Although your grades and activities certainly reflect what we're looking for, we only have a limited number of allowances and we had more than three hundred applicants this year. It was a very tough choice, but unfortunately, we cannot offer you a full-tuition scholarship at this time. Please feel free to pursue other avenues of financial aid. . . .

I swear and close the email. Of course it's bad news. Of course. Why did I think—

"Whatcha doing out here, Sweetly?"

It's Eric Taylor. The Green Squire, most loathsome of Layla's suitors and general, all-around terrible dude. He steps past me, going to the bottom of the concrete steps.

I hold up my half-smoked cigarette. "Duh."

"No, I mean, why are you out here instead of in your section? Is the rumor true? Did Len take you off the schedule and move you to the stable? Is that what his little pep talk to us all was about?" Eric sneers.

"That's remarkably accurate for a rumor. But it's only temporary."

"Sure it is," says Eric. He looks down at the plastic trash

can full of urine-soaked wood shavings, sand, and straw I've dragged down the stairs. "Need some help dumping that?" He nods toward the stable-waste dumpster. I've already emptied one can into it since Len tasked me with stable work.

"I've got it," I hiss. "Why don't you get inside? I'm sure Dalton needs you to run some errand or clean up some horse crap."

"Oh!" says Eric, feigning surprise. "That's what I needed to tell you. I wanted to show you this!"

With what can only be described as a triumphant grin, he whips off his Green Squire tunic. Underneath it is Chris's armor and his extra Red Knight costume.

Stabbing my cigarette out, I stand up. Since I'm on a higher step than Eric, I'm nearly nose to nose with him. "Why are you wearing that?"

"Since your dumbass brother fell off his horse, I'm the next Squire in line. I'm the Red Knight until—or should I say if— Chris comes back."

"That's not fair!"

"Of course it's fair," snaps Eric. "I've been here nearly as long as you. I've gone through the ranks, and now it's my turn."

"What's not fair is that I—and my friends—never even got a chance to try!"

"That's life, Sweetly," says Eric, shrugging. "Now, if you'll excuse me, I've got to get my horse saddled. It's nearly showtime for the Red Knight."

I swear under my breath as he pushes past me. Before he starts up the stairs, he kicks the plastic trash can over, spilling filthy straw and wood chips all over the edge of the stairs.

"Goddammit, Eric. You're such an unredeemable douche-bag. Did anyone ever tell you that?"

"That's for messing up my chances with Layla! Be sure to tell your brother I took his job."

"I hope you fall off your horse!"

"Just like your loser brother did?" he throws back.

He kicks the trash can one more time as he walks away. It goes bouncing into the parking lot, spilling more filth. It's a warm spring night, but there's not a hint of wind. Nothing to sweep the wood chips away or hide Eric's treachery.

I'm so angry, tears rise in my eyes. Stupid, ridiculous tears, even when I want to yell. And hit things. Especially things named Eric Taylor.

I swipe at my tears and get a bunch of sand in my eye.

Dammit!

I'm not even halfway done with mucking out the stables, and now I've got all this mess to clean up. I grab the broom that's propping open the back door and stomp down the stairs. Right as I realize what I've done, the metal door slams shut behind me. Locking me outside, with no way to get back inside except through the front door.

Swearing again, I text Jett.

Kit: COME GET ME? BACK DOOR, BY THE STABLES. I'M LOCKED OUT AND CAN'T GO THROUGH THE FRONT DOOR. PLEASE BRING MY BACKPACK.

His answer doesn't come back immediately—he must've started the trumpeting to announce the King's arrival by now—and so I'm stuck out here. Tucking my phone into my bra strap so I don't miss Jett's text, I begin the slow, terrible process of refilling the plastic trash can with soiled hay and wood chips. Only this time I don't have a shovel. Just a broom and piece of cardboard that was shoved beneath the dumpster.

Revolting.

Using the cardboard like a makeshift dustpan, I get most of the hay and wood chips off the ground and into the can. Of course, I also manage to get a good portion of the nasty stuff in my hair and down the front of my Wench's dress.

Then, I drag the can to the dumpster. It's filled nearly to the top with horse poop, soggy straw, and who knows what else. Flies buzz around it, and after baking in the sun for the better part of the day, its smell has moved from earthy to downright hazardous.

"Get in there," I mutter, as I jam my hip into the trash can and scoot it up my body. It's surprisingly heavy since the straw is dense with horse waste. I stand on a milk crate so I can lever it in enough to flip it into the dumpster.

When the trash can rests on the lip of the dumpster, I shove my shoulder under it and tip it over. It tumbles into the dumpster, spilling out its noxious contents.

I reach in to shake out the rest of the foul stuff inside the can, but as I lift up the container, my phone flies out of my bra strap and goes arcing in with all the mess.

Of course it does.

I lunge forward to catch it, but I'm already off balance. With a yell, I land in the dumpster, face-first in a pile of filth.

"You've got to be kidding me," I mutter.

Words are not enough to convey my disgust and rage, but the fun's not done yet. My phone is nowhere to be found, since the contents shifted as I fell. Reaching into the straw, I sift through the wet straw and clumps of manure, hoping my fingers circle the phone.

Eventually, I find it—now slimy with who knows what—and swear again under my breath.

Righting myself, I wade through the mess, trying to get close enough to the edge of the dumpster so I can boost myself out. With each step, the straw shifts, making me sink even lower as my weight compacts it.

This. Is. My. Life.

How. Very. Not. According. To. Plan.

"Kit?"

Jett stands beside the back door, carrying my backpack. He carefully props the door open with a milk crate. The overhead light shines on his black hair, making it sort of gleam in a tremendously gorgeous way.

For a moment, I consider staying in the dumpster until he goes back inside. But my car keys are in the bag, and I need them to flee home before anyone else can see—or smell—me.

"I'm over here," I call out.

I stash my phone under my armpit as I scramble out of the straw and try to haul myself over the side of the dumpster.

If looks were lightning, then Jett just got struck. His jaw drops and his eyes bulge in his head. "Do I even want to know what you're doing in the dumpster?" He offers me a hand. I take it and he helps me over the inside lid.

"I'm swimming!" I snap as I land on the pavement and shake myself off. "I threw my phone in there, and then wanted to see if I could get it while doing a swan dive."

I can't help the bitchy tone of my voice. It's been a long, long day. And the last thing I wanted was for Jett to see me neck deep in grime, but there you have it.

A huge laugh bursts out of him. "I'm sorry," he says, covering his mouth. "I don't mean to laugh."

"Yeah, ha-ha. It's hysterical. I know. Stupid Kit jumped in the dumpster. Stupid Kit tried to do something right for everyone at the Castle. Stupid Kit tried to actually get her life on track and get a scholarship, but she failed and now she's covered head to toe in horse manure—"

Before I can keep ranting, Jett pulls me into a hug. It's so sudden, and unexpected, I stop talking.

"You really don't want to hug me," I say, as I nuzzle my face into the hollow of his neck.

"I really do," he whispers into my hair. "I'm sorry you're having a shitty day."

I snort, but don't let go.

"Well, okay then," I whisper, hugging him back. My fingers curl into his back and I inhale the scent of him gratefully. "Thank you for bringing my stuff out here."

"Anytime. Happy to rescue the Girl Knight."

"You didn't rescue me," I point out, tilting my head up to look at him. "I could have gotten out of there. You just brought me my—"

His lips are so close. So full. And so tempting. I lean up, standing on my tiptoes. His hand rests on the small of my back. Some part of my brain screams that I shouldn't, but I dive across that invisible barrier. My eyes close. I push my mouth against his gently. His lips open under mine—

"What're you doing?" He pulls away from me with a jerk.

Oh no.

I didn't just kiss Jett.

Did I?

Yes. I did.

And apparently he hated it if the wide-eyed look he's giving me is any indication.

Any shred of hope I had for Jett and me evaporates under that look.

"I'm sorry," I say, covering my mouth with my hand. "I

didn't mean to and you were so close, and I've had a bad day and I just thought . . ."

"We can't, Kit," says Jett. "It can't happen between us. Not like—well, it just can't. I've got to get back inside. Here's your stuff."

He practically flings my backpack at me as he steps away. I glimpse the stunned look on his face, and then he's gone without a look back.

Shit. Shit. Shit.

Today is just a shit day. I've lost any chance of the tournament, my friends are furious at me, I'm literally covered in manure, and Jett just fled from my kiss.

Leaving the empty trash can by the dumpster, I walk to Chris's car. I'm done. Totally, completely done with this day. This week. This job. Everything.

Ugh.

**36**

MAKE IT HOME WITHOUT INCIDENT, WHICH IS SAYING SOME-
thing given the day I've had. As I turn into the driveway, I
keep thinking about Jett's lips on mine. Warm, soft, maybe a
bit hungry. Was I wrong in thinking he was kissing me back?
Even just a little bit? But I suppose none of that matters since
he clearly wasn't into it.

"He doesn't date Serving Wenches," I mutter to myself,
remembering his words from last week. "Or best friends."

Time to go have a good cry over that in the shower.

"Hey!" I yell to Chris as I walk up the stairs. "I'm home!"

He's sprawled on the couch, asleep with the TV blaring in
the background. Tiptoeing over to him, I pick up the remote
and click it off.

"I was watching that," he says sleepily.

"Were you though?"

"Why do you smell like horses?"

"Long story," I say. "Get some sleep. I'll tell you more in the morning. Do you need anything?"

"Nuh-uh. Mom stopped by and brought me lunch. She's on a double, so she'll be home late."

"Okay. I'm going to shower and do some computer stuff. Holler if you need me."

Chris's eyes are already closed and he's snoring lightly. I pull up the small blanket resting on his feet so it covers him up to the chin. For a moment, I pause, considering how very small and fragile my normally tough brother looks.

Then, without stopping for anything else, I head to my bathroom and scrub my hair and body until the hot water runs out.

AFTER THE SHOWER, I SIT DOWN AT THE KITCHEN TABLE AND open my laptop. I kind of towel-dried my hair, but water still drips down the back of my neck, soaking my ratty T-shirt. My stomach rumbles, but I ignore it in favor of the cup of tea steaming on the table beside me. Plucking the tea bag out with my fingers, I squeeze it, and then try to lob the bag into the trash. It soars across the kitchen and then misses by like a foot, smashing into the edge of the kitchen counter and exploding.

Tea leaves and other fragments of who-knows-what fly across the kitchen.

Typical Kit luck.

Sighing, I stand up. My body aches from all the stable cleaning. It takes only a few minutes to wipe up the soggy tea leaves, but it feels like a monumental chore because each swipe of the broom and then paper towel reveals more layers of dirt. We're all working so much that the kitchen hasn't been properly cleaned in months. Starting over in a shiny new apartment is looking more appealing. Mom might be on to something here.

I can't help myself. Cleaning up the tea leaves turns into scrubbing the counters, mopping the floor, and wiping out the refrigerator. When all that's done, and my tea is most certainly cold, I sit back down at the table.

My email has been dinging since I got home—I saw one from the local community college and a few random ones from bloggers asking for interviews—but my phone's nearly dead and still drying from the disinfectant I keep slathering all over it.

Some part of me wants to leave those emails unopened forever. Because if they're bad news, then it's not real until I read it, right? But if they're good news? Or just neutral news? Then it's silly for me not to open them. Plus, I could really, really use some good news today.

Taking a deep breath and putting my courage in the sticking

place, as Lady Macbeth advises, I open my email.

The first is from the community college Chris goes to. It's short and to the point.

Ms. Sweetly,

Congratulations! After careful review of your materials, we are pleased to offer you a full scholarship for your two years of study here. This covers all tuition and a stipend for books and materials. Please reply at your earliest convenience to indicate your acceptance.

Well.

That's good news. And bad news.

I didn't tell anyone—not Mom, not Chris, not Layla, not Jett—that I applied to the community college as a backup. It felt like a betrayal of my plans to even turn in the application, but the scholarship chance also was too good to pass up.

But now that I have it—and don't have a scholarship for Marquette—I almost don't want it. Which is terrible and entitled and I know it.

But I want a school by Lake Michigan. And a new city. And all the adventures waiting for me there.

Deciding not to decide immediately, I drink the rest of my tea in one gulp and click on my website.

Oh no.

Somehow the trolls and legions of men's rights activists (eye roll forever) have found my video.

They've filled up the comments section with their vitriol.

If only this were the Middle Ages, when people would bury their contempt in complex visual allegories like drawing pictures of knights fighting snails (which is a surprisingly common image in illuminated medieval manuscripts). Those pictures—while expressing some strong sentiments by comparing social climbers to slimy garden pests—probably didn't have quite the same impact as a Twitter mob or attacks in comment sections like we have today.

My hands tremble as I scroll downward. What is wrong with people?

The comments on my video go on and on. Disgusting, lewd, angry, outraged. They want to attack me, my body, my friends, and our mission to make things fair at the Castle.

Of course, interspersed with all this awfulness are positive comments, but even a lot of the ones from before have been bombarded by trolls. It's like I must've ended up on some anti-feminist message board, and everyone decided to pile on.

I skim comment after comment, getting sicker and sicker to my stomach.

Biting my bottom lip as I read, I take deep, steadying breaths. I want to hide. Suddenly, having people know my name makes me vulnerable and scared.

I want to reply to each and every nasty comment, excoriating them. I want to take the video down. I want to throw the computer across the room.

I can almost hear what Mom would say to me if she knew:

"This is why you don't put yourself out there, Kit. Why you keep your head low and focus on what you're supposed to be doing, not striving for something that's so far outside your reach."

Which is exactly the kind of talk that made me want to fight as a Knight in the first place. Tell me I can't and then watch me do it. It's also what makes me want to find a way—any way—to go to Marquette over the community college.

"But maybe you should choose your battles," Mom would say. "Your work might not be safe anymore for you and you've got a free ride at another school. Take it. Don't make my same mistakes, blah, blah, blah . . ."

I close the laptop as I hear Mom's key in the door. Not wanting to deal with her in real life, I hurry down the hall to my room, shut the door, and hide under the covers.

Jett texts me when I'm already in bed.

Jett: You feeling any better?

It's sweet of him to ask. To check on me. To pretend like nothing happened between us. To make me forget the fact that none of my other friends—not even Layla—have texted or reached out tonight.

But the thought of Jett, with his lips that need to be kissed and his being a good friend and wanting to make me feel better, just makes me feel worse. I don't want to talk to him when my head's full of all those ugly, hateful comments. And I don't want to try to sort through what it meant that I kissed him and he ran.

So, I turn off my phone. And stay under the covers. Fairly certain I may never leave my bed again.

37

THURSDAY MORNING DAWNS SUNNY, BRIGHT, AND FULL OF birds singing about how great their lives are.

Just kidding.

Who knows what the birds are singing about? Not me. But I'm pretty sure it's not about how great things are because, like humans, birds' lives tend to follow the nasty, brutish, and short model.

I grab my phone off the nightstand and pull my covers back over my head. Still nothing from Layla, Alex, Lizzy, Mags, or Penny.

Opening our Knights group text, I type a quick message.

Kit: Morning friends! I'm sorry again I didn't tell you about what Corporate said. Maybe we can still get together to train? I don't know if you'll be there, but I'll be at Layla's at 3:30 like we planned.

Mags: Can't make it.

Layla: Yeah, we have to cancel. My mom's taking me shopping after school.

What? Her mom is never home at that time of day. And Layla hates shopping with her mom because they always end up in what she calls "fossilized old rich lady boutiques."

A pang goes through me. I knew my friends were mad, but this feels really, really, really mad.

Kit: Okay. Maybe not today. See you all at work tomorrow. And sorry again. xx.

Nobody else replies. All of which is too crushing to think about without some coffee in me. I can't face school and seeing my friends' anger, so despite the fact that I missed Monday too, I decide to skip school today. What's the point of being a senior if you can't ditch days here and there?

I know skipping school is the coward's way out, but I just feel battered from every side.

I mean, I've worked so hard for the chance of knighthood. But what have I gotten from it? Demotion, death threats, and a great big heap of nothing. Who even cares if all these kids are hoping to see the Girl Knight? Suddenly, the whole thing feels stupid, foolish, and unnecessary. Maybe I should just get a job at the mall or something. It would be easy, cut-and-dried, and seriously without the heroic quest aspects. Likely too I'd be able to keep my head down and make enough money for the start of school.

I imagine working at the mall. Folding shirts, peddling facial creams, or flipping burgers at the food court. Each new job makes me cringe worse than the one before.

Also, if I'm being honest, I'd miss the smell of the Castle, the friends I have there, the whisper of anticipation when the lights go out, the roar of the crowd as the Knights ride in. I love it as much as I did the first time I saw the show, and that's enough to make me want to make it better and fairer for everyone. But the question is how? How do I convince my friends to stop being mad? How do I get them to ride out like we planned?

Answers aren't hiding under my covers, but maybe they lie at the bottom of a mug of coffee.

I get out of bed. Last night, my dreams were full of scaly green trolls chasing me through some sort of eerie medieval London-type space, yelling about how they wanted to kill me. My stomach is basically eating itself, and all of yesterday's mess sits heavy on my mind. I wash my face, brush my teeth, and pull on a pair of jeans from the laundry bag. They're wrinkled, but they smell clean at least. A vintage Rainbow Brite T-shirt and my boots complete the outfit. Time for caffeine.

Mom's door is still closed, her snores steady as a lawn mower. I'm not ready to face her yet, so I close my door softly and tiptoe past hers. Coffee is already made, and I pour myself a huge cup.

In the living room, the TV is on super loud and Chris is laughing. I poke my head in there.

"What, in God's name, are you watching?"

On the TV, two dogs are getting married in a swanky church. Women in designer dresses beam at the dogs, and then the two dogs start licking each other.

"I don't know!" Chris gasps, clutching his injured ribs as he laughs. Tears stream from his eyes. "But these two dogs talk, and they're like married now, and they're super fancy . . ."

Beside Chris sits a bottle of pain meds, a cup of coffee, and an empty bag of chips. He's almost at the end of the prescription. It lifts my spirits a bit to see him cheerfully stoned and watching kids' TV.

I plop down on the couch beside him and pluck a few uneaten chips from between the couch cushions. Because it's that kind of day.

"How are you feeling?" I ask after a few minutes of watching the convoluted puppy plot spin out of control. Wrapping my hands around my coffee, I take a long gulp. It's terrible after the flavored chips, but I need it for thinking.

"Great," says Chris. "I can barely feel my ribs, and I think I'll be able to shower today."

"Thank God," I mumble. "No offense, bro, but you're not looking your best."

Chris makes a face and throws a chip at me. I bat it away and it flies back toward him.

"Hey!" Chris looks away from the TV and scrunches his face as if he's trying to remember something. "Why were you so stinky yesterday?"

He looks so concerned that I can't help it. The entire story comes pouring out of me. Starting with Len's speech to everyone, my friends' anger, my demotion to lower stable hand, and falling into the dumpster. I leave out kissing Jett, because there are some things you don't tell your brother. No matter how cool he is.

"I can't believe Len did that," says Chris. "Do you want me to call Penny? I'm sure she's not really mad."

"I'll figure it out. You just rest. Get better."

Chris exhales sharply and then grips his ribs. "I hate being hurt like this. I feel like every minute I'm sitting here, someone else is out there angling for my job."

"Well." I raise one eyebrow. "I'm angling for your job."

Chris laughs at that. I don't tell him about Eric riding out in his armor last night. As we sit there, watching the ridiculous show, one of the nasty comments someone left about my video keeps coming back to me: *Why should anyone care about you becoming a Knight? Does it really matter in the grand scheme of things?*

Before I can think of a good answer to that, Chris drops his phone and groans as he reaches for it. I grab it from him and glance at the screen. It's open to contacts.

There are dozens of girls in the phone.

"Who are all these people?" I ask, moving my finger over Amy, Jenny R., Jenny S., Penny, Sophie, Madeline. "I recognize some of the names from the Castle, but not all of them."

A blush appears on Chris's cheeks. "Well, being the Red Knight has its perks."

"Are you seriously getting numbers at work?"

"You have no idea," he says, laughing. "You know after the show, when the guests come up to us for pictures? I've had drunk women try to get me to sign their bras; they grab my butt when we take pictures—"

"Again, harassment and super not okay."

"Agreed. Most of the Knights just ignore it, but some of us actually say something about it. Even without all that, at least once a night someone gives me a phone number."

"And you put them in your phone?"

Chris shakes his head. "Not all of them. But I'm talking to a few of those girls."

"The secret love life of the Red Knight," I say with a smile. "Teach me your moves, oh wise one."

"Oh, I've got moves," he says. "But I will certainly not teach you them. How are things going with Jett?"

"Does everyone know about that?"

"Well. Not everyone. But Penny texted me last night, saying that she saw you two kissing behind the dumpsters—"

"We weren't behind the dumpsters," I say. I can hear the petulance in my voice. "And it was just a kiss. No big deal."

"Uh-huh," says Chris. He points at the TV. "You should take a lesson from these dogs. The heart wants what the heart wants. You just have to be brave enough to admit it."

I throw a pillow at him. "I'm not taking love-life advice from Chihuahuas or from you. Do you need anything?"

"Donuts," says Chris. "I'd do a handstand for some donuts right now."

"Done."

I wave to him as I hurry out of the house.

WHEN I GET HOME WITH THE DONUTS AND COFFEE, MOM'S walking to the bus stop at the end of the road.

I roll my window down and wave. "Hey, stranger! Want a ride to work?"

She stops by the window and gives me a tired smile. "Hi, hon. It's okay. The bus will be here soon. Plus, I've got a book."

Mom once told me that riding the bus is one of her quiet moments during the day. When she can just sit, read a book, and not worry too much about anything other than getting from point A to B. Every time I ride the bus, somebody's yelling or masturbating or trying to sell me something, but if it works for her, who am I to argue?

"Okay. Have a good day. When you get home, maybe we can talk. I've . . . um . . . I've got lots to tell you."

Mom smiles. "College news? Work stuff?"

"All of the above."

"I'll be on a double tonight, so let's talk tomorrow. Oh, and your brother was talking about going somewhere. Can you take him after school? Just don't let him do too much. He's got to rest."

No need to tell her I'm skipping today. It'll just stress her out.

"Will do. Want a donut?"

"God, yes." I hand her a donut and a coffee.

"Have a good day," I say. "See you tonight."

She blows me a kiss and takes a huge bite. "You too! Oh, and Kit, thank you for stepping up and taking on so much. I know our family isn't perfect, but we're here for each other. That's really all that matters."

She walks away before I can say anything, but all the things I'm not telling her sit heavy on my heart as she disappears up the street.

"I BROUGHT DONUTS!" I CALL AS I COME UP THE STAIRS. CHRIS isn't in the living room, and his blankets and stuff are cleaned up from the couch.

Putting the donuts down on the kitchen table, my eyes fall onto a stack of papers. "Divorce Decree" is stamped across the top page. A note with a lawyer's office name and address is stuck to the top page as well. "Get this signed by your ex

ASAP," it says in scrawled handwriting.

I flip through the rest of the pages. I knew something was wrong! Dad seemed ready to sign the papers at the hospital, but then he just vanished. Clearly, he's not as put together as he tried to make it seem. And this feels like all those times he'd disappeared before. Mom must not have found Dad again, and clearly, she's not made it to the theater where his dragon show is being held. Maybe I can at least fix this part of our lives a little bit.

Grabbing the papers, I wander through the house. Chris is nowhere to be found. Finally, I go out to the shed behind the house.

Chris stands in front of his forge, lining up pieces of metal into rows. He moves slowly, as if every step hurts. On the table by the door sits the enormous chain mail shirt he's been working on.

"What are you doing?" I push the door of the shop open with a loud *thunk*.

Chris looks up and his eyes catch the morning light. The bruises from his fall still haven't quite healed, and his whole face looks grayish purple.

"I've got to work," he says, taking a strained breath. He starts up a blowtorch and lowers his welding glasses. "If I can't work at the Castle, I've got to be able to make some money. This order was due last week." He gestures toward the shirt.

"No way, dude!" I step around the table and turn off the nozzle for the blowtorch. "You just got out of the hospital. You can't be working out here. If you need to do something, go study."

Chris lifts up his welding visor. "I'm done with all my homework. It's not like it's that hard. It's just intro physics, calculus, and my literature classes."

"Fine, Mr. I'm-So-Smart. But I would recommend you don't operate blowtorches while on painkillers. If you need something to do, come with me to yell at Dad. Apparently, he's still not signed these divorce papers." I wave them in Chris's direction. "Maybe we can find him and get them signed so Mom doesn't have to worry about it. And so I can worry about something other than failing at knighthood. At least once they're divorced, I won't have to report his income when it comes to financial aid for school."

That makes Chris put down all his blacksmithing tools and pay attention. "Can I finally confront him for ruining our lives?"

"I'm leaning more toward berating him for being a selfish asshole, but you've got the basic theme."

"Sounds like a plan to me. Though I'm going to need like five donuts for fortitude." Chris follows me out of the black-smithing shed and to his car.

38

I'M NOT SURE WHY I THOUGHT IT WOULD BE EASY TO FIND MY dad. Chris and I drive around the neighborhood near the arena where the animatronic dinosaur show is playing. The area is newly gentrified and has more condos and coffee shops than parking spaces.

"He'd be in some cheap motel if he's here at all," I say as we drive past a row of boutiques next to a tiny bodega.

"I bet he's staying with the show people." Chris points to a group of buses and RV trailers in the parking lot of the arena. "He probably talked his way into one of those and is mooching off them."

I park Chris's car. "Where should we start?"

Semitrailers decorated with the show logo, RVs, and two buses that look like they belong to rock stars fill this part of the parking lot. It's still relatively early and no one stirs.

"Just knock on the first one," says Chris. "Even if he's not in there, maybe they know where he is."

Or maybe they're going to be scary carny folk who sleep with knives under their pillows. Definitely the kind of people who take kindly to early morning wake-up calls from strangers. But the fearless Girl Knight wouldn't let such a thing stop her.

"I've got an idea." I pull my hair back in a ponytail and go back to the car for the box of donuts. "Follow my lead."

Chris tries to shrug, but with his broken bones, it comes out as more of a wobble. He walks a few steps behind me as we approach the first trailer. Taking a deep breath, I knock three times.

No one answers.

I look at Chris.

"Try again," he whispers loudly.

I knock three more times. Still no one.

We try another trailer, which is opened by a very scary-looking dude with tattoos covering his skull. He yells a few choice words at us before we can even ask for our dad.

"Do you even think he's here?"

"We'll try this last row," says Chris. "At least then we can tell Mom we tried."

We knock on every door. A tired-looking woman holding a crying baby opens one. Two of the others ignore us completely, which is better than the one where someone flings a shoe at the door, sending me scuttling down the steps.

With a deep breath, I knock on the second-to-last door. Someone stumbles around inside the trailer.

"What do you want?" demands a gravelly voice, as the trailer door swings open. A hard-lived white woman in a Guns N' Roses T-shirt glares at me. Her platinum hair has gray and brown roots longer than my thumbs and mascara is smudged beneath her eyes. The sickly-sweet smell of last night's booze wafts off her. She looks like an '80s throwback version of Carol Burnett playing Miss Hannigan in *Annie*. Stumbling, still drunk, and mean as hell.

"Um." My voice shakes as I stand there. "I'm a new production assistant for the show, and they told me to bring donuts to the trailers this morning." I open the box with a flourish. Chris ate four on the way over here, so there's just a few left.

The woman eyes me suspiciously and then takes a chocolate-and-sprinkles one.

I stand there for a moment, trying to peer past her. A lumpy couch and a cheap-looking table fill most of the room. But leaning against the wall between them is my dad's guitar. The one he stole from Len and was supposed to give back. I turn around, trying to signal to Chris. The woman shoots me a dirty look and starts to close the door. I put my foot out to stop it.

"Is that all?" she asks, glaring at my sneaker. "Show doesn't start for a few hours, and I'm still sleeping."

My mind goes blank for a moment, and Chris limps up the stairs. "We're looking for Lars Sweetly. Special message from production. Have you seen him today?"

The woman narrows her eyes. "What do you want with Lars? He done something wrong?"

Fear flashes across her face for a moment and her eyes dart to the kitchen table. A mirror and the residue of white, powdery lines covers the table. Something in me—maybe the last thread of hope I had for my dad, which I wasn't even aware I was clinging to—disappears.

"We just have a message for him," I say, trying to keep my voice neutral. "He's not in trouble. I think he might have gotten a raise or something."

"Well, ain't that the shit," says the woman, taking a huge bite of the donut. "Lars! Get your ass out here. Somebody from production wants to see you."

I'm fairly stunned that we actually found him. Chris and I share a surprised look. But I guess even we get lucky sometimes.

Lars stumbles out of the back bedroom, bumping into things and knocking empty bottles to the floor. "What the hell are you yelling about, Janet? Don't you know a man needs—"

He catches sight of us and stops dead in his tracks.

"Kit? Chris? What're you two doing here?"

"You know these two?" Janet finishes her donut and picks up a cigarette out of an overflowing ashtray. She plops it into her mouth and tries lighting it with a cheap plastic lighter. Chocolate smears her fingers, leaving fingerprints on the lighter.

"Get outta the way, Janet," says my dad, pushing past her. "These are my kids. The ones I was telling you about."

"Ahhhhh." Janet looks at us a bit differently now. "What are you here for? He ain't got no money." She laughs at that and turns away from us as the lighter catches and makes the tip of her cigarette glow.

Lars steps outside, still shirtless. All three of us are on a porch so narrow, it couldn't be called anything but a step.

"Well, what do you want?" His voice is defensive and also a little tremulous. He crosses his arms over his bony, pale chest. "You did all this work to find me, but why're you here?"

Chris makes a small, angry noise behind me. Kind of like a snap firework going off, but I find my voice first. "You need to sign these," I say, thrusting the divorce papers at him. "Mom's been trying to find you. What happened to you trying to make everything right?"

A blush creeps across Lars's cheeks, but he crosses his arms. "Things happened, Courtney."

"Kit," Chris and I both say at the same time.

"Fine, Kit, Courtney, whatever. I was going to sign the papers, but some expenses came up and I can't afford all the divorce fees."

The smell of his morning breath combined with the stale

beer and smoke he reeks of make me take a step back. But I'm not backing down.

"By 'expenses' I assume you mean the cocaine on the table in there and the booze?"

Lars runs his hands through his messy, greasy hair. "You've got no idea what it's like to be an adult, Kit. There's so much pressure on you, always. Sometimes, you just need to unwind."

"You're so predictable," says Chris in a dangerous voice. "This is why I didn't want to talk to you at the Castle. And this is why we don't want to have anything to do with you."

Chris is coming in hot, and he moves toward Lars like he might take a swing.

"Your arm is broken." I pull him back. "Simmer down. Why don't you go wait in the car? I've got this."

"I'm not leaving you alone with him!" Chris snaps.

"I'll be fine." I put a hand on Chris's shoulder and turn him away from the trailer. "Be there in just a minute."

He looks up at Lars for one long moment, hatred burning in his eyes. "This is the last time I'll warn you, Dad." In Chris's mouth the word comes out like acid. "Leave Kit, Mom, and me alone. Don't call. Don't try to make up. Just sign the papers and leave. We don't need you and we sure as hell don't want anything to do with you."

"Chris—Son—please—" Lars reaches out for Chris, but then he kind of stumble-trips over his own feet and lands on his knees.

Chris doesn't look back.

Lars looks tired as he watches Chris walk to the car, but he doesn't say anything else for a long moment. He's weak and broken as he kneels there. I have the most unwelcome impulse to hug him and somehow save him from himself.

"I'm sorry I messed up, Kit," he says, standing up. "I screwed it all up. Our family. Your mom. Your and your brother's chances for college. I just wanted to make it better, but old habits die hard, you know?" He turns his arms over. Red puncture marks and purple bruises line the inside of his arm.

"I don't know," I say, keeping my voice as steady as possible, "because I've never bought drugs with money that was supposed to help my family."

The slump of his shoulders and the way he looks toward the trailer, like he's longing to get inside and get this conversation over with, takes all my anger from me. I feel sorry for him. And for what we could've had. But some things just have to be let go.

"Why didn't you give Len the guitar back?"

Lars looks up at me. His face is a wreck now, but in that moment, he looks just like Chris. "I was going to give it to him at the hospital. I swear. But then he was running late, and all those people kept looking at me funny, so I got out of there. I've been avoiding Len's calls ever since."

"You're lucky you didn't pawn it. Len would've had you drawn and quartered."

A funny little sound, like a laugh that's rusty from use, breaks out of my dad. "That's funny, Kit," he says. "Because he thinks he's a King, right?"

I nod. "Exactly."

"Can I have a donut?"

I'd almost forgotten I was holding them. I give him the box.

"Here's what I'm going to do, Dad." His face softens when I say it, but I think we both know I'll never call him Dad again. "I won't bother you anymore. You sign these papers. While you do that, I'm going in there, and I'm going to take Len's guitar and give it back to him. If you try to stop me, I'll call the cops."

He nods. "No need to break down the gate with a battering ram. I'll sign the papers and I'll give you the damn guitar if it means that much. Least I can do after everything else."

I follow him into the narrow, dark trailer, trying not to touch anything. There's the lights-get-turned-off-because-you-paid-the-electric-bill-late poor we are, and then there's the drug-addled-bad-choices poor my dad and Janet are. Janet's hacking cough comes from the back of the trailer, and fruit flies buzz around the pile of dirty dishes in the sink.

"Here you go." Lars grabs a pen off the table and signs the divorce papers. Then, he picks up the guitar. His fingers linger above the strings for a moment, but he hands it over. "Not sure how I'll do this gig without it, but I'll figure something out. I was going to pawn it anyway."

"Thank you for this at least." I feel like I should shake his hand or hug him or something, but I don't. Instead, I dig into my pocket and take out a handful of singles. My change from the donuts. I plop them on the table. "Use it for food or gas or anything but drugs."

I know I can't save him. It's ridiculous to try. But this is what Knights do. Help where we can.

"I'll try," he says, picking up the money. Powdery bits of cocaine cling to it, and his hand twitches to his nose.

"See you around, maybe." I turn away from him, waving over my shoulder.

"Kit," he calls as I go. "Don't let the cold world break you. You're always my little girl."

"I'm not," I say, turning around. "And don't worry. The world won't break me. I'm the Girl Knight after all."

That feels pretty much like the perfect exit line, so I leave it at that. The cheap metal door of the trailer slams behind me.

As I walk back to the car, I swipe away at the treacherous tears that leak from my eyes, getting rid of them before Chris can see.

# 39

LEN'S NOT AT HIS HOUSE. I RING THE BELL FOR LIKE FIVE minutes, but no one answers. I'm so frustrated with him, and my heart still hurts from seeing my dad, that it's all I can do not to knock over one of the half dozen tacky fake Roman statues that line Len's driveway. I settle for throwing a wad of chewing gum into the enormous fountain in his front yard.

I get back into the car. In the passenger seat, Chris holds on to the guitar, but he's not said anything since we left Dad's trailer. We're apparently not going to talk about what happened with Dad. And that's perfectly okay with me.

"Well, Len's either hibernating, dead, or—"

"He's at the Castle," says Chris. He holds up his phone. "Penny had to run over there to work on the schedule and she told me he's been there the entire time, pacing his office and talking to people from Corporate on the phone."

"To the Castle we go then," I say, backing the car out of Len's driveway.

To my surprise, Len smiles when we walk into his office. "Ahh, my favorite niece and nephew." His eyes go straight to the guitar and his jaw drops. "What can I do for you?"

It's disconcerting to think that he's totally forgotten what an ass he was yesterday.

"You're in a good mood," says Chris. He looks suspicious. "What's going on?"

"Maybe there's a sale on toilet paper at the Costco," I say under my breath, knowing how much Len likes to flash his membership card like he's hot shit for being able to shop there.

I help Chris into one of the chairs by the desk.

Len holds up an email he's printed out. "I'm being considered for promotion to the Corporate office in Miami. Despite the initial email they sent you, Kit, someone in upper management really likes what we're doing here for women's rights and becoming more progressive. There's talk that this might be the wave of the future at the Castles. They want me to move to Miami to get their program up to scratch."

I narrow my eyes at him. "You're taking credit for my hard work?"

"No," says Len. "I'm finally getting what I deserve. You already know the Corporate people are coming tomorrow, and although they said no to your proposed scheme, I'm going to authorize you to do a little demonstration. But, just you, Kit. You can ride out with the Knights, wave, and then head back. We'll show them how the crowd loves you, and that should be enough to secure my promotion."

"So, you're giving me permission to ride out as part of the show, but not as a real Knight?" I can't keep the disgust from my voice. "It's all a great big sham of equality?"

"Exactly," says Len. "That's what Corporate wants, so that's what they'll get." He hands Chris a pile of Workers' Comp paperwork. "And here, Chris, fill these out. They should cover your bills. See, there you go. Uncle Len saves the day. Now give me my guitar."

Chris and I share a look. He glances at the guitar. It feels like it should be harder to give something from our dad away, but it doesn't even sting. Or maybe I'm just numb to all thoughts of my dad right now. I shrug and Chris hands it over. Len grabs the guitar, hungrily.

"One more thing, Chris," he says as we turn to go. "My job is going to be vacant, and I put your name in the hat for it. I think you'd make an excellent King and general manager. Plus, you won't have to ride a horse unless you want to."

Chris stops in his tracks. He grips my sleeve with his good arm. "Are you kidding?"

Len shakes his head. "Serious as a heart attack. Make sure I get that promotion and my job is yours. It's full benefits and seventy thousand a year."

Chris looks stunned. "I'll take it."

"He means we'll think about it," I say taking his arm. "And I'll ride out tomorrow. Don't worry. I'll give you a show that won't soon be forgotten."

"Just do as you're told, Kit," says Len. "Think you can handle that?"

Of course I can handle it. In fact, I can do way better than that.

"So, you're going to do something stupid?" says Chris as we walk away from Len's office.

"Most assuredly," I say. "But it will also be grand and bold, and it'll shake things up. If I pull it off, it should help, not hurt, your job prospects."

"I'm not even sure I want this job," says Chris. "Though it is a lot of money. But—and don't tell Mom this—I applied for a transfer to the University of Chicago, and I got in. They're going to give me a scholarship. If I take it, I'll be set up for whatever engineering internship I want. But I'm not sure I can afford to commute and—"

"Chris! Congrats! That's amazing news and we'll totally make it work."

"I think it's what I need to do," says Chris. "I don't want to be Len in another twenty years. But what're you going to do?

Are you really going to let him parade you around like that?"

"If Layla and the others were still talking to me it would be different, but without them, I'm not sure what else I can do."

"Talk to them. Tell them what Len said. I bet they'll want to ride out with you. And Austin and I have already convinced most of the other Knights to let you ride in their places. If we stick to the original plan, you can be the Red Knight, Layla can be Blue, Alex can ride as Yellow, Mags as Purple, Penny as Black-and-White . . ."

"You forgot Green. What's Lizzy going to do?"

"Yeah, Dalton's not relenting." Chris makes a face.

"Maybe we can plan for that. I can always give her the Red Knight costume and ride out as someone totally different. That is, if you know anyone who might have spare plate armor or chain mail in the garden shed."

"Lucky for you I know a guy," says Chris, grinning.

"This could work," I say. "If I can convince the others."

A task that is going to be harder than anything else I've done so far.

## 40

Kit to Knights for Days Group Text: Hi, Knights! I'm sorry I was such an ass. If you can forgive me, I have some news. Reply back so I know you're there.

Kit: Okay, so nobody else is responding. And it's been an hour. Which is fine. I'll just leave this update here. Len's given me permission to ride out tomorrow. (Really, he has. Ask Chris. He was there.) But it's only for a quick loop or two and only as part of a show exhibition. He wants to demonstrate how progressive he is so he can get a promotion and suddenly I fit into those plans. But I was thinking . . . what if we all go out there? What if we stage a coup and have our tournament anyway? The Knights are still willing to trade with us. (You'll ride out as Red, Lizzy, because Dalton's not giving up his spot, because, Dalton.) We know all the moves. And we're awesome. Want to join me?

Kit: Nothing? Really. Okay. Dammit. Friends. TALK TO ME.

Kit: Still nothing. Alright. Whatever. See you all at work tomorrow.

41

I WAKE UP AT 6:00 A.M., ON FRIDAY—THE DAY WE'RE SUP-
posed to all be riding out together and two weeks after I
first took Chris's place as the Red Knight. My phone's in my
hand. And I keep refreshing the group text chain. As if staring
at it would make my friends reply, saying they're not angry.
My fingers hover, wanting to type something—anything—to
make my friends forgive me. But what can I say? Clearly I've
messed up. Badly.

I have to send something. Even though it's super early.

Kit: Hello? Anybody there? Can we at least talk about this?

It's a pathetic attempt, but at least I tried. Hauling myself
out of bed, I go make coffee. Maybe my friends are still asleep.
Maybe someone will write back soon.

By 7:30, when I should be leaving for school, there are still no replies.

A gnawing pang shoots through my stomach, which could be from the three cups of coffee I've just slammed, but it feels a whole lot like something else. Something sadder and lonelier.

Even Layla still isn't speaking to me. Which is like our longest argument in a decade of friendship. Deciding I can't face her, Alex, and Lizzy at school (again, perks of being a senior), I spend the day bingeing the entire *The Lord of the Rings* trilogy extended edition (we only make it halfway through *Two Towers*) with Chris and feeling sorry for myself.

By the time my alarm goes off, telling me it's time to get ready for work, I'm no less motivated. I roll off the couch and flop onto the living room floor.

"I'm not even sure why I'm going tonight," I say with a moan. "I mean, I can't go to Marquette no matter what, so why do I need the promotion to knighthood? And Mom is going to move into a cheaper place soon, so we won't need so much money for the house. And my friends aren't talking to me. Remind me why I need this crappy job anyway?"

"Fool of a Took!" says Chris, sitting up to look at me. He pulls his gray sweatshirt hood up over his head. "All we have to decide is what to do with the time that is given us."

I snort. "You don't get to use Gandalf quotes to boss me around."

"Even the wise cannot see all ends." Chris nods sagely.

"Stop! You're not even doing a good imitation."

He throws a pillow at me. "I did not pass through fire and death to bandy crooked words with a witless worm!"

I roll my eyes and sit up. "Fine. Fine! I'm going."

"Fly, you fool!"

Laughing, I haul myself to my feet. Before I can leave the living room, there's a knock at the front door. I shoot Chris a look, but he just shrugs.

"Coming," I holler as I pound down the steps to the front door. I fling it open and my jaw drops.

Jett stands there, holding a shopping bag and a cup of coffee. He's in his work clothes, with his leather jacket over them.

Suddenly, I'm aware I'm wearing a ratty pair of leggings and a tight "A Girl Has No Name" *Game of Thrones* T-shirt with a coffee stain on it. My hair is in two messy braids, and I can't guarantee I don't have lettuce in my teeth from lunch.

"What're you doing here?"

Jett smiles his easy, familiar smile. It's like coming home to see it. "I brought you coffee. And a Silver Knight's costume rushed direct from Amazon. I figured you needed your own color, since you're redefining things at the Castle."

"Wonderful man." I take the coffee with one hand, longing to put the other hand on his cheek.

"That's not all." He grabs my hand. "C'mon. I'm giving you a ride to work."

"But I have to change," I say, gesturing at my leggings and T-shirt.

"Nope," says Chris, hobbling down the stairs behind me. Somehow he has my purse and phone in his hand. "You're good like that."

He and Jett smile at each other. I narrow my eyes at them both.

"What's going on here? Are you two conspiring against me?"

"Conspiring *for* you would be more accurate," says Jett. "Let's go."

"No clues? No hints?"

"Nope," says Chris. "Just get in the van, and you'll see."

"It's never good when someone tells you to get into a van." I side eye them both.

"Trust us, it's a good thing," says Jett with a laugh as he helps Chris into the passenger seat.

I'm not convinced, but I take my stuff from Chris and clamber into the back of the minivan. Taking a long swig of my coffee (vanilla latte with almond milk, bless you, Jett), I try to steel myself for whatever they have planned.

JETT AND CHRIS LEAD ME INTO THE CASTLE, BUT WE SKIP the break room and our usual haunts. It's still early enough that most of the hallways are empty. Soon, it will be full of the hum and roar of the crowd, but for now the only sounds that fill the halls are horses whinnying and some pre-cooking clatter from the kitchen.

I check my phone. "We're like an hour early," I say. "Did you mess with my alarm, Chris?"

"Maybe?" he says, limping along beside me. He shrugs and throws another Gandalf quote my way: "A wizard is never late. Nor is he early. He arrives precisely when he means to."

Jett snickers beside me and bumps my shoulder with his. It seems we're back to casual BFF contact and there's no lingering weirdness from me trying to kiss him two days ago. At least that's how it feels to me. Who even knows what Jett's feeling when it comes to all that?

"What's going on?" I ask as Jett pushes the door of the Upper Banquet Hall open. Chris limps in before me, and I follow him.

The room is empty except for a round banquet table covered with a white tablecloth. Seven chairs sit around it. In front of the table is a projection screen.

"Welcome to the Round Table," says Jett. "Take a seat. We'll start soon."

"Start what?" I ask.

"You'll see," he says. He takes his laptop out of his bag along with some wires and cameras and other technical-looking things.

I sit down in the closest seat and Chris plops in a chair across the table from me, typing something on his phone.

"Seriously, Chris. What's going on?" I ask. "And I swear if you answer with a Gandalf quote, we're not related anymore."

Before he can say anything, Layla and Alex walk into the room. I give them a little wave. Layla smiles at me—which warms my heart to its lonely, feeling-abandoned-by-my-friends core. Alex just quirks an eyebrow, taking in the room, the screen, Jett fiddling with the tech stuff, Chris, and me.

"What's going on here?" asks Alex, their voice suspicious. "I got a text from Jett that there was something important happening and I had to be here early."

"It is important," Jett calls out. "Have a seat at the Round Table. You'll see when the others get here."

"Round Table?" Alex grumbles and rolls their eyes.

"What's going on?" Layla asks, sliding into the seat next to me.

"I have no idea," I say. "They basically kidnapped me to get me here."

"I'm sorry not to have texted you back," says Layla. "I just needed some time to think. And then Maura and I went out last night." She giggles as she says it, and I smile at her.

"I missed you. And I'm sorry. Like really, really sorry."

"I missed you too," she says. "And I've got LOTS to tell you all about what happened with Maura."

Across the table, Alex rolls their eyes. "You two have been mad at each other for like a day."

"Two days," I correct them. "A very long two days. Are you still mad too?"

In answer, Alex crosses their arms and looks away.

Okay, then.

A moment later, Mags, Lizzy, and Penny walk into the room, talking together. Mags looks like a punk rock mermaid with her hair striped dark blue, purple, teal, and green.

"What's up?" Penny asks, holding up her phone. "Chris has been blowing up my phone all day."

"Everyone, sit, please," says Jett. "Take a seat at the Round Table, where all are equal, and give me ten minutes of your time."

Mags makes an irritated noise, but she sits next to Alex. She doesn't look at me, though Lizzy gives me a small smile.

Jett continues: "Not long ago, I started making what might be the greatest documentary of my career. It started with a video of Kit fighting as the Red Knight, recorded on my phone during what I thought was an ordinary shift at the Castle. But as I worked with you all, it became about so much more than Kit, or her quest for knighthood, or all your hard work in training. It's almost done, and what's emerged is a portrait of friendship and fierceness that go beyond these walls. I've gathered you here to show you what magic you make together. And hopefully to convince you all to fight tonight, so I can finish the film and Kit can finish her plan. And we can all change things here."

Sweet, wonderful, thoughtful, miraculous Jett. I smile at him, resisting every urge to jump up and kiss my thanks. He winks at me, sending my heart ping-ponging in my chest.

"I've got to be on the floor in fifteen minutes," says Penny, irritably.

"And I've got to be taking guest pictures by then for the first show," adds Alex.

"Give me eight minutes," says Jett. "You won't regret it."

"Fine," says Alex. "You have eight minutes."

Jett walks back to the projector, squeezing my shoulder as he passes. Layla pokes me in the ribs once he's past, raising an eyebrow.

"Later," I whisper. She grins.

Jett turns off the lights, and his documentary comes on the screen. It starts with fanfare and then I ride into the arena. He's slowed it down, so my horse gallops dramatically.

"Once there was one Girl Knight." His voice-over comes on as my first video rolls through, now playing at normal speed. "And her struggles inspired people to dream of more." He's interspersed comments from the website with pictures of little girls in knight costumes and kids reenacting my video.

"She had a goal; she had a plan—a four-phase plan at that—but it wasn't enough. Only when the Girl Knight found other Knights to accompany her on this quest was it really underway."

Here Jett's created a gorgeous montage of our training— Lizzy trying the complicated roll off the horse for the first time; Mags and I sparring with training swords and laughing together as we trip over our feet; Penny catching a ring with her garden-rake lance; Layla and Alex jousting with pool noodles in the laundromat; and much, much more.

"It's definitely time for a change at the Castle," says Alex, as the camera focuses on them for a one-on-one shot during our last training session. They wipe sweat out of their eyes. "I've wanted to be a Knight since I started working at the Castle, but it's never been an option for me. Kit and the rest of us have been tirelessly pursuing this goal, and I think we're really going to change things around here."

Layla comes on next, riding her horse right up to the camera: "Why do I want to do this? Because I'm good at it! And it's fun!" She rides off with a laugh, skillfully taking the horse through a series of obstacles.

Jett's interviewed each of us in turn, and there are laughs and cheers for each person's interview.

Then my face comes on the screen. Off-screen, Jett asks, "Why are you fighting so hard, Kit? What is this really about?"

I know my answer by heart because it ran through my head a dozen times last night as I waited for my friends to text me back.

I look right at the camera: "This is about my friends and me getting a chance to be ourselves. It's about fighting against inequality and showing the world that gender shouldn't be a bar for any job these days. And it's about taking a battering ram to the notion that the heroes of the Middle Ages were all men."

"Do you think you'll succeed?" Jett asks.

"I know it," I say into the camera. A smile lights my face.

"With friends like these at my side, there's no chance we can fail."

The film stops there, carried off by some dramatic music. Jett flicks the lights on.

"Oh, Kit," says Penny, tossing a balled-up tissue at me. "You big dork. You made me cry."

I'm crying too. Layla wraps me in a hug. I lean my head on her shoulder.

"You're right," she says. "We can do this together."

"And we should," says Mags. "I'm with you if you still want to run the tournament, like you said in your text chain."

"Me too," says Lizzy. "And I'm sorry for getting mad, Kit. I know you didn't mean to hurt us."

"Group-hug time," says Alex, standing up. Everyone surrounds me, pulling me into a large, sniffly hug. Over my shoulder, I see Jett filming it all and Chris grinning at me.

"Thank you," I mouth to them. Jett smiles again, and I have a sudden image of us kissing for a very long time next time we're alone together.

Clearly, I'm ready to be more than friends. But why did Jett do all this? Is it because he's just the world's best guy friend? Or does it mean more? I thought I'd ruined everything by breaking the rules. But the time and care he's put into this video is more than friendly. Isn't it?

Before I have time to think through the Gordian knot of Jett and me, another phone alarm goes off—not mine this time—and Chris grabs his phone. "I hate to break this up," he says. "But it's time to get dressed for the show."

"Are you ready, Knights?" I ask the circle of amazing friends around me.

"We're with you, Girl Knight," says Layla.

"Until death, victory, or at least the end of the show," says Mags with a sly smile.

42

Tonight there's only one show at the Castle. Normally we have two every day, but Len combined them into one evening show so the Corporate folks would have time to look around and so we could really fill the seats.

Not that we'd have any problem doing that based on how crowded the lobby is.

"Good thing you invited half of Chicago to this show," whispers Jett as we thread our way through the growing crowd.

I grin at him. I've been flouting rules for weeks now. Maybe I can convince him that our Unbreakable Rules are really worth breaking. "Let's talk after the show, okay? About that video and—"

A hand grabs my arm, pulling me away from Jett. "Hi, Kit!" says Isabel, the production assistant from *Good Morning,*

*Chicago!* She stands with an older woman and an adorable little girl, who wears a knight's tunic and has her long dark hair braided into a crown around her head.

"I'm so glad you made it!" I say. "Who'd you bring to the show tonight?"

"This is my mother, and this is my niece, Sofia," says Isabel, smiling as she points to them. "Thanks for putting those tickets aside for us."

Sofia brandishes a light-up sword. "When are you going to ride? Where are the horses? Can I be a knight when I grow up?"

"Soon. The horses are in the back, getting ready for the show. And you can most definitely be a knight when you grow up. Keep your eyes on the arena. We've got a big surprise planned tonight."

Layla, Alex, and Mags wave to her, and Sofia's eyes widen.

"If you have time," says Isabel, "maybe we can grab a quick interview after the show? Bettina wanted a follow-up, so we'll be filming tonight."

"You got permission to film?" I ask skeptically.

Isabel points toward a cameraman standing at the edge of the Great Hall, filming the crowd. "Your boss seemed quite keen, in fact. He said you'll be riding out with the male Knights as part of a special exhibition."

"He's got part of it right. But we've got a bit more planned. See you after the show!"

"Go, Girl Knight!" shouts Sofia.

I wave to her, and Jett and I keep walking. We stroll right past Len, who's too busy kissing up to the Corporate folks—two women and a young guy, all of them in nice suits and carrying clipboards—to notice us.

"We're really into changing our image here," says one of the women.

"I couldn't agree more," says Len, chuckling. "Time to take this place out of the Middle Ages and move it into the twenty-first century. I have a special surprise planned for you tonight. Our very own Girl Knight is going to ride out with the other Knights for the first part of the show."

The two women exchange a wary look. I roll my eyes with them. They're certainly going to get more of a show than that.

Chris, walking with the help of Penny's arm, leads us away from the crowd and to the Knights' locker room.

"Are we supposed to go in there?" asks Lizzy doubtfully. "I don't think they're going to just welcome us."

"Think again," says Chris.

Penny pushes the door open and we follow her into what looks a lot like a normal locker room, except for the colorful heraldic banners that divide the room into each knight's section. The last time I was in here, when I first fought as the Red Knight, I was in too much of a hurry to pay attention to details. Now, I take it all in. Costumes hang from racks, and there's an entire wall of weapons. Of course, there's also a lingering smell that's a combo of BO and horses, and the showers look suspiciously like those in the high school gym locker room.

"Welcome!" says Austin. He stands with the Yellow, Black-and-White, and Blue Knights. "We're here to help you get suited up and settled on the horses. If you have any last-minute questions, let us know."

"I have a question," calls out Alex. "How are you all so cool with this? Won't we be taking shifts away from you if we get hired as Knights?"

Austin shrugs. "Some of us have been wanting to move on to different jobs—I actually have a degree in finance, and I want to work downtown."

"And there's more than enough work to go around," adds Chris. "It's exhausting doing two shows a night. I'd love to cut down to just one."

"Same," says the Yellow Knight. He's a white guy in his midthirties who's been fighting as a Knight since before Chris started. "I'm getting too old for two shows a night."

"Plus, it's just the right thing to do," adds the Blue Knight. "All of us feel that way. Except for Dalton. But he quit this afternoon, so that's kind of a win."

The other Knights laugh, and we laugh with them. It's like we're one big happy knightly family.

I look around the room. There's someone standing in the Green Knight's area, getting dressed. His faux chain mail hood is pulled up over his head, but when he lowers it, his red panda mullet hair is visible to all. I groan.

"Is Eric riding out tonight?" I ask Chris.

"As the Green Knight. He's the only one who wouldn't give up his spot."

"Of course," says Layla, rolling her eyes. "It's okay though. I can't wait to pulverize him out there. Do you know the kinds of photos he was texting me before I blocked his number?"

I scowl. "I'm very comfortable with all of us going through the routines we practiced. And also making it our personal mission to defeat Eric Taylor."

"Hear! Hear!" Mags and Alex say together. Eric shoots us a death glare and continues getting ready.

There's a loud trumpet of fanfare, telling us it's ten minutes until showtime. We all hurry to get dressed.

"Showtime." I put my helmet on. "Let's go storm the Castle."

43

"WELCOME ONE, WELCOME ALL! TONIGHT WE HAVE A very special show at the Castle!"

Somehow Chris has finagled his way into the MC's role tonight. His voice booms out over the loudspeakers after the last bunch of fanfare has ended. Len and his court, including Jett, are already in the royal box. Layla, Alex, Mags, Penny, Lizzy, and I wait in the arena hallway. Our horses whinny, nervous about the new riders. Eric Taylor, in full Green Knight gear, doesn't bother hiding his scorn as he twists around on his horse to stare daggers at us.

"You are going to make fools of yourselves," he says.

"Maybe we should've practiced on these horses," says Lizzy doubtfully, as her horse shakes its head. She looks wobbly in the saddle.

"Steady, Silver Knight," I tell her.

She insisted I ride out as the Red Knight, saying that way people will recognize me from my video, so we pulled her costume together out of what Jett ordered for me online and other bits and pieces from the locker room.

"You can always quit," scoffs Eric. "I'm sure they won't miss one more Girl Knight."

"We're more of a gender spectrum of Knights. And I'm going to relish knocking you off that horse," says Alex loudly. "Think Roller Derby meets the Middle Ages."

"You've not got much more experience out there, Eric," calls out Layla. "Try to stay on your horse."

Eric blanches at that thought. Before he can say anything, Chris calls out: "First, fair folks, we have the Green Knight!" Chris sounds almost bored and the crowd cheers lightly.

Eric digs his heels into his horse and gallops into the arena.

"Wish me luck," says Layla, who's up next. She pulls her helmet on and sits up tall in her saddle. The Blue Knight's tunic is big on her, but she holds the reins steady, looking like she belongs there.

"You've got this." I smile at her.

"Next, let's give a boisterous Castle welcome to a fierce warrior who's better at horsemanship than anyone in the far reaches of the kingdom, THE BLUE KNIGHT!" Chris's voice is louder this time and he revs up the crowd.

Layla's grin is electric as she digs her heels into her horse.

She rides into the arena, confident and radiant.

We cheer with the crowd as she does her first loop.

"Next up, all you folks over here in the Yellow section, make some noise for your champion, the very tough, very talented, very tenacious Yellow Knight!"

Alex pops their helmet on their head and grips the reins. They ride out to loud cheers and do a flashy circuit around the arena.

Next is Mags, fighting as the Purple Knight. Then Lizzy as the Silver Knight. Then Penny—looking amazing in the Black-and-White Knight costume with her hair streaming silkily down her back.

Finally it's my turn. My horse—the ever trusty Shadow-fax—and I are alone in the dusty hall that leads to the arena. For a moment, it's two weeks ago and I'm waiting for my first gallop into the arena.

But this time, excitement, not nerves, grips me.

Chris riles up the crowd and I can feel the buzz of their voices from here. "Last, but never least," he practically screams into the mic. "You've seen her videos. Now it's time to see her fight again! Ladies and gentlemen, KIT SWEETLY, FIGHTING AS THE RED KNIGHT!"

I kick my horse forward and ride out into the dazzle of the arena. Screams and cheers surround me, amplified a thousand times in the large space. I guide Shadowfax around the arena in a loop, past my grinning friends and a scowling Eric.

"Time to start the show," Chris yells into the mic. "First, let's joust!"

HORSES GALLOP DOWN THE PITCH. ERIC JOUSTS AGAINST Mags. She bites her lip, steadying her hand. Although we have the moves and who-wins-what choreographed and planned with each other, Eric's a wild card. Our primary objective tonight is to stick to our own routines and knock him down as many times as possible.

Which should be fun.

Mags steers her horse down the pitch, lance balanced so precisely it almost skims along the top of the tilt. Eric's arm shakes as he holds the lance, but his mouth is set in a grim line.

They smash together with a great *thud*. Eric sways in his seat for a moment and then he slides out of the saddle. Mags's section goes wild, shouting for her and waving their purple banners.

Eric's horse goes riding off, and he slinks to the side of the arena.

Layla faces Alex next. They grin as their horses run toward each other. As they did with pool noodles at the laundromat, Alex and Layla come together, their lances barely missing each other. They do two more rounds and then Layla unseats Alex, as they've practiced dozens of times.

Next it's my turn, and I'm supposed to ride against Penny, but somehow she's slipped into a round with Lizzy. Once they battle, Eric lines up his horse again. So, okay then. Me versus Eric. We're doing this. I settle my lance against my side and Shadowfax and I fly toward Eric.

It feels like déjà vu—me versus the Green Knight in the arena—but I knock him off his horse on the first try. This time he doesn't slink away. This time he charges toward me, swinging his sword. It's not technically time for ground fighting, but if Eric wants a fight, I'm game.

Before I can leap out of my saddle, Lizzy and Layla are at my side. They chase Eric to one side of the arena, and both of them do the complicated dismount and roll that Lizzy's been practicing for so long. Lizzy charges Eric first, but then she steps aside, so Eric and Layla can swordfight.

Layla's smaller than Eric, but she's faster and not shy about tripping him. They fight, swords clattering into each other. Layla sweeps out his feet and then Eric's on the ground.

The Blue section erupts in cheers as Layla stands over Eric, hands over her head. She yells her triumph and we cheer with her.

We put on a magnificent show. The crowd is totally into it and they roar their approval as Penny catches all the rings with her lance, Alex dominates the melee, knocking all of us down, and Lizzy pulls off a fancy horse trick that I didn't know she'd been practicing.

I even manage to throw a favor to Jett.

He grins at me, and I swear my heart turns to pudding in my chest.

There's a grand fanfare when we're done, and then all six of us slide off our horses and turn toward where the people from Corporate sit. Chris hands me the mic and I wave to the crowd as we all take our last bows.

"Hello, Chicago! I'm Kit, the Girl Knight!" I shout to the crowd. "We hope you enjoyed the show! People of all genders have been fighting for centuries, in places all over the world. But you've not heard their stories. Here at the Castle, we think it's high time for a change."

Layla, Alex, Penny, Lizzy, and Mags wave from their horses. The crowd goes wild, and the five of them grin so widely I'm certain their faces will hurt tomorrow.

I introduce each of them, and it warms my heart to see a bunch of Girl Scouts on their feet, screaming and cheering for us.

"We're the new face of the Castle," I say. "We hope you enjoyed the show and for now, good night to you all!"

We all bow one more time, except for Eric, who stands on the sidelines scowling. Then we ride off.

# 44

"**T**HAT WAS AMAZING!" LAYLA SAYS ONCE WE PUT OUR horses away. We head out into the Grand Hall to greet the crowds. Squires, stable hands, and Wenches cheer for us as we pass.

"You were perfection out there!" I wipe my sweaty hair out of my eyes and laugh.

"I can't wait to do that again!" says Penny.

"No one is doing that again," thunders Len, pushing through the crowd. His face is red. "Kit, I gave you—just you—permission to ride out. All of you except Eric are in—"

Before Len can say more, Isabel pushes through the crowd. Behind her is a tall, skinny dude carrying a huge camera. The light of the camera shines on us and Isabel puts a microphone in my face.

"Tell me, Kit, what inspired you to bring others into the arena?"

I put an arm around Layla, who puts one around Alex, who puts one around Penny, who puts one around Mags, who puts one around Lizzy. Other members of the Castle staff rush in, cheering and buzzing with excitement.

"Ask my friends here how it's felt to watch cis men get all the glory for so many years," I say, handing the microphone to Layla.

She, Penny, Alex, Mags, and Lizzy talk about how they've wanted this for so long, how exhilarating it was to be out there, and how they can't wait to do it again.

Isabel turns to Len, who's finally made his way to us. "And you, King Len, what did you think of the performance?"

He pulls at his beard, his eyes shifting between the Corporate people and us. I lift an eyebrow at him expectantly.

"Well, erm—"

Before Len can say more, one of the women from Corporate steps in front of him. "I'm Alisha Day, head of Castle PR and brand management, and we just wanted to put our full support behind these Knights! They are a magnificent part of our new show, which we'll be unveiling soon at the Castles throughout the nation."

My eyes meet Len's. His are wide with surprise, but then he shrugs. He's a company man through and through, so if Corporate says this is how it goes, he'll go along with it. He gives me a thumbs up, and I can't help the smirk that splits my face. Way to jump on board at the last minute there, Uncle Len.

I return the thumbs-up, hoping he at least got the promotion he wanted.

My friends and I spread out to talk to the guests and get our pictures taken with them. My mom comes up to me and pulls me into an enormous hug. "Thank you for getting the divorce papers signed," she whispers as she squeezes the air out of me. "That was incredibly chivalrous."

"Mom, stop, you'll make me cry," I say, beaming at her.

"I'm serious," she says, wiping away a tear. "I'm so proud of you. And even though I know you're going away to school next year, you'll always be my baby."

I roll my eyes a bit at that. Moms. Good grief.

We take a selfie together, and then I tell her the news I've been sitting on for too long. "Speaking of college I've been meaning to tell you: I got into Marquette."

"Oh, Kit! That's amaz—"

"But I'm not going. It's too much money, and I got a full ride to the community college. I'll be going there in the fall."

She pauses for a moment. "Are you sure? We can figure out something else. I'll have the money from selling the house and Chris's medical bills will be covered."

"We'll talk more about it later," I say. "But my mind is made up. This is a better fit in every way. And it means you can still chase some of those dreams of yours."

She hugs me again. "Love you, Kit-Kat. Don't stay out too late. I've got tomorrow off and we should do something fun. Just you, me, and Chris."

I wave to her and then sign an autograph for a small girl wearing a Red Knight costume. As I talk to fans, smile for pictures, and laugh with my friends, some small part of me still mourns letting the Marquette dream go. But maybe that's just one version of my dream. Maybe I can find a new path that will help me end up where I want to.

Once all the guests are gone, Len comes out of his office, wearing civilian clothes. The guitar Chris and I gave him is strapped to his chest. The Corporate folks are long gone, but only after getting contact information for me and all the other Knights and promising to have contracts for those of us who want them.

"One night only, final Ninja after-party!" Len yells. "Drinks are on me because I just got promoted, and we're going to celebrate!"

The Castle staff lets out an enormous cheer and someone switches out the medieval soundtrack for some EDM.

The bar opens up, and Castle staff keep hugging Layla, Penny, Alex, Mags, Lizzy, and me, toasting us with shots someone's pouring. Layla's yelling at Eric, and then she gets tackle hugged by Maura, her pink-haired girlfriend. Penny and Chris are laughing near the break room. Alex, Lizzy, and Mags are showing a bunch of Wenches some moves.

Jett moves through the crowd, grinning as he approaches me.

"You were great out there." He picks me up in a sweeping, swinging hug.

I hug him back, squeezing him hard as my feet leave the ground, not wanting to let go. "Everything worked out according to plan! I can't believe it."

"I can," says Jett. "You're a force, Kit Sweetly."

He puts me down and presses his forehead against mine. Gently, he pushes a piece of my hair behind my ear. The touch sends heat through me. Feeling exceptionally brave, I tilt my head and push my lips against his. His mouth opens and the kiss deepens as our bodies press together. And it's good. Oh. So. Very. Good.

Loud cheers and whistles surround us. Because of course our first real kiss is in front of the entire Castle.

I pull away, breathless. "I thought you weren't into me. Or that you didn't date Serving Wenches."

Jett gives me the smile that makes the edges of his eyes crinkle. "I've been into you since the first time we met. But I didn't want to screw it up and lose your friendship. So I said that about Serving Wenches, hoping you'd realize I was more into Girl Knights."

"You literally fled after I kissed you on Wednesday."

"I panicked. I'm sorry. But I'll make up for it." He kisses me again, this time slow, sweet, and lingering. It sends hummingbirds zipping around my belly.

"GET IT, KIT!" shouts Layla. I glare at her, but then burst out laughing.

Jett doesn't look at all embarrassed. "I bet you're starving. Let's get pancakes. Want to meet me at your mom's restaurant in half an hour?"

"You have yourself a date," I say. "Just let me change first."

**45**

IT TAKES ME LONGER THAN EXPECTED TO SHOWER, CHANGE, and say goodbye to everyone at the Castle.

"I'll give you a thirty-minute head start," says Layla. "But no guarantees we won't show up. I'm famished after all that riding. Being a Knight is a real workout!"

Maura whispers something in her ear and Layla laughs wickedly. She waves to me as they walk away.

"SORRY I'M LATE," I SAY AS I SLIDE INTO THE BOOTH ACROSS from Jett.

I want to sit next to him, like the adorable white-haired couple behind us, who lean over to share a magnifying glass as they do a crossword puzzle. But I don't. Some distance feels necessary as we figure out whatever this is between us.

"I ordered already," says Jett.

Right as he says it, Dot, a red-haired server who's worked with my mom since I was in junior high, puts down plates piled high with pancakes, bacon, sunny-side-up eggs, and two cups of coffee. She's an unabashed feminist who wears a "We Can Do It!" button on her uniform and has sleeves of tattoos full of political slogans from the '60s.

"I see that," I say to Jett, pouring sugar into my coffee. My stomach grumbles.

When all the food is on the table, Dot tucks her tray under her arm. "You all need anything else, Kit?"

"Just some sugar." I hand her our empty sugar container. She snags the one from a table next to us and hands it to me.

"Thanks, Dot," I say, pouring more sugar into my coffee.

"No problem, sweetie." She stands there a moment longer, and then she clears her throat. "And congratulations on your big night. Your mom told me all about your campaign, and she just sent me a video from tonight. I've always loved horses and my granddaughters have been begging to go to the Castle for years. I've never had the money to take them just to see a bunch of men fight, but after your performance, I think we can go see the famous Girl Knight and company."

I smile at her. "I'll leave some tickets for you at the front desk next weekend. Try to sit in my cheering section. I'm riding as the Red Knight at least through the end of summer."

Dot squeezes my shoulder affectionately and then turns to Jett. "You've got a real special girl here, you know. Better be good to her."

Jett smiles. "I will."

I blush to the roots of my hair. "Get out of here, you. I've got breakfast to eat and a boyfriend to talk to."

Dot gives me a knowing look as she walks away.

"I see your strategy is to butter me up with breakfast food before we move on to matters of the heart," I say, slathering jelly and butter onto toast.

Jett rolls his eyes. "Bad jokes are not the way to my heart."

I hold out the ramekin of butter. "Really? No? Too much?"

"Too much. Now, won't you come over here and sit with me, so we can give that old couple a run for their money?"

I pour half the jug of syrup onto my pancakes. "Somebody's feeling confident this evening."

"Somebody just got called your boyfriend," he says with an easy grin. "I want to make this the most unsurpassably cheesy romantic breakfast of your life."

I laugh. "Fine, fine. But you're not having any of my pancakes."

Jett scoots over as I slide into the booth next to him.

"This is so weird!" I turn to try to look at him as I take a bite of pancakes. "I can't really look at you while I eat. And your elbow keeps jabbing me and—"

Jett leans in and kisses me.

I give him a playful push away. "You can't do that every time we're having a conversation."

"But I've waited so very long to do that," he says. "And you're lovely when you're complaining like my grandma."

"Ha-ha. Eat your breakfast and leave me in peace."

Jett laughs and cuts into his own pancakes. "So, have you decided what to do about Marquette?"

I give him the quick rundown on Mom's late mortgage payment, the divorce, the money from my website, and getting a full ride to community college.

"I keep trying to come up with a plan so I can have it all, but without taking out tons of student loans. There's no way I can make the money appear for Marquette's tuition. Even if I keep working at the Castle on the weekends, it's not enough."

"So, stick around," says Jett. "Go to community college for two years, then move on to something else."

It hurts a bit, but I know he's right.

"But, the lake, Jett! And the kite festivals! And all that cool stuff in a new place!"

"We can still visit Milwaukee," he says. "We can go up there and hang out all the time."

"I know we can visit, but it's not the same." I sigh and take a piece of bacon. It coats my fingertips in grease, reminding me of the marvelous fact that the German's have a word—*kummerspeck*—which translates to "grief bacon." It refers to the weight you gain when you've been eating your feelings. As I devour the piece of bacon in two bites, I can almost taste my sadness along with the salty porky deliciousness.

Grief bacon: here meaning the literal bacon Kit consumes as she says goodbye to her dream of going to Marquette.

"It might not be the same," says Jett. "But you never know, it could be better."

He's right about that too. Of course.

"I think I know that on an abstract level, but it feels like I'm failing if I let the Marquette dream go." I eat another piece of grief bacon and refill our coffee cups from the metal pot Dot left on the table.

Jett leans into me, his steady warmth and presence enough to chase my sadness away.

"It's not failing if you stay here, Kit," says Jett softly. "Things happen. Other things don't work out. But you can still make a good life. Even if it's not part of your plan."

"I know that," I say, shifting so I can look at him. "But I can't help what I want."

"But do you still want the things you did before?" Jett's eyes don't leave mine.

I look away, letting out a long breath. "I don't know. It used to be so clear. I wanted to be so much more than the girl I was. When I was twelve, I used to stand in my backyard at night and chant 'more, more, more . . .', though I could never see the path to what that more would look like. It just seemed like everybody else was having a better time or that it was easier for them. My life was full of if-onlys, and that made me miss things. Good things. I know that now. Just like I know I want to be with you. Even if it's just for the summer. Or maybe it will be longer, I don't—"

This time, when Jett stops my monologue with a kiss, I don't complain. He tastes like syrup and coffee and his own delicious self.

"We have our whole lives ahead of us to worry about this not being enough," he says, when we finally stop kissing. "Let's see where this summer goes. And let the rest take care of itself. Will that work for you, my Lady Knight?"

I smile as I look at this beautiful boy whom I've loved for so long. "That will be enough for me."

We kiss again, our mouths lingering together, breathing each other's air for a moment. Jett's hand threads through my hair and I—

"GET A ROOM!" crows Layla as she, Maura, Penny, Chris, Alex, Mags, and Lizzy walk toward our booth.

I blush and pull away. "More of that later?" I whisper to Jett.

"As you wish," he says, his mouth right beside my ear.

The promise sends a shiver of anticipation down my spine, and I'm suddenly ravenous for the next time we're alone together.

Layla and Maura squeeze into the other side of the booth.

Penny, Alex, and Mags pull up a few tables, making one long table that fills the back half of the restaurant. The bacon disappears, and Layla orders ten more plates of pancakes and sides.

"My treat!" she declares. "A feast for the Knights!"

We all cheer, our voices rising excitedly together. The food arrives, and the conversation flows back and forth from tonight's performance to changes at the Castle to graduation to summer and then college plans.

Underneath the table, Jett squeezes my hand.

It's all pretty damn perfect.

And that's when it hits me: This is really all I want.

A life with the people I love.

Together.

Eating shit tons of pancakes.

Bravely facing whatever the future holds.

# Acknowledgments

MAKING A BOOK IS NEVER A SOLITARY ACT, AND I'VE BEEN lucky enough to be supported, encouraged, and buoyed by so many people on my long, twisting road to publication.

Thank you to Kate Testerman, my wonderful agent, who pulled me out of the slush, chased me down on Twitter, never stopped believing in my books, and entertained all my ideas. I'm grateful always for your optimism, generosity, friendship, and enormous knowledge of all things publishing.

Thank you to Ashley Hearn, my delightful editor who sent me an email about KIT that made me cry in a drive-thru line. Thank you for immediately getting exactly what I was trying to do with these knights, for your brilliant notes, and for laughing so hard your sides hurt.

Thank you to Lizzy Mason, dear friend, first champion of KIT, and amazing publicist. I'm so glad we finally got to work together and thank you for always believing in this book. Hugs you fiercely.

Thank you to my copy editor, Juli Barbato, whose keen eye caught so many things I missed and who asked all the right questions.

Thank you to the amazing Page Street team who helped KIT ride into the world: editorial assistant Tamara Grasty;

editorial intern Hanna Mathews; production editor Hayley Gundlach; editorial manager Marissa Giambelluca; editor Lauren Knowles; designer Rosie Stewart; publisher Will Kiester; and the wonderful sales team at Macmillan. I appreciate your hard work and vision for this book so much!

Thank you to all my writing friends—how can I thank you all enough?

Thank you, Noelle "Peanut" Salazar: Has it really been the better part of a decade since we had bagels together at PNWA? Thank you for all the friendship, encouragement, and laughs over the years.

Thank you, Megan England: wonderful friend, co-mentor, and potato chip universe co-creator. I'm so glad we stumbled into each other's lives. Let's meet in real life soon, yes?

Thank you to my Sisters of the Pen: Cindy Baldwin, Amanda Hill, and Ashley Martin. I'm eternally grateful for our conversations about all things and for all the love and support.

Thank you to my Pitch Wars 2015 family: Joan He, Leigh Mar, Katniss Hinkel, Jenny Ferguson, Margaret Owen, Julie Artz, Courtney Gilfillan, Joanna Hathaway, Kristen Ciccarelli, Mike Mammay, Sarah Madsen, Lucy Goacher, Jenny Chou, and everyone else in our '15 group. It really is impossible to quantify how much your messages, texts, emails, CP reads, and getting to read your stories have meant over the last few years.

Thank you to Brittany Cavallaro, for all the advice and

encouragement over the years. Thank you to Hafsah Faizal, for the friendship and commiseration. And, thank you to my KT Literary fam: Jessie Hilb, Carrie Allen, and Jessica Bibi Cooper. Your books have kept me reading late into the night. Thank you for keeping me afloat and laughing through the submission process.

Thank you to Mike Lasagna for his tireless enthusiasm for KIT and for his friendship; thank you to my wonderful street team, The Round Table, for all their hard work in getting the word out about KIT; and, thank you to all the booksellers, librarians, and bloggers for the blurbs, early reviews, and excitement about KIT. I am so grateful to you all!

Thank you to the friends who've been with me through so much of my life and without whom a book like KIT could never have arisen. Truly, this story is a love letter to you all: Thank you to my BFF Ashleigh Bunn for the packages, the visits, the walks, and for working so hard to build bridges of understanding when things got tough in our adult lives. Oh, and also for Gatlinburg. I'll be thanking you for that until we're ninety. You were magnificent.

Thank you to Liana Bowen, who listened to so many of my ideas on so many walks and who always wanted to know what I was working on next.

Thank you to the original Overshare Circle, Lindy Russell and Luke Anderson.

Thank you to my many other friends, who've shared so much

of their own lives and stories with me: Kim Donohoe, Andrea Dula, Melanie Richards, Cheryl Clearwater, and Sarah Banck.

Thanks also to all the friends in the autism community who understand what it is to balance our particular parenting journey with everything else in life and to the autistic adults who've taught me so much. Thank you especially to Lyn Jones, Shannon Rosa, Anna Yarrow, Chris Lacey, Patti Moore, and Ryan Mulligan.

Thank you to the Merrimans, especially those of you who have who been part of my writing adventure: My parents for giving me love, education, and a sense of humor, and always letting me read what I wanted. Margaret, youngest sister and biggest fan who's read all the books I've written and swears that some of them are her favorite books ever. (Good grief, love you.) Kim, sister and bestie. My favorite birthday present ever, who's been there always, cheering me on, and showing up with burritos. Kathleen, whose books I loved reading. I'm so happy you're passing your love of stories on to the students you teach. And, Mark, fabulous and opinionated friend. Thanks for telling me first. We'll always have a bottle of gin at our house waiting for you.

Thank you to my Grandma Merriman, librarian, endless talker, and voracious reader, who fueled my love for books with her own many stories. I'm fairly certain KIT would've made you cackle and I'm positive you would've been proud I made a real book. I wish you were here to read it.

Thank you to my Grandma Rightmyer, whose heart is bigger than the family she's grown. I'm so grateful for all your letters and your love.

Thank you to my wonderful in-laws, Greg and Kathy Pacton, for watching the boys, for always asking about my books, and for giving us so much support through the years.

And thank you to the three people in my immediate family who make every day challenging, fun, and interesting: Thank you to Liam. For being exactly the person you're meant to be and for all the snuggles. Thank you to Eliot, a dreamer like me, whose fan art and encouragement kept me writing in those months when I wanted to give up. I can't wait for the world to read your stories someday. And thank you to Adam. Great love and best friend. Who talked to me first on that snowy night so long ago. Who's been there through it all. Who's always supported me and this writing dream. Who sends me out to write. Who keeps me laughing. Who's cried with me in good times and in bad. I couldn't do any of this without you. I love you.

# About the Author

JAMIE PACTON GREW UP MINUTES away from the National Storytelling Center in the mountains of East Tennessee, and stories have always been a huge part of her life.

Although she's been writing since she was a kid, after college, Jamie spent a long time working as a server (including a few years at a '50s-themed restaurant, where she had to do lots of dancing in costume), a nanny, a pen salesperson, a bookseller, and many other jobs that will certainly find their way into books someday.

Jamie currently teaches English and writing at the college level, and she's written for national and local magazines about parenting, autism, and writing. When she's not writing books or teaching, Jamie's usually reading, exploring the world with her family, wandering through a museum, drinking coffee, or rattling off history fun facts to whoever will listen. *The Life and (Medieval) Times of Kit Sweetly* is her debut novel.

Learn more about Jamie and her books at jamiepacton.com.

You can also find her at @JamiePacton on Twitter and Instagram.